More than qualified at thirty-something to fulfil a vague ambition of becoming an author when she grew up, Wellington-based Donna Wright swapped the harsh, fluorescent lights of the corporate world for a desk lamp, and wrote her first novel, *Spinning the Bottle* (Black Swan, 2002).

Wright was born to an army father in Corby, a staunchly anti-Tory, Midlands steel-working town. She spent her early childhood in Germany before returning to the UK. Itchy feet as a teenager — and a monetary bribe to leave home — resulted in 29 addresses (not counting poste restantes and C/Os) in twenty years, the last ten moves occurring to and within New Zealand. Her only dependants are three ageing pets with enormously expensive dietary requirements.

As part of her research for *Mumbo Gumbo*, Wright self-funded two trips to New Orleans and Haiti, experiencing everything from hurricanes to mambos, rum punches on the verandah at the Oloffson to Grenades in the underworld of Saturday-night Bourbon Street.

MUMBO GUMBO

DONNA WRIGHT

BLACK
SWAN

National Library of New Zealand Cataloguing-in-Publication Data

Wright, Donna, 1964-
Mumbo gumbo / Donna Wright.
ISBN 1-86941-607-4
I. Title.
NZ823.3—dc 22

A BLACK SWAN BOOK
published by
Random House New Zealand
18 Poland Road, Glenfield, Auckland, New Zealand
www.randomhouse.co.nz

First published 2004

© 2004 Donna Wright

The moral rights of the author have been asserted

ISBN 1 86941 607 4

Text design: Elin Termannsen
Cover design: Katy Yiakmis
Cover photographs: women – Getty Images; hotel – Donna Wright
Printed in Australia by Griffin Press

ACKNOWLEDGEMENTS

I consider myself blessed to have had help, advice, friendship, and frequent outright kindness from the following people:

Mum and Dad for continuing to bail out my sorry financial ass despite my being thirty-something; Brad Richards — a.k.a. Prof. Amerifilter™ — for reading *first* first draft and coming all that way; Kathleen Mackie, Megan Coleman, Shelly Simpson, Paul O'Neill, Helena McMullin, Victoria Scott, Alison Anelzark, Fiona Wright and Anthony Patete for being worth their weight in gold; Jayne Klein for her target-audience crash-test read-through; Harriet Allan for being one of the nicest — if not *the* nicest — publishers in the business; Jane Parkin for her magical editing; Barbara Robichaux for being New Orleans' best tour guide and doing her city proud; Karin Maher for being the world's most understanding personal banker; Dr John T. O'Connor of the University of New Orleans for pointing me in the right directions; Sean Hubar for practically paying *me* to stay in his condo on St. Charles; Kevin Rablais and Jennifer Lavasseur for being friendly faces; Rodney and Wanda Rablais whose southern hospitality was such that I put on half a stone in two days; Brent Simpson and Michelle Barber for introducing me to the best margaritas in LA and making me miss my plane; Sheriff William C. Hunter of the Orleans Parish Prison for his time; Liesl Picard of the Latin American and Caribbean Center of Florida International University for her saint-like patience;

Dr Terry Rey of FIU for his field notes; Dr Eduardo Gamarra of FIU for being a good sport and sort; Dr Jean-Robert Cadely of FIU for his Kreyol; Neil Van Dine for sharing his knowledge of Northwest Haiti; and finally, once again demonstrating why Louisiana is America's finest state, Joshua Clark of Light of New Orleans Publishing for being easily bribed with VB into clanger-checking.

Anyone I've forgotten should let me know so I can kick myself.

"Oh, massa mighty!"

"What do you mean by mighty, Pompey?"

"Why, Massa, you look noble."

"What do you mean by noble?"

"Why, sir, you look just like a lion."

"Why, Pompey, where have you ever seen a lion?"

"I seen one down in yonder field the other day, Massa."

"Pompey, you foolish fellow, that was a *jackass!*"

"Was it, Massa? Well you look just like him."

(From *Slave Cabin to the Pulpit: The Autobiography of Rev. Peter Randolph: The Southern Question Illustrated and Sketches of Slave Life.* Boston: James H. Earle, 1893)

CHAPTER 1

JUST ABOUT CHOKE on my beer when I see that girl on the TV. Shock make me mess on myself like I don't got enough laundry with two kids, two grandbabies and every one of they daddies a goddamn fool don't help out none. I set down front of the TV after dinner, see if I cain' catch a movie or something interesting to take my mind off things, and WWL News got Dennis Woltering raising his baboon brows over the police treatment some girl on the receiving end of down in the Quarter. Couple Eight District gorillas manhandling her something awful, beating on her like she some kind of riot-control exercise.

I ain' the faintest notion why they arresting her, seeing nobody expecting y'all to behave at Mardi Gras and anybody with the sense they born with get the hell out of town until the damn thing well and truly over, but that girl make a break for it. Folks cheering and clapping and making way for her, but the police can move despite all the gear they got attach to themselves, and they *dive* on her. Tear

her sweater clean off, and even Stevie Wonder could see she ain'
wearing no bra even with WWL fuzzing her boobies out. One of the
policemen snap some cuffs on while she trying to cover herself up,
and that when I see the sign all red and puckered on her left
shoulder like my ancestor Angélique say in her journal — the very
same sign she say I suppose to look out for.

'You want me to fetch you another beer, Mama?' Hoover say.
He sweet like that.

'And some towels so I can clean up, baby,' I tell him, my heart
still pumping away like crazy from all the adrenaline now everything
starting to come true.

'Why don't you just hook yourself on up to the icebox?' Jolie
butt in where she ain' got no business. 'Save on the carpet.'

Got a bad-ass mouth on her like her daddy. Folks call him
Almanac Jack because he got a answer for everything. Fifteen when
she had her twins. Seem she smart enough to get out the trailer
nights without me knowing, but not smart enough not to get knock
up. She been running around like Lolita since she made twelve and
ain' a goddamn thing I could do about it. Nuh-uh. Fast as I sew
something up you be proud to wear to church, she shoplifting strap-
less bras out of the Wal-Mart down on Lafitte.

'I wear you down in a minute you don't quit with that mouth
of yours,' I warn her.

'Mama say you is a acofrolic,' Little Sammy say to me, eyes all
bright and round with mischief.

Even her babies dissing me now because they see she don't
respect me none.

'Shush! Cain' y'all see I tryin' to watch the TV here.' But it too
late. Woltering talking about some strippers in the Quarter got a
robbery scam going.

I got ceiling-to-floor mirror tiles on one wall of the trailer, and

I see Jolie rolling her eyes just about all the ways to the back of her head when Hoover hand me a fresh beer and some towels over. Hoover's daddy glue them tiles up. Man so bone-idle wouldn't wipe his own ass if he had to reach even a inch further, but somehow he got the energy and crazy-ass notion in his head to stick mirrors on my walls. Say it make the place look bigger but, nuh-uh. Busy is what it look like. Even when you on your own you feel like you got company, goddamn reflection always staring back at you.

'Alco*hol*ic,' Jolie say, putting her boy right.

'For your information,' I tell her, patting myself down with the towels, 'I ain' a drunk, and if y'all live to make thirty-eight as poor as me your whole life, y'all goin' be damn grateful you ain' givin' five-dollar hand jobs to Texans out back of the casino for crack money.'

''Stead of drinkin' two six-packs of beer a day in front of the TV, you mean?' Jolie say back with unnecessary unkindness.

I look over at my eldest, meanest child, my heart breaking for her because I know she resign to her future already, and she cain' help being so piss before she even make twenty. I ain' never been in a position to change that for her, but now I seen that white girl with the slave branding Angélique describe in her journal, it make me believe Angélique right about the gold she say belong to me too, and I don't always have to be worrying all the time about no bills I cain' pay. Jolie's eyes defiant though, and my temper get the better of me.

'Don't think I don't know,' I say to her. 'I hear you sneakin' out of the trailer durin' the night. It startin' to make you look ugly.'

DESPITE CONSUMING FIVE sleeping tablets in the last thirty-six hours, most of them with glasses of complimentary airline wine, I've racked up only four hours' sleep when the phone goes.

My head throbs as I sit up and feel my way up the greasy lamp base to the switch. The bulb has been painted with lilac nail polish, probably to tone down a wattage unflattering to the kind of people who would rent a room like this. The cool bluish light has a crime-scene effect on the room and I half expect stains on the bedcover to glow. The phone smells like it's been swabbed down with water left over from cleaning the floor.

'Hel —' *Hil.*

Just one vowel-mangled syllable and I know it's the editor of *Kerb*. 'It's not even light yet, Elizabeth. Hang up, you torturer.'

'Oh, I'm sorry. Did I get you out of bed?' *Bee-ed.*

'Why are you calling this early?'

Outside, there are at least four sirens going by on the street.

'It sounds like *Third Watch* over there,' she observes.

'No shit.'

Elizabeth waits for the noise to abate before continuing. 'Has Mozzie got in contact with you yet?'

'No. Why would he?' I whine, latching on.

Having worked with Mozzie on a number of occasions for just about every magazine in New Zealand and Australia, I now know Mardi Gras is going to suck. The man is rude, charmless, sarcastic, up himself, and only nice to women he wants to sleep with. And he has an unerring ability to hone in on a person's weak spot, which he never then gives a chance to scab over. This is the first time since *Cleo* made him Bachelor of the Year in '01, and his already inflated ego practically exploded, that I've had the misfortune to get stuck with him on a job.

'Who's your buddy?'

'No,' I whine again. 'You said Lewis.'

'Lewis is sick.' *Suck.*

'Jesus Christ, Elizabeth. Did it have to be Mozzie?'

'Look on the bright side.'

'You've just damned me to the dark side of the moon and you know it.'

'Oh, stick a flag in it. He's not that bad.' She laughs unbecomingly into my disapproving silence. 'Well, if he doesn't call — he may still be sleeping — you're meeting him at the Monteleone around nine.'

'Monteleone? When I'm stuck in a motel out on Airline Highway? Why didn't you just book me into a prison? There's razor wire blocking every exit in this place. I heard gun shots last night, and that was just getting out of the taxi. The *driver* hit the ground.'

I hear the clatter of the Christine Rankin earrings as she shrugs. 'So I'm thinking something along the lines of Mardi Gras' underbelly. You know — what's really going on behind all the glitter and bright lights. I want you to get shots of the police action and underage girls lying in gutters in their own vomit. That kind of thing.'

'Nice.'

'You *play* nice. And something else.'

'What? I have to carry his bags?'

'You're meeting a local there, too — Floyd Simeon. A genuine Cajun no less. He's going to show you around.'

'He can show Mozzie into the middle of the Mississippi.'

'Act professional,' she snaps, and hangs up.

It takes an hour in unbelievable traffic to hit the Quarter, the taxi driver turning to punch me on the arm every time he spots a New York registration plate — 'Goddamn Yankee bastards give me a ache in the ass for a month every year' — and the grand marble lobby at the Monteleone is packed. It's only just after nine in the morning, but the guests are dressed to the nines and partying, champagne corks popping all over the place. I ask a desk clerk to call Mozzie's room for me, only to be told that Mozzie isn't ready to

13

receive guests yet: I'm to wait in the lobby for him and he will be down shortly. Instead I fight my way through the crowd to a brocaded barstool in the Carousel Lounge and charge a coffee to Mozzie's room.

He turns up just as I'm finishing my fourth coffee, with no breakfast yet, and the gilded carnival bar has done twenty-two revolutions of the room on its underfloor rollers.

'Rough flight?' he asks.

After some initial heart palpitations while my defence system kicks in, I notice he hasn't changed much since the last time I saw him — hitting on a visiting Panamanian supermodel at the Qantas Media Awards — except for his hair being longer and white-blond from a Sydney summer. Still on the skinny side of athletic, he has Arctic Circle blue eyes that are acid bright with a brutal, slicing intelligence, applied for the most part in tormenting others. You rarely see it coming and it hurts for days afterwards.

'We can't all fly first class on Air Broomstick,' I say.

Mozzie takes his time responding as he sizes up the talent in the bar. Finally, seeing nothing to his liking, he flicks his attention back to me. 'Fancy a drink?'

'It's your tab. Make mine a double.'

He calls the bartender over and orders some drinks. 'Up yours,' he says, raising his glass.

'Ditto.'

He smiles. 'Laura Delacross. A veritable virago of the vocal volley.'

'Mozzie Russo. A wanker. No alliteration necessary.'

He ignores this — water off a duck's back — and takes a sip on his drink. 'So how's New Zealand these days?'

'Great since you moved to Australia.'

He makes no show of having heard me, his eyes following the

progress through the bar of a glamorous Grace Jones-looking woman, her boob job a perfection not diminished in any way by the skin-tight electric-blue velveteen sheath dress she's wearing.

'She's a transvestite, you moron.'

'Still rather do her than you,' he says.

'You'd have a better chance.'

He looks at me for a moment, and just as I think I'm in for a punishing rejoinder he smiles and says, 'Another?'

On an empty stomach, the last drink has gone straight to my head. 'Aren't we supposed to be working?'

'Later. I need to get a handle on the vibe first.'

'Sure you do, Faulkner. Get me something to eat as well.'

I get talking to a kid from Idaho while Mozzie orders the drinks. Idaho's in New Orleans with 'a whole bunch' of college buddies, and none has slept for the forty hours they have been in town. They're done up as a rock band: long teased-out wigs, garish KISS make-up, tight leather pants padded out with socks, sporting cardboard guitars and cheap, glittery sunglasses. He admits to doing some speed: 'I'm not missing a goddamn second of this freak show.'

Mozzie hands me a fresh drink and a bowl of complimentary pretzels, and introduces himself to Idaho, telling him to watch out for me as I have a thing for college boys.

Changing the subject, I ask him, 'Have you heard from some local guy called Simon yet?'

'Who?' he says.

'Maybe it's Simone.'

'Still who?'

'It's something Elizabeth arranged. Or some*body*. He's supposed to turn up here some time this morning.'

'I haven't seen him,' Mozzie shrugs, before turning to engage Idaho and his friends in conversation.

The Idaho boys are receptive to his sense of humour, and gradually the rounds get faster and more outrageous. A jazz band starts playing, and after a good three hours of mixed shooters it seems a brilliant idea to hit Bourbon Street. We leave en masse, the Idaho boys sharing their strings of Mardi Gras beads so Mozzie and I have some too. Outside on the street there's a deafening, oppressive roar from a million high-spirited voices. I'm surprised the Quarter isn't imploding from the weight of all the revellers. Merciless wintry sun glints off metallic festival leis, blinding us as we make our way down Royal Street, which isn't easy because it's like Courtenay Place on Friday nights, times a thousand. Young women yell at Mozzie and the Idaho gang from drape-festooned galleries, flashing their tits when they've got the boys' attention. Mozzie tells me to take pictures. I tell him to write something, then, 'Oh shit. I left my camera at the Monteleone.'

'A good soldier never loses his gun,' he says. 'It's unprofessional.'

'You should be glad it's not a gun.'

'Hurry up. We'll wait here for you.'

By now every sorry-bastard drunk from the night before has dragged himself back out on the streets, which have become a blur of bright feathers, fake jewels, face paint and scanty fancy dress, though it's not much more than fifteen degrees tops. The sun is starting to look jaundiced behind a rapidly descending, cool layer of cloud.

Back in the Carousel Lounge, I can't tell which was my barstool because the bar has rotated God knows how many times in my absence. I approach some big black guy using a straw to drink though a Saddam Hussein mask. Saddam's ensemble runs gaily to a red velvet pirate's jacket with epaulettes and fancy buttons, a frilly red Tom Jones kind of shirt, red leather trousers, a red bandanna tied pirate-style around his head, a huge gold loop dangling from one ear and, to top it off, a sabre hanging from his waist. Even his boots are red. It's an effective outfit, but my camera is missing.

I tap him on the shoulder. 'Excuse me.'

'My pleasure, baby,' he says, rich and deep, swivelling around to look me up and down.

'Have you seen my camera? I may have left it under your stool.'

He shakes his head. 'Sorry, baby. Don't know nothin' about no camera.'

'Are you sure?'

'Yes, I am.'

'Okay then. Thanks.'

I squeeze past him to talk to the bartender, but as everyone else wanting his attention is holding out what is implicitly understood to be a tip, he ignores me. Saddam holds out a couple of fifty-dollar bills and the bartender's over in a flash, practically saluting him.

'Yes, sir?'

'You seen this lady's camera?'

'No, sir, I have not.'

Saddam turns to me and shrugs. 'Buy you a drink?'

'Sure,' I sigh, estimating what's left on my credit card for a new camera. 'Surprise me.'

He orders me a Lullaby, whatever that is, and offers me his hand. 'You got a name I can use, baby?'

'Laura. And yours?'

'Prince le Kreyol. And I got to say there some fine lines on you, Laura. Mmm, yes, there is.' Because of the mask I don't know what's going on with his face, but I'm pretty sure he's giving me the glad-eye. 'I sure like to work some magic on you, sugar. What you say we go back to my room?'

'Well, Prince,' I say, snatching my hand back and pretty much downing the spicy warm Lullaby in one so I can get back to Mozzie and the Idaho boys, 'thanks for the drink, but I've got someone waiting for me.'

His laugh rumbles through my chest and the next thing I know I'm woozy as hell and Prince is carrying me up some wooden stairs into a long, narrow room that smells of butcher's waste and rum. Shutters covering the small window opposite the doorway muffle the Mardi Gras din outside. He leads me across the dark and fetid room — I can't feel my legs working, let alone fight him — and lays me down on a single mattress that reeks of dogs and stale night-sweats, singing quietly in a language I've never heard before.

'*Lè destine rive*
Pou chans retounen nan vi mwen
Se san mwen, se swè mwen, se dlo nan je mwen
Ki sòti nan tout tribilasyon Ginen an.'

He lights a candle and his gigantic shadow looms eerily into the dank corners of the room, its walls stained with leaks, plaster crumbling away in wet chunks. Prince starts removing my beads and sweater, and my limbs are so heavy and useless I can't fight him off. He undoes the button and zip of my jeans, then hooks his fingers inside the waistband, removing them in one tug.

'Hush, *bèl ti fi*,' he soothes, rolling me over onto my stomach and unhooking my bra.

'Get off,' I slur, unable to stop him, my tongue lolling around like a dead thing. Whatever Mickey he slipped me was enough to paralyse my body into absolute compliance, but not enough to numb the horror of what could now ensue. 'Don't hurt me. Please.'

'I ain' goin' hurt you, baby,' he says. 'Jus' givin' you a little *lagniappe* to take home with you. We good like that in New Orleans.'

He picks up a long wire from beside the tin candleholder and holds it in the flame. '*Lagniappe* jus' somethin' for nothin', baby, jus' somethin' for nothin'.'

'Please don't,' I say, as the glowing tip of the wire is coming at me, but he laughs, and I hear my skin sizzle as he fries an agonising pattern onto my shoulder. The stench of my own flesh burning makes me gag, and the stench of my own terror makes me piss myself.

Almost immediately Prince gets off the mattress and throws me my clothes.

'There a basin and soap over there so you can wash up.'

'Thanks,' I manage, assuming it best not to appear ungrateful.

'That Lullaby goin' wear off in jus' a little while, baby,' he says, blowing the candle out, throwing the room back into darkness, 'and then things is really goin' start happenin'.' He pauses briefly at the door before leaving. '*Au revoir, Mademoiselle* Delacross.'

After I hear the last of his footsteps on the stairs it seems to take ages before I can move again, and feel around for the matches to relight the candle. My thighs are wet with rapidly cooling urine, so I stagger over to the tin basin of water on the floor of a mildewy, dark corner and clean myself up as best I can with the sliver of soap. Still drugged, I find dressing a confusing, uncooperative conflict between brain and body, and I struggle to get my jeans over my head for minutes before I realise what's wrong. Finally I pull my sweater and shoes on, and stumble down the stairs into the Quarter, running smack bang into Mozzie as I hit the sidewalk.

He takes one looks at my dishevelled appearance and says, 'Did you just get laid? Have I been waiting here for over an hour so you could get laid?'

'Did you see a big black guy come out of here?'

'No,' he says, offering me a hand up off the sidewalk.

'Dressed like Captain Scarlet?'

'Still no.'

'Wearing a Saddam Hussein mask?'

'How am I not making myself clear?'

I turn and lift my sweater to show him the burn. 'Look — some fucking weirdo just burned me.' Unfortunately, in doing so I also expose my breasts to a group of men masquerading unflatteringly as Swan Lake, who make a series of lewd suggestions, all of which involve no fewer than three people and some kind of sex toy.

Mozzie pokes the burn, which is too numbed by alcohol to feel like much more than a throb. 'What the hell have you been up to?'

'What the hell *is* it?'

'It's a flower — no, a *fleur-de-lis*, maybe. It's quite cool, really, mate. Where did you get it done? I might get a *Playboy* bunny while I'm here.'

'Cool, my arse,' I say, dropping my sweater again. 'Some wacko drugged me in the Monteleone and *completely* against my will carried me to the room at the top of those stairs there, and — what?'

Mozzie has been nodding his head for some time, as though receiving confirmation of something disappointing but inevitable. 'I think you better lay off the sauce for a while.'

'It's true,' I tell him.

'Come on,' he says, taking my elbow. 'Let's get something to eat. Maybe you'll sober up.'

'Where's the Idaho boys?' I ask, struggling to match his pace.

'Where *are* the Idaho boys.'

'If it makes you happy.'

'They got bored waiting. So did I, but I thought it best to have photographs that augment my impressions.' Mozzie comes to a standstill and raps me on the forehead with his knuckles. 'For — *hello* — continuity.'

We buy lucky dogs off a street vendor and get most of the ketchup and mustard jostled all over us as we fight our way through the Quarter and enter the first bar we come to on St Ann Street. It's chock-a-block with drag queens batting trowelled-on eye make-up at huge guys in leather who look like they haven't showered for months. When a guy who's easily as good-looking as Viggo Mortensen finishes stripping on the pool table, we start a doubles game with a straight couple from Nebraska, Carly and Bill, who seem to be wondering what the hell they were thinking coming to New Orleans for Mardi Gras. She's all pastel make-up and neutral-coloured, natural-fibre clothing, and he's dressed like he's never been out-of-state before. Mozzie is perfectly charming to them considering the middle-America material he has to work with. Bill loosens up after a few beers courtesy of Mozzie, but Carly's inherent Presbyterianism seems to be exacerbated by alcohol and she becomes stiffer and more brittle by the second. Bill, a goofy, good-time smile on his face, slaps her playfully on the back and tells her to relax. 'Come on, honey. We came here to have fun, didn't we? Chill out a little.'

She's not pleased: a look like that can kill.

Mozzie goes off to buy more drinks — non-alcoholic for me — and I ignore Carly and Bill who are bickering about problems they brought with them from home. When Bill downs the beer Mozzie brings back for him, Carly stomps off to the toilet, slamming the door hard enough for everyone in the bar to look over. Someone yells, 'Pussy-whipped!' and lobs a beer bomb, which hits me full in the face and drenches my hair and sweater. Just as Bill is trying to pat me dry with his bare hands, Carly exits the toilet and lunges at me like it's my fault her husband's an idiot.

The cops turn up just as I've got her in a self-defence headlock and Bill starts yelling that I started the fight, so it's me the cops drag outside. It's pandemonium out on the street, with everybody shouting and cheering and the cops using way more force than is necessary considering I'm not putting up much resistance. When one of the cops rips my sweater off, straight away I catch sight of that bastard Mozzie literally wetting himself with mirth. Then I'm topless, handcuffed, and in the back of a New Orleans police car.

CHAPTER 2

IT HARD TO read Angélique's writing, and not just because of the paper being all old and fade don't help none. It hard to read because it wrote in French. Had Jolie go shoplift a French dictionary seeing as she so good at it and it ain' like we got the money to go waste on no books. I been through a word at a time since I dig that damn journal up, waiting until the kids sleeping so they don't know what going on. Sometime I just plain cain' read Angélique's handwriting, though there a lot of words I cain' get because the dictionary don't see fit to tell me. Sometime her choice of words don't make no sense, like *because for what?* instead of just plain old *why?*, so I just guessing at a lot of what she saying. The edges crumbling away and the last few pages so stain I cain' read them, and damn if they ain' the most important ones with the actual whereabouts of the gold.

Cain' make up my mind where to start telling about the journal — how I know it in the flower bed out the front of the Phoenix Motel in the first place, or how a whole bunch of gold hidden somewhere in Saint-Domingue that rightfully mine. Seem to me I best off starting with my mama because she the first one to be telling me about unnatural goings on, and I sure wouldn't bother with reading some filthy-ass old journal in a language I didn't understand less I had a damn good reason to go to all the effort involve.

My mama's name was Bella and she born right here in St Luc Parish, August 15, 1942. Well that not entirely true. She was found on the steps front of St Joseph's Convent other side of the bayou when she just a newborn baby no more than a few hours old. The sisters at St Joseph's raise her up until she make eighteen, then she got a option of joining them or staying they maid, and Mama decide she ain' going be nobody's help no more. She decide she going be a sister and spend some time as a apprentice.

But the very night she marry God, she get herself a honeymoon visit from a god she ain' expecting. Nuh-uh. She tell me a color man dress all in red wearing a mask so she cain' see his face turn up in her room and scare the hell out of her. She hollering away expecting the other sisters going come run in the room and save her, but the man say they cain' hear her so she wasting her breath. Mama say his voice make her legs go weak on her, and next thing he stroking on her and kissing on her and he taking her nightgown off and she ain' fighting him none because she say nothing ever felt so good before then or since. She ask for his name afterward, and he say, Prince le Kreyol, and he wanting a child from her because it be old Guinea magic settling a score. Mama ask when he coming back because she just have herself the best night of her entire life and she plan on repeating it a bunch, but Prince say he done what he came to do and it didn't matter what potions she drank, she going have a baby girl nine months from now.

Mama didn't leave St Joseph's in the morning like you expect, nuh-uh. In the cold light of day she think she just have a sexy dream, so she carry on praying and counting rosaries and lighting candles and what-have-you it is sisters keep themselves busy with. She keep on believing Prince le Kreyol was just a dream right up until she have to leave St Joseph's in a hurry because the other sisters notice she got a baby on the way and they all yelling biblical insults at her.

Mama a fine-looking woman back then, and in no time she had herself a job waiting tables in a color roadhouse out by the oil refineries at St Luc. Even while she pregnant Mama got a bunch of men hitting on her. One man came in every day for two months to ask her on a date, and eventually she agree to go out with him because he seem like the kind, quiet type, with good manners. She soon find out he make her laugh and he don't mind the fact of me on the way. Mama not stupid about what her life going be like as a unmarry color mother, so she count her blessings and go jump the broom with him a few months after I come by and she can fit into a wedding dress.

I wish I could say they love story had a happy ending, but Mama so disappoint with her new husband on they wedding night she up and move back to St Luc first thing in the morning. Mama say Prince le Kreyol ruin her for life, showing her heaven like that, because she never found a man afterward could even lift her off the ground.

Mama just shy of making twenty-two when she go back to St Luc, and times even harder back then than they is now for a color woman with a baby and no husband to show for it. She smart enough to keep her wedding band on her finger though, and she take to wearing widow's weeds, telling everybody her husband die on a oil rig. She moving back home with her little orphan baby see if she cain' get herself a job and someplace to live. Somebody take pity and give her a job at the new grocery store just open and the owner got some rooms out back he let Mama have for cheap. She allow to keep me in the store with her long as I don't eat nothing she don't pay for.

Times was good for a while but after a few years Mama get a itch need scratching, and every last one of them good-for-nothing bums she drag home don't do nothing but leave her so frustrate she screaming like a demon on the inside. Harder she try scratch her itch, the more it burn, and more she develop a taste for liquor from hanging around with white trash wanting themselves cheap pussy that they ain' too picky about.

They liquor ain' never enough to calm the itching though, so she start sneaking it from the store. Soon the owner start to hear things about her too and he notice his liquor going missing. He don't want no thieving nigger whore running his store so after he give her a beating, he fire her, and we back out on the street again.

Now I ain' saying mine was the worst childhood a child ever had to suffer but it sure could have been a bunch easier. Thanks to my mama, there ain' a damn thing can go in no place a man and a woman got, in any position you care to think about, that I don't know about. Saw everything in them two little rooms out back of the store, and I ain' never took up much interest with sex myself because of it. Seem to me it just a whole bunch of undignify groaning and sweating and a baby you cain' afford at the end of it. I sure would pay a lot of money to forget some of the things I seen Mama do trying to relive that one night at St Joseph's with my daddy.

Now Mama cain' get no job because everybody know she trouble and to watch out for her. She get by selling her ass on the street but she ain' happy and seem like she getting meaner and meaner every day. She getting dirtier and uglier too because we living rough and not eating right and her boyfriends starting to expect it for free like they doing her a favor fucking her up against walls stinking of they urine. One day a white lady from the church come right up while we setting out in La Salle Square, and she recall Mama from when she was at St Joseph's.

'Sister Poupet,' that white lady say to Mama, 'you ought to be ashamed of yourself neglecting a child like that. It's not as if you haven't fallen far enough from grace already.' That white lady tell Mama she got exactly a week to get her shit sort out or she going tell the authorities about us to take me away. That a slap in the face to Mama, possibility losing her kid like that, and she swear right there and then she ain' never going so much as go near another man or his liquor again. She beg the white lady to help out, and the church get us on welfare and into a brand-new trailer-home they rent out cheap to poor families, and finally I get to go to school at age twelve. All the other kids thinking I's dumb because I cain' read yet like they can but, nuh-uh. I was catch up and outsmarting them inside of three months.

It sure a fine church trailer me and Mama living in back then, everything spotless shiny new. We thought we's living in a palace. Never thought the arrangement be a permanent one though and I still going be living in the damn thing some twenty-six years later. The church put the trailer on blocks when the springs rust through and they understand I ain' moving no place else because of it. One time they even go build me a porch so I can set outside on a nice evening but they didn't think to enclose it, so soon as the sun go down anybody setting out there is eaten alive.

This trailer the first time me and Mama got a front door to call our own and ain' nobody coming in less we want them to, which we had occasion to be grateful for a whole bunch more than once. Mama still getting her urges but she know the church going be watching and making sure she don't sin against God a second time. She start making moonshine in the trailer and drinking it in secret so she drown out the hunger for a man ain' never going show up. I don't know if the first bunch of liquor ready in three weeks or not, but twenty-one days exactly is how long it take her to start drinking and never stop. And when she start drinking again is when she lock the door and draw the blinds, and when she start telling me about how Prince le Kreyol is my daddy and how I special like Jesus.

Back then, far as I concern — right up to when Prince le Kreyol show up in the trailer on the fifteen-year anniversary of when her liver quit working — she just take a little too much of the communion wine at St Joseph's and her mind so steep in liquor it confuse the janitor with a religious experience. I use to think, 'Some mysterious god going call on her, my ass.' Mama never *that* good-looking even before she a mean old drunk.

'YOU OKAY THERE, darlin'?' a woman with horrible perfume and a black eye asks. 'You were screaming.'

I groan when I realise I'm wearing orange prison overalls — OPP stencilled across the front — and I didn't just pass out in a bus station.

'Aw,' the woman says sympathetically, her breath a blast of bourbon. 'Looks to me like you been drinking too many Hand Grenades down in the Quarter, huh? Them things is lethal. The tourist board got a responsibility to let people know about them. They oughta carry a health warning, amount a people I see just about kill themselves on the damn things.'

Between waves of nausea I hear some commotion with keys and sensible shoes, and next thing some female guards either side of me are saying, 'Come with us, please, Ma'am,' and dragging me up off the bench towards the door.

My extensive bruising reminds me of what I'm in prison for — oh, God, fighting with the police as well as with Carly — and the events of yesterday bloom wide open in my memory via a sequence of painfully acute recollections, not the least of which is arriving here with a blanket over my head. Fingerprinting and mug shots aside, the most startling incident of all is Prince le Kreyol burning me. And the lying, stealing bastard must have seen the *Property of Laura Delacross* tag on my camera, because he knew my surname and I sure as hell didn't give it to him.

'In here, Ma'am,' one of the guards says, and I'm led into a room that contains a table and several AA-meeting-looking chairs, some guy with alligator accessories he probably killed for in the swamps, and Mozzie.

Mozzie grins. 'And how have you enjoyed the hospitality of the Orleans Parish Criminal Sheriff's Office Intake and Processing Center?' he says.

I look beyond him to the sight of my bleary-eyed, puffy-headed reflection in the two-way mirror. I'll need a twelve-hour uninterrupted coma just to look my age again. 'How much do you think I enjoyed it, idiot?'

From the expression on his face, I know he can't wait for what he is about to tell me next. He knows I know it, too. 'You made the news, mate,' he gloats. 'Most of Louisiana had the privilege of seeing your pixellated bazookas on prime time.'

'When I get out of here I'm going to kill you,' I tell him, sitting with some relief on one of the chairs.

'As these lovely ladies of the law are my witness,' he smiles.

I look at the prettier of the two guards — sheriff deputies if their badges are any indication — he's referring to. She has a brutal perm, no neck and an ATM slot of a mouth. 'How come he's here? What's going on?' I ask her.

'We're releasing you, Ma'am. You're in here on wrongful arrest. These two gentlemen took the security film from that bar you in on St Ann Street in front of Judge Bronner. Seems like the fight ain't your fault, so he signed your release papers. We're letting you out. Sorry for the inconvenience.' She hands me a pen and asks me to sign the release form on the table.

'What if I refuse?'

'Then we going to book you on resisting arrest.'

'Okay,' I say, signing with a flourish.

'I'll go fetch your belongings,' she says after I give her the pen back. 'You care for a shower before you go?'

Visualising a garden-hose-like stream of cold water, cracked dirty soap and concrete that smells of disinfectant, I decline. She returns in minutes with my clothes and shoes. My sweater is in tatters and God only knows where my bra is.

'Get real,' Mozzie snorts, when I look at him. 'This is Ralph Lauren. No way.'

'Here, take this, you,' Alligator Dundee says, removing his hat to reveal a head of thick dark-blond hair. *Take dis.* He unbuttons and shrugs off his shirt to reveal some nicely arranged meat on his bones, and he goes to the bother of pulling the inside-out arms back through the armholes of the shirt before handing it to me.

'Won't you be cold?' I ask, taking the shirt from him.

'*Mais*, I'll probably freeze my ass off,' he says, 'but I won't be able to drive with you half-naked in my truck.'

There's a laid-back-as-hellness about him I immediately like. His shirt smells nice too.

Hoover, Little Sammy and Whitney all spoon up like the last three Little Injuns on the sofa bed out in the lounge. I been lying wide awake for hours in my room listening to Jolie tossing and turning in hers, and sure enough I eventually hear her sneaking out. I been in this trailer so long I know exactly where she putting her feet from the creaks. Through my drapes I watch the glow of the pipe she sucking on before I get up out my cot and put a robe on, and tiptoes over to the front door so she don't know I coming after her. She jump just about twenty-something feet in the air when she see me, then she try to wave the smoke away like it don't reek of burning shit out here with not a breath of wind.

I try not to be accusing. 'Where the brains you was born with, fool, smoking that shit?' It cold enough out here to make my breath puff out in clouds as thick as her smoke.

It take her a couple seconds to recuperate herself, then she back with that mouth of hers. 'Well, at least they ain' drownin' in the bottom of a Colt 45. Here,' she say, offering me the damn pipe, 'why don't you try some? Might change your life.' Her voice ain' got no hopefulness at all, and when she laugh and take another draw just to spite me I get scare and slap her, because sooner or later I going lose her to drugs and I don't know how else to stop her. She drop the pipe and just about cough her lungs out through her mouth. I ain' never seen my child look so ugly as she does right at this second with her drug-dumb eyes and drool hanging from her mouth. She make to pick the pipe up again.

'Oh, no you don't,' I warn, kicking it the hell out her reach. 'You got two babies in there you oughta start bein' a mother to, instead of a crack-whore.'

'I ain' a whore,' she inform me, like she wouldn't even care none if she was.

'No? How you affordin' it then?'

'Let's just say I's in the loop,' she laugh, but there ain' no humor in it. Then her eyes all glassy and black like she imagining the worse thing that could happen. 'Them babies better off without me.'

Lord, but I slap her again just to stop her talking. 'You want another one? You want me to smack you again? Well, you just carry on with that self-pityin' shit and I goin' damn sure oblige you.' The babies start up inside the trailer because all the hollering going on is scaring them, so I drop my voice. 'I brought you up to know better than sneakin' out at night so you can kill yourself with drugs and leave your orphan babies for me to take care of. Nuh-uh. You got that all wrong, girl. And look how mean you gettin'. You ain' exactly givin' any love out to the world.'

Her bottom lip start quivering then just like it always done since she a baby and about to cry and I suppose to make things better. One of her tears run hot and wet over the back of my hand as I stroke her cheek where I smack it before. 'I don't know how to quit, Mama,' she say, all soft like she use to talk. 'There jus' never seem enough reason to.'

'Sugar, your babies ain' enough reason?'

She quit with the crocodile tears then and pull away, curling her lip at me like I some kind of hypocrite. 'You right, Mama. I swear to God I goin' switch to drinkin' beer ever' night of the week. Get drunk instead. What you think?'

'You ever go hungry?' I say, but she got me going on a guilt trip already, damn her. 'You ever go without shoes on your feet?'

'*FUCK SHOES*!'

She scream that last part at me with all her might, and her hollering set dogs off even outside the immediate neighborhood. Right there and then, feeling bruise from the wrath of a child who hate me just for having her in the first place, I decide to get the ball rolling before my children ruin themselves with drugs and resentment. Hoover due to start high school in the fall and then it only a matter of time before he make Jolie seem like a angel in comparison.

'I plan on changin' that,' I tell her.

'Huh?' she say, wary 'cause she ain' sure if I kicking her out.

'You know how to hot-wire a car?'

Might as well be asking if she know how to make a phone call the look she give me.

'You drive too?' I ask her.

'Enough.'

'Well, go get something nice,' I tell her, 'then call back here and pick me up when you're done. We got some business in New Orleans to take care of.'

CHAPTER 3

ALLIGATOR DUNDEE'S TRUCK is the size of an armoured personnel-carrier, and takes up nearly three parking spaces. Even with three adults and his weird-looking dog sitting up front, there's still room for one more. The dog has long ears, tight curly orange fur and happy but droopy eyes. It decides it wants to sit next to me and pants whatever it last ate — probably reptile jerky — in my face. The truck starts up with an earthquake-like rumble and Alligator Dundee pulls out onto the deserted street. He notices me shivering and turns the heater to high, then leans forward so he can see around Mozzie and the dog. 'Where's your hotel at?' he asks. He has very light grey-green eyes and is blond in a weathered autumnal way — not precision-cut and Nordic like Mozzie — the russet stubble on his face complemented nicely by a permanent tan. The corners of his mouth and lines around his eyes betray him as someone who does a lot of smiling and squinting in the sun.

'Hotel,' I laugh, mostly to myself. 'I wish. Just drive down

Airline Highway until you see the Gulag about five blocks down from the overpass.'

'Why don't you stay with me at the Monteleone?' Mozzie says.

'Because I'd rather move back home with my parents, *pregnant*,' I tell him.

The dog settles across my lap. It must weigh fifty kilos.

'Suit yourself,' he says. 'Elizabeth booked me into a suite. If I'd known she was going to I'd have offered sooner.'

'A suite at the Monteleone?' Alligator Dundee whistles, checking the rearview mirror as he changes lanes. '*Mais*, you must be some good writer, you, for Elizabeth to spend all those *beaucoup* bucks.'

Finally his presence makes sense. 'Are you that Simon guy?' I ask him.

He takes one hand off the steering wheel and offers it to me with a genuine, easy smile. 'Floyd Simeon — at your service, Ma'am. And that dog there making himself comfortable with you, he goes by the name of Genius.'

Genius wags his tail at the mention. Floyd has a good confident handshake: manly without being frightened of hurting me. His slow, amused Southern accent is tinged with something distinctly regional. '*Mais*, that damn dog smart enough to join the Spanish Army since they drop their IQ requirement. I printed the entry test off the Internet, me, and offered him a yes-no option to each question. One bark for yes, two barks for no. One hundred percent correct that dog get. The Spanish Army would enlist him as an officer. Go on, ask him anything you want.' *Anysin*.

Mozzie rolls his eyes and sighs rudely.

'Get out of here,' I tell Floyd, smiling so he knows I know I'm being had but I'm prepared to go along with it.

'*Mais*, you get out of here,' he says, pretend serious. 'If that dog got lost he could write his own registration number in the dirt, then just sit down and wait for the dog-catcher. Go on, ask him something.'

'Ask it to clean its teeth,' Mozzie says.

'Hey, Genius,' I call, to get the dog's attention, and he looks up at me with the same good-natured gaze as his owner, except more alert, maybe. 'Is Michael Jackson a sausage short of a link?'

The dog barks a warm, possible digestion-problem *yes* into my face.

'Not bad,' I nod at Floyd.

'I told you,' he smiles. 'That's one smart dog, him. Try something harder.'

'Okay then, let's try a geography question. Genius — your starter for ten: is Helsinki the capital of France?'

Genius barks twice.

'*Mais*, you're even not trying, you,' Floyd says. 'That dog knows the brand name of every dog food in America. He can spell them backwards, him.'

If Floyd didn't dress like he wasn't just about to jump off the boat and fight something, he would be seriously hot.

'Jesus Christ,' Mozzie mutters.

'You try spelling Eukanuba backwards,' I tell him.

'The dog,' Mozzie sighs, 'is just listening for clues in the tone of your voice that you're too stupid even to know you're doing. He *wants* to please you. It's what dogs do to make sure you keep feeding them.'

'Genius?' I coo, cupping the dog's face with my hands. 'Is Mozzie a big annoying bad-tempered bastard?'

Genius barks once and Floyd fights a grin, turning away so Mozzie can't see.

'Who's a clever doggy woggy then?' I say, patting the dog's head.

'Could you people mangle the English language any more?'

Mozzie says, dropping his head into his hands. 'Please, stop talking. You're giving me a headache. And you,' he says to me, 'have a breath mint, for Christsakes. You smell like a wino.'

Floyd winks conspiratorially at me and tunes the radio in to some hideous, fiddle-twanging Cajun music.

'I hope the headache's something inoperable,' I tell Mozzie, and wind down the window because it's now too hot.

The conversation doesn't pick up again so I just stare outside, grateful for the silence. I wish I had my camera so I could take shots of the trees, top-heavy with strings of Mardi Gras beads, along the parade routes, and the sheer tonnage of discarded plastic and paper lying on the streets. Small armies of cleaners are working away in the drizzling, cold dawn, piling up bags of trash on the sidewalks for the trucks to take away before the tourists wake up and begin another assault on the city.

Out the front of the motel there's a homeless person with a plastic bin liner over his head taking a dump in the bushes under the motel sign. The truck's headlights illuminate him perfectly. We watch him run down the street, trying to pull his pants up.

'Looks like to me,' Floyd says, ' you don't want to look a gift horse in the mouth.'

'Give me five minutes to get my stuff together.'

JOLIE ARRIVE BACK less than a hour later, chewing like crazy on some gum, and with a shiny-ass SUV that no more been off road than my trailer. The twins ain' quit screaming since she left and they show every sign of continuing on if she leave again. Hoover refusing to be left behind on his own, too, so I agree to let them ride along. They all squish up asleep together by the time we hit the I10 heading to Baton Rouge. The SUV got a furry-ass object hanging from the interior mirror smell like something for cleaning your bathroom with, so I toss it out the window. Jolie go through all the CDs in the glovebox until she give up in disgust and find some of that hip-hop music she like on the radio. She take a quick look back over her shoulder to make sure the twins is okay.

'You plan on tellin' me what we's up to now?' she ask me, when she looking straight ahead at the road again. She a bit wobbly on the steering now we doing seventy.

'Nuh-uh.'

She look over at me, frowning.

'Keep your eyes on the road, baby.

'Nuh-uh?'

'You goin' think your mama is crazy if I tell you.'

She swerve over a lane, and the SUV start slowing down. 'I got news for you,' she say, pulling over to the side of the highway.

'Aw, Jesus. Don't tell me we run out of gas already.'

'No, we got plenty gas,' she say. 'I just ain' drivin' a inch further till I know why we driving down to New Orleans in the middle of the night.' She fold her arms across her chest, determine to wait me out. It so late at night only the big trucks going, and they tailwinds shaking the SUV around like a hurricane.

I ain' never learn to drive a car or possess the first clue how to start one up, so she got me over a barrel. 'Okay,' I agree. 'I tell you what you need to know when this vehicle is movin' again.'

'Okay,' she say, turning the ignition over. 'Start talkin', crazy lady.'

She go pulling back out into traffic then and nearly get us kill by a damn police car of all things. Less than a couple inches is all between a lucky escape and a tragedy. The car flash its lights and turn on the siren. Jolie know to pull up behind and not go on no high-speed car chase. 'Crap,' she say, as a policeman come toward us with a flashlight. 'What we goin' do now?'

I turn around and look at Hoover. He setting there wide awake but struck dumb by the turn events is taking. 'Smack the babies,' I hiss at him.

'What?' he ask like he ain' hearing me right.

'Smack the babies. Quick, before that policeman get here.'

'I ain' smackin' them,' he say, outrage by the idea.

Thank God one of my children got the brains they born with though. Jolie catch on to my idea and she unhook her seat belt to smack the babies herself. The slaps sound like gunshots going off in this confine space. The twins start screaming because they ain' done nothing wrong, and by the time the policeman knocking on the window they howling fit to burst.

The policeman shine his flashlight round the interior before he beam it right in Jolie's face, just about blinding her. He mime her having to roll the window down, and then he frowning at the volume of the babies' hollering when she does what she told. 'You got your driver's license and registration, Ma'am?' he holler to make himself heard.

Jolie start lying as easily as her daddy, making me think it genetic. 'Sir, my babies sick and I rushin' them to they pediatrician. I ain' thinkin' straight and I left home with nothing but my keys on me. I just had to pull over before because I thought one of them was dyin' back there. You goin' arrest me?' Butter would freeze in her mouth.

The twins screaming like devils now they so piss with Jolie smacking them for nothing other than just sleeping quietly.

'Aw, no, I'm sorry, Ma'am,' the policeman say, stepping aside. 'You want me to escort you there?'

'That sure is kind of you, sir,' she tell him, 'but I don't want to cause you no bother. I know the way to the hospital with my eyes close, so I just as soon not waste your time. I know how busy you

37

must be, and I mean — ' she smile, jerking a thumb behind herself — 'you can hear for yourself they both plenty alive right now.'

The policeman seem kind of disappoint we don't need him but he lets us go about our business with no further interference other than telling us to take more care driving. The first twenty minutes I spend trying to get the twins back to sleep. Poor kids too scare to in case they get smack again, but Hoover sleeping too by the time we exit Baton Rouge and no more than a couple hours from New Orleans at most.

When the traffic thin out again and Jolie don't have to concentrate so hard, she say, 'Well? You goin' tell me why we headin' down to New Orleans?' Her face is lit up by the headlights of a oncoming vehicle and I see she just as nervous as me. And she ain' even got a clue what coming yet.

'Mind your grandmammy?'

'Mind her? That mean old bitch is my earliest memory. She smack me six ways to hell every chance she got.'

'Know she use be a sister at St Joseph's?'

Jolie's jaw drop open and she lose her gum. 'Huh?' Then she laugh her head off. 'Grandmammy a sister at St Joseph's? Hell, they must have been desperate or somethin'. I thought sisters suppose be nice people.'

'It ever occur to you she might have been at one time?'

'Not even for a second.'

'Well, she was,' I say firmly, leaving no doubt as to the truth.

Jolie pick her gum out her lap and start chewing on it again. We ain' been receiving no clear signals on the radio for a while so she turn it off. 'So what happen?'

'What happen is she met my daddy.'

Jolie look over at me wide eyed because she ain' never heard talk of my daddy before now. 'You know who he is? You meet him?'

'Just the one time.'

'Did he beat her? Is that why she so piss all the time — because of him?'

'Hardly. She only meet him the one time herself.'

'She was rape?'

'No, she wasn't rape,' I say, slapping Jolie's leg. 'She was — *seduce*.'

'And bein' charitable Christian women, St Joseph's go throw her out when she got knock up with you.'

The thing I admire the most about Jolie is her mind always one step ahead of everybody else, but the thing making me the saddest is she trying her damn hardest to bring it back into line.

'Yeah, well, you know. You cain' blame them — a pregnant bride of God ain' exactly a good look for a convent.'

'So when did you meet him?'

'About a year ago. He show up at the trailer one night while y'all sleepin'. He dress the same way as Mama describe him to me — that how I know he was my daddy.'

Jolie shake her head. 'Mama — you didn't think to wake nobody up and let them know they granddaddy was in the trailer?'

'Sorry, baby, I didn't get no chance to. One second he in the trailer, the next he — poof — gone.'

We just pass through Ascension, which make us about almost there.

'You don't think that was a little strange?' Jolie ask.

'Strange? Well, let me see. A man I never saw before, dress like a lunatic, show up in the trailer without me hearin' him comin', and I wake up to find him setting on my cot in the middle of the night. Course I thought it a little strange. Had to change my sheets afterward.'

'*Exactly* what night he show up?' Jolie say. The wheels

39

turning in her head trying to figure things out like always.

'Last summer. On the anniversary of when your grandmammy die.'

'That the day you was drinkin' beer from when you wake up in the mornin' until you pass out in the evenin'?'

'I cain' grieve on the day my mama die?'

'She die sixteen years ago. Get over it.'

'See how you get over it when I die,' I tell her. 'You never get over losin' your mama, no matter how bad she was.'

Jolie crack her gum in reply and don't talk for a while. Then she say, 'What you and your daddy talk about?'

'He the one do all the talkin'. I woke up with his hand over my mouth and him tellin' me to go dig some journal up.'

'What journal?'

'The one I found where he told me I would.'

'Why ain' I seen it?'

'Because I been hidin' it from y'all while I finish translatin' it.'

'So that the reason you had me go steal you a French diction-ary,' Jolie say, nodding to herself. 'The journal in French, ain' it?'

I smile at her. 'You should be a detective, baby.'

'Who wrote it?'

'Let me see — your great-great-great-great-somethin' like that grandmammy.'

'What she have to say?'

'That we goin' be rich.'

Jolie laugh. 'Is that right? What? We goin' win the lottery or somethin'? Some rich-ass relative we never heard of goin' die and leave us they fortune? Your daddy die? Is that it?'

'Nuh-uh. It a bit more complicate than that.'

'Is that why we goin' down to New Orleans for? To get rich?'

'We goin' down find that girl on the news last night.'

'What girl?'

'The one they arrest down in the Quarter.'

'Why her?'

'Because of that *fleur-de-lis* she got. The damn thing is a sign from the journal.'

'A *fleur-de*-what?'

'The brandin'. On her shoulder. You saw it too.'

'Yeah, for a second,' Jolie say, sounding exasperate. 'Same as you. And anyhow, brandin' is big at the moment. Everybody havin' it done. Probably just a coincidence.'

'Nuh-uh. I know she descend from Captain De la Croix.'

'Captain who?'

'De la Croix,' I tell her again. 'He the man that take our ancestors from Africa. And that girl some kind of clue to findin' a fortune belong to us.'

Jolie shakes her head. 'You don't even know where it is?'

'Not exactly. I got a pretty close idea though.' I'd have a better one if I could even find Saint-Domingue on a map.

Jolie quiet for about five minutes and eventually when I cain' stand the silence no more I ask, 'So, you goin' help me or what?'

'Still drivin' ain' I?' she shrug. 'But how we goin' find that girl in the middle of New Orleans durin' Mardi Gras with a million extra people down there?'

JOLIE ALREADY KNOW her way to the Intake Center on account of some of her ex-boyfriends spending time there. We park on Perdido Street opposite the prison about three in the morning, and I keep an eye on the front of the building while Jolie and the kids get some sleep. Must be around five when some big-ass old swamp-cracker truck pull up and two detectives get out. The driver upstate Cajun by the look of him, and the other one dress like a Miami drug

41

dealer. A couple hours later they come back out with the girl I see on the news. She wearing the Cajun's shirt now and him with just a vest on in this weather.

'What you pokin' at me for?' Jolie grumble.

'That the girl. That her. Take a look.'

'You sure?' Jolie ask, adjusting her seat upright again.

'Only one way to find out,' I say, as the three of them take off in that big-ass truck. 'Reckon you can tail them?'

Jolie prove to be a natural at it, and she hide the SUV down a side road one block down from where the truck pull into some run-down motel look like the sort Jimmy Swaggart use to spend some of his leisure time in. When they rolling again we follow them into the Quarter, until the truck disappear into the Monteleone's parking facilities on Bienville. We drive around until we find a meter close by with some credit left on it.

'What we goin' do now?' Jolie ask, killing the engine.

'Well, Hoover and the babies goin' stay right here,' I say, handing over a twenty-dollar bill, 'and you goin' to buy some *beignets* and Cokes for everybody's breakfast.'

She ask, 'Where you goin'?'

I pull the switchblade out my bra that get me my own way on a number of occasions. 'To find that girl. Like I came here to do.'

THE BACK OF the Monteleone mostly got color people working, so nobody pay me no mind. I locate the laundry and find me a maid outfit that don't fit by about two sizes too small. Somebody leave a cleaning trolley lying around with a security pass attach to it and I's polishing a big mirror in the lobby when the girl and the detectives take a elevator to the ninth floor. I push the trolley into the elevator when it comes by again and listens by all the doors on the ninth floor until I hear them talking. The detectives decide they going get themselves some breakfast down in the restaurant but the girl staying behind in the suite and ordering room service. I hide in the linen closet until they gone, then let myself in with the security pass. The place is cram with antique furniture and big luxury-ass sofas. The coffee table must be a couple hundred years old and they got a vase of flowers sittin' right on it with no coaster. The shower going in one of the bathrooms, so I sit down on the bed that fit for a queen outside, and eat the fancy chocolates on the pillow while I wait.

MOZZIE'S SUITE IS on the ninth floor, with a good view of the Quarter on one side and a partial view of the Mississippi on the other. A steamboat berthed close by whistles the same shrill, irritating tune over and over. Mozzie throws his jacket into one of the bedrooms, and says, 'Laura, don't even think for a second you're coming down to breakfast with us looking like that. It's embarrassing. Order some room service and do whatever it takes to make you look human again.'

Floyd helps carry my bags through to the other bedroom, then leaves me in privacy while he borrows a sweater from Mozzie, and the two of them head down to the restaurant. I unpack my toiletries and arrange a few clothes on hangers before ordering a tomato juice and cheeseburger from room service, then have a couple of Panadols before hitting the bathroom.

Using the huge wall-mirror to inspect my shoulder, I take a good look at the throbbing *fleur-de-lis* — its three bulbous points traced out in a thin, charred line of flesh — gingerly inspecting the burn for signs of infection. It seems clean enough, but I swab it with an antiseptic pad that hurts like hell. That Prince le Kreyol randomly chose me out of probably a million people to *assault* deeply depresses and unsettles me — I mean, why me? Why not someone else? — as does realising I got off lightly considering I was completely incapacitated by a seriously deranged psycho.

As I'm gently but stiffly patting myself dry after a quick shower and shampoo, I hear someone moving about in the bedroom.

'You guys didn't take long,' I yell through the door.

'Room service, Ma'am,' a woman replies.

'Thanks. Just leave it on the coffee table,' I tell her.

When she doesn't appear to be in a hurry to leave I assume she's hanging around for a tip, and search through my discarded clothing. As I open the door slightly to hand over the five dollars I've found in Floyd's shirt pocket, I'm so surprised to make eye contact with the exact same rare eye colour as my own, it takes a couple of seconds for the knife the slack-jawed black maid is brandishing to register. Then I slam the door shut and wonder how much more insane New Orleans can get.

CHAPTER 4

I SNATCH THAT five dollar off her before she slam the door in my face, then we both quiet for a minute, me just about having a heart attack with realizing she got identical eyes to me and my entire family. Couldn't tell *that* from the TV.

'What do you want?' she holler through the door, trying to sound like a tough-ass.

'I want to talk to you.'

'What about?'

'We got some destiny need figurin' out.'

'I don't even know you,' she say. 'Go away before I call the police.'

'The phone out here in the lounge,' I tell her. 'Come and get it.'

'There's one in here,' she say. 'And if you're not gone in ten seconds I'm calling 911.'

'Good luck, darlin'. I cut the wire.'

'Oh.'

I just about stab myself with my own knife when the intercom buzzer go off, it give me such a scare. Anybody think I was shoplifting it so damn loud and accusing.

'Don't make a sound,' I tell the girl. 'Or it goin' be the last one you ever make.'

The buzzer go off again, so I creep over to the front door and put my eye up to the peephole. A color maid with a tray is waiting outside, looking piss because I taking so long to answer. I press the talk button on the intercom. 'You mind leaving it outside, honey?'

'You got to sign for it, Ma'am,' she say.

'One moment, please,' I say pleasantly as you like. 'I ain' dress yet.' Then I go running through the other rooms till I find a towel and rip the maid outfit off. My bra and panties so worn out they just rags and there ain' no way a maid going believe I belong here with them on show, so I get rid of them. The towel don't quite go all the way round and my bare ass expose for all the world to see.

Just like I plan though, when I open the front door to the maid, that girl come running out her bathroom and she trip on the Bell South directory I leave just outside the bathroom door. Damn thing so thick only way of getting over is by hurdling. I sign the room-service slip, take the tray, give the maid the five dollar as a tip and lock the door again before the girl even hit the floor. Then I toss the tray aside and jump on that girl before she even know what happen to her.

WHEN I HEAR the impostor maid open the front door to the real maid, I make a split-second decision — too linear to be called an escape plan — to run for it, but it all goes horribly wrong. Instead of hurtling to freedom, I trip on something the size of a briefcase just outside the bathroom door and hurtle towards the carpet. Face-down in the pile, heavily winded and groaning with pain, I take a while to realise the impostor maid is sitting astride me *naked*. She pushes my face further into the carpet while she reaches for her knife, then pulls my head up by the roots of my hair so she can hold the blade to my throat. This angle, apart from making my spine feel like it's going to break, and cutting off my oxygen, affords a good view of the blood splattered all over the walls of the lounge. I make an animal noise I didn't know I could do.

'Don't scream,' she tells me.

'Can't breathe,' I gurgle, images of arterial blood spray alternating with spells of dizziness.

The naked maid gets off my back but then quickly crouches in front of me, keeping the knife against my neck. 'Now you get up nice and easy,' she warns, 'or I goin' cut your head off. Don't go gettin' no fool ideas about fightin' with me. I gut you open in a second.'

We rise together, my legs shaking and uncooperatively lead-like, until we're standing face to face, apparently as spooked as each other about our identical eye colour — an orangey gold, which Mozzie reckons is the same colour as bats' eyes — and one I've never seen in another human before. Apparently my birth even caused a rough patch in my parents' marriage when my blue-eyed father doubted for a stupid instant my hazel-eyed mother's absolute fidelity.

'Lose the robe,' the maid tells me after I've got my breath back. She doesn't take her eyes from mine for a second. 'And turn around.' She gets fed up with me fumbling with the belt and tugs it open herself. 'Now lose the robe like I told you,' she says, standing back in all her terrifying, naked glory.

After I shrug the bathrobe to the floor, she tells me to lift my hair off my neck and turn around again. She becomes silent, except for heavy ragged breathing, which I pray to God isn't any indication of mounting sexual excitement. Then she prods my shoulder and demands, 'Where you get the brandin'?'

I flinch away from her and she pulls me back by my hair. 'Ow!'

'You got three seconds before I cut you a new smile,' she says, holding her knife to my throat again.

'Prince le Kreyol did it,' I shriek, and urine runs down my leg for the second consecutive day.

She shoves me away when she realises what the splashing is.

I TELL HER to put the robe back on and fetch me a beer from the mini-bar. 'Get yourself somethin' too,' I say. She hand me a Abita, and she got the shakes so bad I can hardly take the damn thing off her. I so dehydrate from my nerves I finish it before she even got the ring-pull up on her can of 7-UP. 'Prince le Kreyol, huh?'

'Yes,' she nod, all scaredy-eyes. She keep looking between me and the mess on the walls.

'Relax. It just tomato juice.'

She laugh, but stop when she catch my eye and look scare again.

'When you run into him?'

'Yesterday.'

'That before you get your chicken-brain self arrest?'

She nod again. She ain' taken so much as a sip on her drink yet she so scare of me. She perch on the edge of that sofa like a wild animal don't know how to set down properly.

'He say anythin' to you?'

'Not really. Just some stuff about things happening soon.'

'What things?'

'Just — things.' She shrug by way of apology. 'That's the word he used. *Things.*'

Seen enough courtroom TV not to ask a leading question. 'If you had to take a guess at Prince le Kreyol's favorite color, darlin', what would that color be?'

'Red.'

'And can you describe him for me, please.'

'I don't know. He was wearing a mask.'

'Was he color?'

'Red?' she say slowly, somewhere between a question and a answer.

'No, you fool. Was he black, like me?'

'Of course. Black. Sorry. Yes, he was.'

'Well, we definitely talkin' about the same man,' I say, twirling my knife round in one hand while I give myself a second to think.

'So, am I free now?' she ask.

'Hell no, sugar. Fact you ought to go take another shower and put some decent clothes on. You and me is takin' a little trip together.'

I CAN SEE Mozzie and Floyd sitting in the plush seats of the restaurant as the maid guides me out the Monteleone with one arm around my shoulders and her knife in my side. Mozzie is taking notes while Floyd does the talking, a Dictaphone and a couple of empty coffee cups and some plates in front of them. *Please look at me*, I scream on the inside, and Floyd stops mid-sentence, frowning as though he senses something amiss. He actually starts turning in my direction before a waiter turns up to clear their breakfast debris and blocks the sight of me being hustled out of the hotel against my will — my second abduction in as many days.

Keeping her knife in my side, the maid takes a couple of rights and a left on to Chartres, walking what seems like half its length before she pulls me over to a small red Jeep. As soon as she opens the passenger door, an attractive young black girl in a white leather jacket and long matching nails, again with the same orangey gold eyes, says, 'What the hell take you so long? We been waitin' in this vehicle almost a hour for you.'

'Well, you ought to be nice and rest up then, huh?' the maid says.

Then she tells me to get in the back, but I can't work out how to make the passenger seat go forward and she impatiently pushes me aside to do it herself.

'Hoover, get on over the other side,' she says to a teenage boy sitting in the back seat with a couple of toddlers. 'Take one of the twins on your knee so this girl got room to set back there with y'all.'

Again I consider making a break for it, but the maid must have read my mind because she prods me with her knife, and says, 'Nuh-uh. In the back.'

After a bit of reshuffling we all fit in the Jeep and the young girl driving takes off, tearing through the congested streets of New Orleans like a maniac. The rain is persistent and dark, the outside world visible only through the small portal she clears for herself in the breath-misted windscreen. Hoover and the toddlers, a boy and a girl, are staring with huge, astonished eyes, also identical to mine, like they've never seen a white person before. Hoover is wearing a puffed rapper jacket and jeans that reveal the best part of a pair of cartoon boxer shorts. If I catch him staring at me, he looks away and scratches his corn rows in a way that reminds me of Stan Laurel.

'Is that beer I can smell?' the driver asks.

'So what if it is?' the maid says. 'I was thirsty.'

'That why water was invented. You ought to try it sometime.'

'Baby, if I hear another word about beer come out of your junkie-ass mouth, I — hey, look where you goin'!'

The Jeep brakes sharply and I wait for the sickening thud of impact, but there is only the wet shriek of tyres coming to an emergency halt. The driver gesticulates her apologies to someone I can't see and stalls the Jeep a couple of times before we take off again.

'Maybe now,' the maid says, 'you keep your damn eyes on the

road instead of answerin' me back all the time. You only just miss that poor old lady.'

The driver is too shaken to respond and nobody talks for ages, by which time we are long out of the city and all I can see are rain-lashed highways and dense swamps. Strangely, their sheer grey monotony quells my terror somewhat, though God knows the passing country looks good for dumping a body in. I start wiping the condensation from the window beside me so I can read the road signs, but the maid catches me out.

'I see you looking anyplace but the back of my neck,' she tells me, 'I goin' kill you. Understand?'

Her threat shocks everyone into silence, until at last, after what seems like hours, the boy Hoover says, 'I could eat the asshole off a skunk, Mama. When we goin' stop?'

'I could use the bathroom too,' the driver says.

The maid turns around in her seat to smile at the toddlers. 'You two darlin' sweetpeas hungry?'

'Uh huh, Gran'mammy,' they agree.

'Well, okay, then. Let's go find us somethin' good. What about you?' she asks me. 'You want somethin' to eat?'

I'm so ravenous I'd fight Hoover for the skunk.

'Don't try anythin' stupid,' she warns as we pull into a whole village of fast-food places.

We go through three different drive-thrus before everyone has what they want. The cashiers look so bored with their jobs, so over the general public, they couldn't care less if we drove though naked and bleeding. And I'm still not convinced that that's an unlikely scenario. We drive to the back of a deserted car park without a single McEmployee noticing anything strange, and pull up under an oak tree next to a fast-flowing river. I wash down a giant roast-beef-and-gravy roll with a chocolate milkshake, taking cautious sips in case I get the chance to run, while the Jeep's occupants regard me with varying degrees of confusion, anxiety or — in the driver's case — disinterest. The toddlers get covered in honey from their McNuggets, and the maid tells Hoover to take them back into McDonalds and get them cleaned them up. The driver, who seems to be the twins' mother even though she doesn't look old enough to have left school yet, just sips on a Diet Coke, staring sullenly into the relentless rain, gnawing on gum like it was a competition.

'Jolie?' the maid says, to get her attention.

'What?'

'You ready to get movin' again?'

'Sure, Mama. Let me know when you got the horses saddle up.'

The maid shakes her head and sighs. Then she turns to look at me and asks, 'You goin' introduce yourself any time soon?'

'Laura Delacross,' I say, not sure if I'm supposed to shake hands.

'Delacross ain' exactly how I would choose say it. That French, though, right?'

'No idea, sorry.'

The maid's gold eyes are complemented perfectly by cocoa skin, but are wary and tired-looking. She's carrying enough extra weight to make her skin fold over on itself in places like her neck and belly, but the weight lends to her the lush, inviting plumpness of a good couch. Her hair could do with a decent cut, and it wouldn't hurt her to have her eyebrows shaped, but she has an exotic, full mouth and huge cheekbones that mean she'd be beautiful if she made the effort and didn't carry herself like a fifty-year-old. I have to say the family's teeth aren't great by American standards. Even Jolie is missing a side tooth, a gap that adds about a decade to her pretty but sulky-princess face.

'Well, please to meet you anyhow, Laura,' the maid says, like the situation is perfectly normal. 'My name is Renée Poupet and that my eldest daughter, Jolie, doin' the drivin' there.'

Jolie cracks her gum. 'Only daughter, you fruitloop.'

'Don't mind her,' Renée says to me. 'I brought her up with the pigs and she don't know any better.'

'You the pig,' Jolie snorts with a kiss-my-arse tone to her voice, pulling on the door handle and shouldering open the door.

Renée grabs one of Jolie's wrists to prevent her leaving. 'Where you think you goin', baby?'

'I need to use the bathroom. I got to — uh — powder my nose,' she smirks.

'Nuh-uh,' Renée says. 'Set back down, baby. You ain' drivin' while you trash out your head.' *Tray-ash.*

'How you think I was plannin' on stayin' awake?'

I sense some psychological horn-locking going on between them, and it takes Renée a while to disentangle. 'Make that your last time or I goin' make it your last time for you.'

Jolie smiles a victor's taunting grin before she disappears for ten minutes.

Back on the highway, the twins get as far away from me as they can and drop off within minutes. Hoover puts a protective arm around each of them and soon his head lolls forward as he joins them. Soft snoring from Renée indicates that she's fallen asleep too. I surrender to my tiredness and hangover, flaking out with my neck at a right angle.

I WAKE WHEN we pull up outside a rusting, mildew-covered trailer sitting on blocks in the middle of a paddock of waist-high weeds and leafless, drooping trees that have been rendered uniformly grey in the miserable gloom. My neck is killing me.

'How that for timing,' Jolie says, tapping the Jeep's display panel. 'The gas light been on for the last five miles.'

53

'What that on the door?' Renée asks as she undoes her seat belt. It's pelting down outside, and she squints through the rain as though trying to see a celebrity past a crowd.

I briefly glimpse what appears to be a piece of paper thumb-tacked to the trailer door before Jolie turns the wipers off and the windscreen is completely blurred by a torrent of rainwater. 'Look like somebody leave us a message,' she says.

'Who goin' leave us a message? I live in that damn trailer over a quarter century and not once has nobody left me no message on the door.'

'First time for everythin'.'

'Things don't change that suddenly for the best, darlin'.'

'And to think some folks say you ain' a positive influence in our lives, Mama,' Jolie marvels, as Hoover starts passing the twins over. Jolie and Renée take a kid each and bolt for the trailer, leaving the Jeep doors wide open.

I glance over at Hoover, not sure what I'm supposed to do. He smiles sheepishly and scratches his head again. 'Mama won't hurt you,' he says. 'She couldn't even kill the chickens we had one time. Heck, she even had proper Christian funerals for them all when they die of natural causes.'

Although this information doesn't so much comfort me as make me visualise my decomposing body in a chicken cemetery, the sight of the active cellphone sitting snugly in its little plastic car accessory on the dashboard does.

'WHAT THIS SHIT?' I say, ripping a official-looking notice down from the door, disappoint it ain' personal. Only had two hand-written letters my whole life and they just come to the wrong mailbox. Rest all welfare checks, bills and warnings from various government agencies like they ain' got themselves nothing better to do than waste they time and postage on me.

'Move out my way so I can get the door open,' Jolie tell me. 'The babies gettin' soak out here.'

'Listen to this, sugar — the church threatenin' to evict us. Goddamn prayin' motherfuckers turnin' us out in the street. The hell they is. Nuh-uh. I got news for them. They ought to be thankful somebody *willin'* to live in they rusty-ass piece of crap and pay rent for it.'

Jolie roll her eyes and push me aside to unlock the trailer door. 'Well, you ain' been payin' no rent or the church wouldn't have a problem with us, would it?' She put Little Sammy down before taking Whitney off me, who hollering because I holding on to her too tight. 'Now look what you done,' Jolie say.

'Grandmammy's real sorry, darlin',' I say, bending to kiss Whitney's tears away. 'I didn't mean to hurt you none. Here, you smack Grandmammy's hand so you feel better. Go on. Bad Grandmammy. Ow! That hurt, girl. You goin' be *strong* when you grow up.' Whitney happy then, and quit crying, the baby teeth of her smile already letting me know she going be needing dental work later on we cain' afford.

The trailer cold and damp-smelling on the inside, and first thing Jolie do is light the gas heater. It make the lounge seem nice and cozy — inviting, instead of one hundred fifty cubic feet of beat-up charity-shop junk and other folks' throw-outs.

Hoover and the De la Croix girl turn up in the trailer right behind us, and because of the damn wall mirrors it feel like twelve people cram in here now. Hoover go straight to the icebox and help himself to a Coke. 'Mama? Can I play with my Gameboy?' he say.

'Sure, baby. Do me a favor though and play in my room. And shut the door behind you.'

The twins want to play, but Hoover won't let them and they

start yelling they heads off. Hoover stay firm on it though. I think he looking forward to some privacy nobody cain' hardly get in here.

'You babies goin' take a nap,' Jolie tell them. They determine to stay up but she drag them kicking and screaming into her room. 'You okay out here, Mama?' she say before she shut her door.

'Just fine, darlin'.' The white girl ain' looking too fine though. Look worse than a week-old plate of stew need heating up. 'Ain' nothin' to do out here for a while. Get yourself some rest.'

Jolie take another look at the girl. She frowning and I can tell she trying to figure shit out. 'Unplug the phone and give it here for safe keepin',' she say.

'Nice thinkin', baby,' I smile.

RENÉE LOCKS THE trailer door and drops the key in her cleavage. 'You want a beer?' she asks me.

'Have you got something hot?'

'Probably got instant coffee someplace. You take cream?'

'Yes, and sugar, thanks.'

While she searches through her badly organised cupboards for coffee and sugar, I look through the dusty blinds of the kitchen window to the pristine-condition Jeep sitting out in the rain with its doors wide open, the leather upholstery getting soaked. If Renée's trailer is anything to go by, there's no way she can afford to disregard an asset worth hundreds of times the entire contents of her home. The Jeep has to be stolen.

While the water is boiling, Renée pulls the ring off a Colt 45 and gulps the entire contents down. 'Oh, that good,' she burps, and reaches for another can. She wipes a relatively clean mug on a filthy towel to make my coffee, then crosses the trailer and takes a seat in a La-Z-Boy that's seen better days. 'Set down,' she tells me. 'Make yourself at home.'

As I walk over to sit on a low sofa-bed covered with a synthetic throw depicting a peaceful woodland scene with deer and birds, I get a good look at myself in the mirror tiles. In the soft light of the gas heater, my hair looks brunette instead of red, and is obviously averse to Louisiana weather if the afro it's arranged itself in is anything to go by. I haven't had a decent meal in days, and weight is plummeting off me already. Underscored by sagging, dark bags, my eyes are so bloodshot they look like an accident with a pair of scissors. My walk is shuffling and stiff. I look thirty years older.

I groan with both pain and relief as I sink down on the sofa.

'I hear you, honey,' Renée says, extending the footrest of her La-Z-Boy. 'I feel like I been awake for a week I so exhaust from my nerves.'

The La-Z-Boy is right in front of a bay window and I watch an old white lady with a golfing umbrella and about twenty lapdogs of one kind or another go by on the badly maintained dirt road running parallel with Renée's paddock. The dogs are tied to a shopping trolley, which the old lady is utilising as a canine-powered Zimmer frame.

Renée catches me looking, and says, 'That crazy old bitch eat out of other folks' trash cans so she can afford to feed all them dogs. Couldn't give her food poisonin' if you try.'

'Is she homeless?'

'Nuh-uh. She got herself a place her daddy built over by the Injun museum. Everytime a hurricane come in I think that poor neglect house of hers goin' blow over, but it always standin' there the day after.' Renée jumps up suddenly and hammers on the window. 'Get out of my yard, you bastard dogs, before I come out there and kick your hairy little crappin' asses off my property!'

'You know, you probably should hide the Jeep,' I say to her.

Her head swivels in my direction.

I'm reasonably certain now she's not the type to hurt me — in fact she seems intent on making me feel more like her guest than her abductee — but a woman who has threatened you with a knife probably isn't taking her medication and is almost definitely prone to extreme mood-swings. Other than it's got something to do with Prince le Kreyol, I can't even begin to guess what she wants with me, especially as our identical eye-colour is a coincidence she wasn't expecting any more than I was. The cellphone out in the Jeep is my only chance of escape now Jolie has taken the telephone in her room, so I give it my best shot. 'Someone's probably looking for it.'

She stares at me for a few moments, her lips pursed in thought, before she says, 'You right.'

'I'll hide it around the back of the trailer,' I offer, trying to hide my sudden shaking.

'Damn,' she says. 'I goin' have to get wet again.'

Damn, I think, because it hadn't occurred to me that she'd want to come too.

I MAKE THE girl walk ahead of me and we both sitting in the SUV before I allow her to drive it round the back of the trailer and park up nice and private where nobody can see it. When she turn the engine off, I got my door wide open before I think to ask for the keys.

'Catch,' she say, tossing them too hard. The keys go flying out the door and land in a puddle of water.

'Next time just hand them to me,' I tell her, going after them.

'SORRY ABOUT THAT,' I say to Renée when we're back in the trailer. 'Sometimes I just don't know my own strength.'

She locks the door and hides the key on her person again. 'I goin' get me a sweater. Set back down on that sofa and behave yourself. Maybe I fix us somethin' to eat after. There anythin' on TV you like to watch?'

'Sure. Probably.'

She turns the TV on and leaves me with the remote control. I start surfing through channels but as soon as her bedroom door is closed I pull the cellphone from my waistband. I have absolutely no idea what number directory services is, so I go through the cellphone's options until I see the last number dialled — Woody — and call it.

'Yo, Trenyce, baby. Wassup?' Woody sounds like he's talking around a brick.

'Uh, this isn't actually Trenyce,' I whisper, 'and this is going to seem like a strange call, but just let me explain —'

'Where Trenyce at? She okay? What you whisperin' for?'

'She's fine. And I've just got a bit of sore throat.'

'So why you callin' me for?'

'We're at the scene of an accident and Trenyce is taking care of someone, which is why I'm using her phone. We need to contact the injured party's husband and he's staying at the Monteleone down in the French Quarter. You couldn't look the number up for me, could you?'

'Sure. Hold on. No problem — jus' give me a second.'

I hear him flicking through his phone directory before he says, 'Here it is. I got it. 800-MONTELEONE. Can I talk to Trenyce now?'

'Sorry. She can't come to the phone right now. I'll get her to call you back as soon as she can. Bye.'

I quickly dial the Monteleone and ask to be put through to Mozzie's room.

'Hello?' he says.

'Mozzie,' I whisper. 'It's me.'

'Who? Linda Blair? What the hell happened in this room? Did you actually *piss* on the carpet?'

'Shut up for a minute and listen. I've been kidnapped. I think —'

'And I think you owe me three hundred bucks for getting your exorcism cleaned up.'

I can hear Renée moving about in her room and the sound of a metal coat hanger clanging against the back of her door. 'Mozzie, listen to me, some madwoman abducted me from your suite at *knifepoint*. Now she's holding me hostage in her trailer.'

'Well you *sound* convincing,' he says, dubious as hell but not dismissing me altogether.

'Mozzie, I really, really, really need your help. I'm not kid —'

Renée's door handle starts to turn.

'Shit.'

'Where are you?' Mozzie says.

'In a ratshit trailer near some Indian museum about three hours from New Orleans. Find me and get me out of here.'

I disconnect the call and hide the cellphone under my thigh just in time. Renée comes back into the lounge wearing a thick Starsky kind of cardigan and fluffy slippers. 'You warm enough?' she says.

'I'm a bit cold,' I say.

While she fetches me a blanket I switch the cellphone off altogether, then sit and watch TV with her until the cavalry arrive.

THE KIDS BEEN up a couple hours and we all had ourselves a supper of frozen pizza. We been watching a old *Lassie* movie for about a hour when we hear the sound of a vehicle that nobody expecting, and I see that big-ass cracker truck with the detectives pull up right outside my front door. They got a dog with them look like something from *The Muppet Show*.

'Goddamn. How the hell they know to come here?' I throw Jolie my knife. 'Quick, take that girl in your room and keep her quiet. Hoover, you babies — don't y'all say a word about Laura to those detectives, okay? She hidin' from them because they bad men.'

When the detectives knock on the door I open it and smile, all friendly and helpful as can be. 'Lord, what so important you gentlemen out on a awful night like this?'

'Ma'am,' the Cajun say, 'we are looking for one Miss Laura Delacross. We have reason to believe, us, that you know the whereabouts of her.'

'What, me? Laura who? I don't know nobody by that name.'

'Is that so?' he ask. 'She got the same color eyes like you.' Seem like he just going stare at me for ever, but then suddenly he say to his partner, 'Mozzie, take a look round the behind of the trailer.'

Mozzie raise a eyebrow but does what he told even though he don't like being order around, and the Cajun just staring at me until Mozzie come back with a long strand of kinky red hair.

'Mate, look what I found,' he say, and smile at the Cajun. 'In a 2001 model BMW X5, would you believe?'

Damn, them detectives is good.

The Cajun look from that strand of hair to me and vice versa a couple of times. 'I think you got some explaining to do, you.'

MY ONLY HOPE of still getting the gold now the detectives is catch up with me is to convince them to come in on my plan. Well it ain' strictly a plan yet but it sure is the beginning of one.

'Come on in out the wet,' I tell them, 'and find yourselves someplace to set. Might as well bring your dog in too.'

They take a seat at the dining table that ain' got two legs the same length and smile at Hoover and the twins. The dog act like it live here its whole damn life and go straight over to the heater and lie down, start licking itself.

'Jolie!' I holler. 'Come on out here and bring Laura with you.'

'Mozzie, thank God,' Laura say when she spot him in the lounge.

'Put the knife down,' I tell Jolie, 'and let the girl go.'

Laura rub her arm where Jolie was holding on, and smile at Mozzie. 'I never thought I'd say this,' she say, 'but I am seriously delighted to see you right now.'

'You're not harmed, Laura?' the Cajun ask her.

'No, I'm okay. She didn't hurt me.' Then she give me the evil eye all right. 'Just scared the freaking *bollocks* out of me.'

'I apologize for that,' I tell her. 'But I didn't know how else to get you here.'

'You could have tried asking nicely,' she reply, a bit sharp if you ask me.

'Why do you want Laura so badly, you?' the Cajun ask me.

'Yeah, Mama,' Hoover say. 'What goin' on? How come that girl *is* here? And you said they is bad men.'

I look from Hoover, to Jolie, to the girl, to the detectives, and they all staring at me waiting for a answer I ain' sure how to give. So I decide to let them work it out for theyselves. 'Anybody here read French?'

'*Oui, moi,*' the Cajun say. '*Pourquoi?*'

'Well, y'all get yourselves comfortable then,' I tell them, then go to fetch Angélique's journal from the box under my cot.

'What's this?' the Cajun say, unfolding the cloth I got it wrap in.

'It's a journal. One of my ancestors wrote it and it explain everythin'. You mind readin' it out loud so everybody can hear?'

CHAPTER 5

Le Phénix Plantation, St Luc Parish, Louisiana

THE YEAR IS 1806 and I am writing this journal for some future family of mine to find one day, maybe in twenty years, maybe in two hundred. Whoever you are what has found this journal, within these pages you're going to learn the whereabouts of a fortune what belongs to you. However, first you should know its awful, bloody history because that wealth was crushed from a thousand wretched lives like so much cane juice, and it will bring you nothing but torment and misery unless you use it wisely.

When the time is right, your father will lead you to this journal. Have no doubts that you were meant to find it, because it was decided long before you were born. Read what I write now with the utmost care, because when you have read everything there is within these pages, then it will be up to you to put right plenty of injustice.

I begin with the words of my mother.

THERE WAS ALWAYS singing and music in Guinea. The people was happy and friendly, not like after when they was taken away and forced into slavery. When I was a baby my mother sang lullabies to me, and when I was older she taught me work songs so I would enjoy my tasks. Song and dance was everything to us, as much a part of our lives as food.

My favorite task was when my mother and the other wives took our laundry to the river what ran through the village. The babies and small children was placed in the shade of the big trees along the riverbank, and the mothers and most big girls sang to them from the river while they scrubbed the clothes. My father belonged to a *dókpwê* and I liked to take drinking water to the fields so I could watch the men help my father to plant his crops. The men worked in teams and competed with each other to sing the best and most loud songs. Some of the men was musicians and later, at the feasts what my father's wives prepared to say thank you, they played their instruments and everybody danced and sang until dawn.

There was many compounds in the village what was surrounded by a mud wall more high than my father. The paths of the village twisted around everywhere. There was plenty of secret places to meet boys, although we wasn't supposed to do that. There was five houses in my father's compound, and I lived in one house with my mother and two brothers. Most of the time my father lived at his own house, but sometimes he liked to stay the night with one of his wives. My mother was his third and favorite wife and he liked to spoil me because of that, but he was kind to his other children also. My mother was the best cook of all the wives, and her dishes was so tasty they made your mouth water before you even took a bite to eat.

In the compound there was lots of goats, chickens and pigs. It was the work of the small children to look after the animals and weed the compound. The older children collected firewood for cooking, and drew water from the well what my grandfather dig with his own *dókpwê*.

All of my father's children was given three palm trees when they was born. We was allowed to keep the profit of our trees, but for a long time my brother, Alinhonû, tricked me and told me the juice of my trees was sour. Then he sold the wine and oil for himself. I didn't discover he was cheating me until I was big enough to climb the trees and taste the juice in the calabashes for myself. When my father learnt of Alinhonû's cheating, he made Alinhonû sell his goat at the market and give me back my money.

Every four days there was a market in the village square and all my father's wives had a stall there. The first wife sold his crops, the second wife sold his honey, and the fourth wife sold his eggs and milk. My mother inherited many palms from her father and she made plenty money at the market selling the wine and oil. From when I was a little girl she woke me before dawn to help her at the market. She showed me how to roll some cloth, like so, to carry the calabashes on my head, but I never learnt not to spill the red oil, and all the people in the village called me Tumé like the red, shiny berries what grew on the river bushes. Before we left the compound for market we always stopped by the sacred tree what Legba lived in and promised to come back with something nice for him if we sold everything. When we sold everything, my mother bought him some green bananas and sweet *líxâ*, and left them in a raffia sack in his tree.

'MISTER,' WHITNEY SAY, 'is Legba a monkey?'

Everybody laugh except for the Cajun who act impress. 'That's a very smart question from a little girl. Seems to me that a tree is a very good place for a monkey to live. *Mais*, I think Legba is like the

65

snake in the Garden of Eden. But he lives in everybody's tree.'

'Is he living in one of our trees?' she ask, so serious she seem wise beyond her years.

IT WAS POSSIBLE to buy anything what you wanted at the market. In one section the women sold linens and cottons what had been dyed with berries and the wings of beetles a man brought from upriver someplace. In the more shady part of the market was the women what sold the live animals and poultry, the meat and the river fish, and by the entrance was vendors of pots and dishes. Opposite the market entrance you could buy mats and ironwork. The women what sold the vegetables and fruit was the most noisy. All day long they sang about how fresh and juicy their limes and banana and papaya and figs was. Some other women sold cakes and tea, and some cut hair or sold jewelry. The tax collector always came to the market as the women was setting up their wares and he took cowry shells from the women based on what they had to sell. The women wasn't friendly with him and they made rude faces to his back. The tax collector was scared of the woman behind the live animals what sold monkey skulls, charms, roots and herbs, and he never asked her for some money.

Before the market started the women made shelters from poles and mats before the sun was too hot. The market was always crowded and busy, but it was worse in the afternoons. Even more people came then because they knew that any wares the market women had left over was taxed again at the next market, and the women was more willing to bargain then. Sometimes my mother didn't sell everything, but she always made sure to sell my oil and wine before hers. When she didn't sell everything she would tell me to ignore Legba in his tree, and not to give him even a peanut.

In the evenings all my father's family sat together in the

courtyard. Sometimes my father would visit with some friends, but most of the time they came to his compound because he was such an excellent host. The wives taught the girls sewing and weaving, and my father taught the boys how to carve calabashes and stools. When the rains came my father would sit under the eaves with all his children and tell stories. The most little children used to cry when he told them about the half-monkey, half-baby spirits in the forest what would eat them if they left the village without a grown-up. The story I liked to hear best was about my ancestor who was plenty smart at solving riddles. Everybody knew about him because there was no problem he couldn't solve. One day some important people came to him and said a man had been murdered but they couldn't find his killer. Even the priests didn't know. My ancestor thought about this for a little while before the answer came to him. Then he told for them to cover the dead man in ashes and lie his body out in a private room. Everybody had to go to the room and kiss the body, but first my ancestor started a rumor that the dead man was going to shout out when his killer's lips touched his dead body. One by one all the people went into the room and came out again with ashes on their lips. Finally, the last man to go into the room — the dead man's cousin — emerged with no ashes on his lips, and my ancestor knew he was the killer because he didn't kiss the body.

One day my mother told for me to take my father's meal to him like always. On the way to the fields as I was walking along the path that went by the river, the boy, Sosú, stopped me there.

'It is many years since we last played together, Tumé,' he said to me. 'What a beautiful woman you have become.'

I took a good look at him and saw he had grown into a fine, handsome man, and for the first time I felt a warm feeling in my body I never had before. I didn't talk with Sosú though, because my father would beat me if he knew I talked to a boy without my mother's supervision.

As I walked away, Sosú called to me, 'See you tomorrow.'

The next day, when I took my father's meal to him, my heart was beating very fast like drums, but there was no sign of Sosú anywhere. It was the same thing the next day and the next day and the next. Finally I didn't care about Sosú no more and I wasn't even thinking about him when he appeared suddenly from some bushes where he was hiding. He frightened me so much I dropped my father's meal.

'Look at that,' I scolded. 'My father is going to be very angry with me now.'

Sosú smiled and handed me a fine calabash, carved with all the birds of the forest. He told for me to open it, and inside was a clay pot of sweet almond oil.

'Will you be my wife, Tumé?' he said.

I was so frightened I ran all the way back to my mother. When she saw Sosú's gifts to me, she asked me if I wanted to marry him. When I blushed she said it was best for me to marry him soon because some man more old than my father had been enquiring about me. My mother prepared a better meal for my father and she went to his fields herself. When she came home she told me that Sosú's family was invited to my father's compound to seek approval from our ancestors for a marriage.

My father's compound was very busy for the next few days as everybody swept and cleaned, mended and cooked. My father polished the best and most high stool for the priest himself because he didn't trust anybody to do a better job. On the afternoon of the feast my mother prepared a special perfume bath for me. She told for me to add some of the almond oil what Sosú gave to me, then she washed me very carefully before plaiting my hair with beads.

Afterwards she dressed me in a soft white cloth, and my father gave to me an ivory bracelet what belonged to his mother.

'Remember to act reluctant in front of Sosú's family,' he said to me, 'like you don't want to leave here. Nobody wants a daughter-in-law in a hurry to leave her own family.'

'JOLIE, IT GETTIN' late. Why don't you put the twins to bed in your room tonight?'

I remember what coming up soon in Angélique's journal and better they sleeping while the story still seem like it might have a happy ending.

'That a great idea,' she say, for once understanding the look I give her. She pick the twins up, one on each hip, and carry them off to her room. They eyes can hardly stay open and she got them settle in minutes.

WHEN THE NIGHT started to cool, people began arriving at our compound. First the priest and his drummers, my father's brothers and their wives, cousins, and finally Sosú and his family. They brought gifts for my ancestors of tobacco, a goat, a chicken, vegetables and some cloths. I held onto my mother's belt and kept my eyes down, not speaking a word. One time when nobody was looking Sosú brushed his hand over my wrist and that warm feeling came back to me again.

The priest told everybody to kneel before presenting a jug of pure water to the points of the crossroads, where the world of the living and the spirits of the dead are joined. Then he said for Sosú to bring forward the chicken for Legba what has to be fed first or he don't let nobody cross. The priest placed the chicken by a bowl of roast corn on the altar and poured water from Legba's tree to the corn. As soon as the river was complete, the chicken ate some kernels, so everybody knew that Legba wanted the chicken. The priest wrung the chicken's neck and gave it to my mother to prepare. Everybody talked quietly and the air was smoky with burning feathers.

My mother made Legba some roast chicken with sweet potatoes, and the priest shook his rattle until Legba came to eat his food. Legba is a slow, old man with sore bones so everybody had to wait patiently until he was finished. Afterwards Legba sucked his fingers and belched. The priest asked Legba if he had enough to eat and Legba said plenty. He felt warm and strong now, Legba said. He was very satisfied and in a good mood. The priest, in return, asked Legba to open the crossroads and let our ancestors come through, but they wouldn't come until the goat what Sosú's family brought was killed and cooked for them.

When the food was ready and everybody was dancing to the drums, the ancestors began to come in the heads of the living so that they could eat. When my grandfather arrived, right away he wanted his pipe and some Guinea beer, and he didn't shut up about either until they was brought to him. My aunt what was killed by a snake wanted the jewelry what belonged to her, and then she was happy and dancing for a long time. The ancestors got plenty to eat and drink, and they enjoyed the music very much. Damballa, what is the most ancient of the ancestors and belongs to everybody, showed up, which was a good omen because Damballa sheds luck the same way a snake sheds his skin. When the priest asked the ancestors for their blessing so I could marry Sosú, they gave it willingly.

Some days afterwards my family went to Sosú's compound with gifts for his ancestors what they was very pleased with, and they also approved of a wedding. Sosú's family had almost finished building a house for us, and I had everything I needed for my dowry, when my father died suddenly in the fields. We didn't even have time to ask Ghede, lord of the dead, not to dig his grave.

My brothers brought my father's body back to his house, but first they tied up his head with cloth so his three drops of essence didn't leave his mouth and be used for bad magic. When the priest arrived at the compound, right away he went to where my father lay, surrounded by his grieving family. The priest said some prayers and shook his sacred rattle while the women cut my father's nails and hair. Then the priest placed the trimmings in a pot so that my father's spirit could use it as a throat until he was ready to visit in somebody's head. Afterwards, the wives wrapped my father's body in white funeral cloth and lit oil lamps for the watch.

All night my father's friends, family and neighbors came to pay their respects. They knelt on black funeral mats, alongside his family, and wailed with grief just as loudly. His *dókpwê* gave the wives seven hundred cowry shells to help pay for the funeral what was the next day.

The gravedigger dug the grave very deep so my father's spirit could take many gifts, some for himself, but most for the ancestors what expected something nice also. Everybody brought plenty liquors, fine pipes and tobacco, embroidered cloths, goats, chickens and cowry shells, signs of respect, to my father's funeral. While the women prepared my father's favorite dishes, his friends and *dókpwê* played some games and made jokes so his spirit would be happy when it left. Then when everything was prepared, the priest killed a goat for the ancestors, and in return asked them to give my father's spirit an easy passage.

At the graveside the mourners placed their gifts on top of my father's body, and the priest blessed my father to enjoy everything in death what he enjoyed in life. He asked the ancestors to make my father very welcome and keep his spirit safe among them. After the grave was stamped down, my father's best friend revealed that my father wanted Tègbèssou — the middle son of his second wife — to be new head of the family, so it was Tègbèssou who added one cowry to the calabash what contained the count of the ancestors. Nobody was ever allowed to know that number.

Tègbèssou took the responsibilities what my father gave to him very serious. He accepted all of my father's wives as his own, and offered to care for his mother the rest of her life. But of course he didn't want to lie with the other old wives any more than he did with his own mother, and before we even stopped wearing black sashes for my father, he took the girl, Chádási, for his wife. He didn't even ask the ancestors if they was happy about that. Right away my father's wives didn't like Chádási, but she was number-one wife now and they had to hold their tongues. Chádási liked to look at her own reflection a lot and she refused to help the other wives with any work. She slept until the afternoons, and then she would lie out in the shade of the trees and shout at the children to bring cool drinks. Everybody in Guinea knew that people who sleep late are up to no good at night. All the time she wanted gifts from Tègbèssou even though his mother was still preparing all his meals.

When he came home, she would say, 'What did you bring for me, Tègbèssou, eh? Something nice? Ah, a bracelet, so beautiful, thank you, my love.'

The other women was sure that Chádási had brought strong magic with her what made Tègbèssou love her against his will.

When we finally stopped wearing mourning sashes, Sosú came to our compound to let Tègbèssou know that his family had built a hut for me, and they was ready for a wedding. Chádási came out from her house then to see what was going on. It was the first time she ever saw Sosú and she made big eyes at him.

'Tumé is a lucky girl a handsome man like you wants to marry her,' she said to him. 'But we only just had a funeral and a wedding here. We don't have the money for another wedding right away. Maybe after the rains you come back and we can give you a day then.'

I saw her words made Sosú sad like me, but Chádási insisted I must have a big wedding to marry a most fine man like Sosú or we would insult him. Where was my pride? Did I want him to think we had no respect for his family?

The rains came and went but still Chádási didn't offer a day for my wedding, and when the ancestors' feast came round she refused to spend any money at all. She said it was my fault they didn't have much to give the ancestors that year, because of my big, selfish wedding. Chádási would only allow the ancient chickens and old vegetables covered in rat *caca* and mould to be used in the feast. She told for us to use the sour palm wine left over from market day. She didn't invite Sosú or his family to the feast, no drummers, no neighbors, no friends, because what did we have to feed them for also? If she didn't have to pay for my huge wedding, then she could feed everybody plenty.

The first ancestor to arrive at that shameful feast was my father. The pot with his spirit shattered into more pieces than the stars, and right away he came into my mother's head. He snatched his cane from Tègbèssou and started to beat him with it. My father was the most angry I'd ever see him.

'Not even a year I've been dead and you dare to feed me rotten, fucking yams, you ungrateful little bastard. And what made you think you could go ahead and get married without asking me if I approved? Eh? I could have told you she was bad for the family. Where are your manners and respect? Don't you know how hungry we are? We've protected your crops, your health and your animals all this time, until we are weak from that, and you give us the chickens what the dogs don't even want. And where are all my

73

friends? Eh? Where is my *dókpwê*?' My father kicked over the calabash of palm wine what Chádási offered to him. 'I make a nice compound for you all to live in and you give me snake piss to drink. How dare you insult me this way.'

The women and children was screaming, and it took all of the men to stop my father from beating Tègbèssou to death. When my mother come back in her head, as soon as she knew what was happening, she ordered Tègbèssou to kill all the goats and pigs at once. Even Chádási helped the women prepare a huge feast to say sorry, but the ancestors was so angry with us they didn't come to eat. To punish everybody they sent the slave raiders to our village at dawn.

CHAPTER 6

THE RAIDERS HAD plenty fierce dogs and guns. Some men made me watch while they raped my mother. She begged them to stop, so they cut out her tongue and threw it to one of their dogs. When they was done with her they just left her to die like an animal. Some of my brothers tried to fight with the raiders but they set their dogs on them and laughed when the dogs fought over the meat. All the animals and the people of the village was screaming, and there was blood every place you looked. The raiders killed all the old people and little babies —

'TIME FOR A break,' I say. 'Who want a beer?'

Only Mozzie take me up on my offer.

While the Cajun and Hoover take the dog out for a run now it finally stop raining, Jolie check up on the twins and Laura pay the bathroom a visit. There only me and Mozzie left, and he having a good old look at himself in the mirror tiles, leaning back on two legs of his chair just about to break if he ain' careful.

'What district y'all from, Officer?' I ask him.

'Do you think me and Banjo out there are cops?' he laugh, setting all four legs of the chair down on the floor properly where they belong. He take his first sip on a Colt 45 and shudder. 'Jesus, this beer is strong.'

'You ain'?'

'No, mate. Too handsome. I'd be wasted.'

He is sure full of himself. 'So what business you got with Laura?'

Mozzie take a long swallow on his beer, then he burp, cool and relax while he take his time responding. 'Under the circumstances, that's probably a question I should be asking you.'

The man got himself a point there. 'You her boyfriend?'

'He's his own love interest,' Laura say, tossing me a mobile phone as she come back out in the lounge. 'That belongs in the Jeep, by the way.' She take the same spot on the sofa as before, and pull the blanket up to her chin.

Hoover arrive back with the Cajun and his dog the same time Jolie decide she going grace us with her presence again. She look worn out and mean with it.

'The twins okay?' I ask her.

'Yeah, they sleepin'.'

The Cajun take the journal and make himself comfortable between Hoover and Laura on the sofa, then he shake hands with Hoover. 'Excuse me, I didn't introduce myself. Floyd Simeon. Pleased to meet you.'

'Likewise. Hoover. Who your friend over there?'

When Mozzie don't take the lead and introduce himself, Floyd say, 'That's Mozzie. *Mais*, he came all the way here from Australia, him. First class, too, like a movie star. Imagine that.'

Mozzie the closest Jolie ever get to first-class anything except for a first-class disappearing act for a daddy, and she perk right up at that information. 'You right with that beer, baby?' she ask him, 'or you ready for a fresh one?'

THE RAIDERS TIED all the rest of us together in the village square. The leader had sharp teeth like his dogs and deep scars on his face from smallpox. He ordered his men to bring all the spirit pots from the temples, and laughed and taunted the people each time he broke one. Some of the pots contained spirits of the living, and a priest died from fright when he saw that his spirit was no longer protected. Everybody begged the leader not to break the pots because the spirits would be wild and probably some *sorcier* would use them for bad magic against people. The leader told the people to shut up or he would set his dogs on them.

When the raiders had all the valuables and money they could carry, they put torches to our houses and fields before they marched us all together along the same path as the sun. For a long time we could see black smoke rising from the ashes of our village. When we left the shade of the forest the sun was at the most hot of the day, and a boy said to the raiders that he was very thirsty.

The leader pissed into a gourd. 'Here,' he said to the boy. 'Here's some water for you. You drink this.'

'I don't want that,' the boy told him, and the leader said the boy wasn't grateful. He whipped the boy so bad he couldn't get up from the ground. They left the boy alone there for the wild animals and vultures to finish.

The raiders gave us no water all day, and some of the people became very dizzy and weak. The men shouted at us and they beat anybody what couldn't keep up with them. They said they was going to sell us to some white *djabs* to eat. One time we stopped, and the raiders ate some bread and goat cheese, but they gave us nothing. They sat in the shade of some trees, while we had no shelter and some people was getting sick. It wasn't possible to sleep when everybody was weeping and moaning, and I wanted to die. I didn't want to live without my mother and I couldn't see any of my family or Sosú among the other prisoners. I didn't know if they was dead or alive and I never did find out. I couldn't believe my father wanted to punish me like that.

'I'm sorry,' I said to him. 'I'll make it up to you, I promise. It is Chádási what wants a big wedding, not me, Father. Don't treat me like this, please.'

But he gave me no sign that he heard me.

The raiders didn't give us anything to eat but some fruit and berries what we found along the way, and we only had water when we crossed some rivers. It took more than four days of walking to reach a big town next to a huge lake wider than my eyes could see. One of the raiders said it was called the *Atlantique*.

Maybe twelve people from my village had died already from the march by the time we came to that town with earth of yellow stones no bigger than grains of salt. The path to the town was lined with the skulls of enemies, and the trees had many powerful charms tied up in the branches to keep harmful spirits away.

I'd never seen so many people before as that town had. There was people everywhere, every different size and shape like you could think. Some of the women in the town was wearing rich cloths of more colors than a rainbow, what shimmered like rivers. They wore rings with sparkling stones on their fingers, and gold bangles on their wrists. There was carts and oxen everywhere, transporting thousands of barrels this way and that, some piled high with strange furniture, some loaded with big bales of fancy cloths like the women wore.

The raiders took us to a prison what had a moat around it and we could hear the people there crying and screaming before we even arrived. The prison had rooms one on top of another all around an open yard. The walls of the prison was the same color of yellow like the earth. Some prisoners shouted for us to help them, and some others shouted to escape if we could. 'It is true about the white *djabs*,' they said. 'We saw them when they came here to pick what ones of us to eat.'

The leader of the raiders talked a long time with the guards at the prison, until they gave him some money what he seemed pleased with. He didn't even look once at us as he left, because he had his money and we didn't exist no more. His men was laughing and making some jokes about the pretty women they going to find in town that night.

After the raiders left, the guards told for us to remove our clothes and they beat the prisoners what refused to do that. More people was crying now, even some men. I'd never been naked in front of strangers before and I was so ashamed. The guards took what jewelry they wanted from us and burnt our charms. One man had a wound on his face what didn't smell any good, so a guard scooped out the dead flesh with a hot knife and flicked the pus into the fire. I was more hungry and thirsty than ever before in my life but I was frightened to ask for anything. I was glad when the guards gave to us some kind of watery gruel that didn't taste of anything. Then the guards ordered the men into the rooms on the ground of the prison and the women had to go into the rooms on top.

The rooms was filthy with shit and piss everywhere you looked. The smell made me so sick I couldn't keep the gruel in my stomach. Some women talked to me but I couldn't understand their *langaj*. There was some pallets for sleeping but there was so many women in the room not everybody could lie down. Anyway it wasn't possible to sleep because as soon as night fell the guards came and

79

took what women they wanted, and raped them in the courtyard where everybody could see. Some of the women didn't come back.

In the morning the guards made everybody go to the yard and they ordered us to clean the prison rooms with some lime juice and water. Afterwards they sent some prisoners back to the rooms, and then they shaved all the hair from the rest of us. They told for us to scrub our skin with water and some coarse fiber. Some of the guards pinched the women's nipples and laughed. They beat any women what tried to stop them. Finally they told us to make our skin shine from some palm oil what they gave to us.

For some time we sat huddled together in the hot sun until there was some knocking at the gates of the prison. I almost died from fright when some white *djabs* came into the yard. They had no color, white like milk, with long hair and black, rotten teeth. Some of the white *djabs* had yellow hair and eyes like the sky. The hair of the leader was red like a sunset, and his eyes was almost the same color as honey. The *djabs* smelled like they never bathed, and their clothes was very strange. The hat of the leader was fixed with a great white feather and, like all the *djabs*, he wore black shoes with shiny brass buckles. I thought they was made from skins of Guinea people.

The guards brought stools for the white *djabs* to sit, and shortly afterwards came the sound of many horns. The guards ordered us to kneel with our heads to the dirt as a Guinea man wearing the most fine rich cloths and jewels was carried into the prison by four slaves, each supporting a corner of his litter. The Guinea man wore gold slippers and a feathered hat like the leader of the white *djabs*. Some more slaves shaded the Guinea man from the sun with embroidered parasols, and others whisked away the pesky flies. The leader with the red hair stood up and took his hat from his head. He spoke the same *langaj* as the Guinea man and gave him six gold cups as a gift.

The Guinea man didn't seem so happy with the cups, so the white *djab* gave him another gift of a pocket-watch, what was the first machine I saw. The Guinea man was very happy then and he made some sign that it was okay for the white *djabs* to pick what ones of us they wanted. Later I found out the white *djabs* paid for us with their weapons and brandy.

I never thought I would know humiliation like what happened next. One by one the guards brought us before the white *djabs*. Two of them looked at our teeth and gums, prodded our bellies, made us jump in the air, and they put their filthy fingers between the legs of every single woman. There was nowhere the white *djabs* didn't think to look.

When they picked a prisoner they wanted, they made some marks in a book. Then they burnt a sign like a flower on our shoulders with an iron heated to white in a fire. Some guards held the prisoners still while they did that. It was the worse pain of my life, but I didn't scream.

For many nights we was in the prison and every day some new prisoners would arrive, always brought there by Guinea raiders. Afterwards the white *djabs* came back and picked what new ones they wanted. One day some raiders brought a giant Guinea man. He bore the scars of a prince and it took plenty guards to control him. When the important Guinea man came back to meet with the white *djabs* again, the prince refused to kneel to anybody, so the guards beat him and the prince couldn't get up for a long time after. Even though every day more prisoners came to that prison, there was plenty room because plenty prisoners died from fevers. The dead bodies was just thrown away like trash.

On the ocean it was possible to see a big ship with masts tall as trees what belonged to the white *djabs*. They moved about the ship like busy ants, and from dawn to dusk it was possible to hear the noise of carpenters from there. Some Guinea men in canoes ferried wood and supplies to the ship many times a day. At night I saw the lamps of the prostitutes what visited the white *djabs* in their tents next to the ocean. Some of the *langaj* of the women in the prison I could understand now, and I heard news that lots of the white *djabs* was dying from Guinea fevers also.

One morning suddenly all the prisoners with the sign of the *fleur-de-lis* was ordered to the yard. The white *djabs* was there, and they shackled all the prisoners together by the ankles then marched us to the edge of the ocean what was boiling and wild and angry. It seemed like hundreds of Guinea men was helping the white *djabs* to steal us. Wave after wave crashed down on the yellow earth like falling trees, and there was so much noise the *djabs* had to shout to be heard.

Not only was the prisoners terrified of the ocean, we knew we was leaving Guinea now, and everybody was screaming and crying and begging for the white *djabs* not to take us away. Some men struggled from their chains, but the guards caught them and beat them. The prince fought them the most, and even the white *djabs* was scared of him. When maybe three hundred prisoners was there, the guards forced the women into the waiting canoes first. Some Guinea men rowed us into the waves, and the canoes was tossed around like little sticks. The women was too crazy frightened to think about leaving Guinea no more. One of the canoes was turned over in a huge wave, and because the women was tied together they couldn't save themselves and they drowned. The white *djabs* was very angry about that. When we came next to the white *djabs'* ship I saw a beautiful woman with the body of a fish carve from wood at the front, what must have been the spirit of their ship. Some Guinea men tied ropes around our waists so we couldn't jump into the ocean, and they made us climb a rope ladder what the white *djabs* threw to them. My legs was so weak and trembling I thought I was going to fall and be eaten by the big hungry fish below.

When all the women was on the ship the white *djabs* untied us and made us go below into a small dark room. Nobody could even sit up down there, but the *djabs* made over forty women fit in a space the same size as my house. When they closed the hatch there was no light and some women started to moan and cry. I don't know if I was more sad or more frightened then.

For many hours we could hear the men fighting and the heavy drag of chains on wood. There was no air in that room and I was faint from no water. Suddenly the whole ship rumbled and trembled like thunder and there was many loud bangs like lightning. The ship's timbers was creaking and groaning so loud I thought the woman-fish spirit of the ship was coming alive.

Nobody had been on the ocean before and all the women was sick from the motion. It seemed like we was in that little room for days. We only had a bucket for a toilet and it always spilled over. One woman was shitting blood and she moaned day and night from the pain and fever. Sometimes we could hear the men in the next room, but the white *djabs'* wall was so thick we only heard screaming and shouting.

When I was sure we would all die in that room, the white *djabs* pulled back the canvas from the hatch and told for us to come up on deck. The light hurt my eyes and it was a long time before I could look. Even then I saw only ocean in any direction and no sign of Guinea. When the *djabs* found the woman with the flux, she was thrown overboard to the sharks.

The white *djabs* had built a high wall across the ship and although we could hear the men on the other side it wasn't possible to see them. There was always much shouting and whipping from that side, and we knew the men was still shackled because we heard their chains grumbling along the deck. The white *djabs* had their weapons pointed at us all the time. They made the women kneel on the deck and then a white *djab* what spoke some *langaj* like me told us to use the platforms around the ship for our toilet. The *djabs* beat and whipped the prisoners what didn't understand until they did. Then when everybody was finished the *djabs* showed us how to draw buckets of water from the ocean. Everybody was so thirsty they drank some of the water, but it didn't taste like Guinea water and it made us sick. The *djabs* laughed at this. They had cold eyes and looked at us no different from the way they looked at the coils of rope they used for stools. When we had plenty of ocean water the *djabs* ordered us to scrub our room top to bottom. Maybe thirty buckets each woman had to draw that morning and we was very tired and weak. Afterwards the *djabs* told for us to come up to the deck again. They made us kneel and threw the rest of the ocean water over us. Not even cool well water ever felt so good to me, and in my head I thanked them for that.

When all the prisoners was clean the *djabs* gave to us some buckets of millet and fava-bean gruel. The food was horrible but we was starving and we fought over it like dogs. The *djabs* was laughing and some looked disgusted, but I never saw one of those men wash his hands before a meal so they had no right to do that. One woman was too sick from the ocean to eat, so the *djabs* beat her. When she still wouldn't eat they forced some food in her mouth until she was choking. I thought they was going to kill her, but the leader of the white *djabs*, Captain De la Croix —

'LAURA, ARE YOU okay?' Floyd ask her.

'No,' she say. 'Would you be? Look, the hairs on my arms are standing up. De la Croix, Delacross. It's the same name but anglicized. Red hair, eyes like honey — you figure it out.'

'Yeah, that some creepy shit,' Jolie agree. 'Glad it ain' me got that *fleur-de-lis* on my shoulder. I rather find 666 tattoo on my head.'

'What make you think you won't if you go lookin'?' I ask her.

'Just because you got it tattoo on your ass,' she say back.

CAPTAIN DE LA Croix showed up and shouted at the men what was beating the woman to stop. I soon learned the captain and his officers always wore fine clothes because they never really did any work that I could see. For a long time De la Croix stared at us like we was goats for sale at the market, then he ordered some men to bring the women drinking water.

After the women had enough to drink, De la Croix made some signal for a *djab* with a big box to make some music like cats fighting. The *djab* what speak my *langaj* ordered us to dance, and beat the women what didn't dance quick or happy enough. Seem like that was De la Croix's favorite time and he always watched us dance for some amusement. Sometimes the *djabs* made us jiggle crudely like Ghede. They would laugh and jeer as they pinched our asses and rubbed their *zozos* up against us. The captain laughed the most.

Every morning was the same after that — the same millet and fava beans, drawing plenty water from the ocean, cleaning our room, a little drinking water, and some dancing. Anybody what got a fever the *djabs* threw away. The *djabs* didn't seem to beat us so much when we knew what we had to do. Sometimes the *djabs* shaved our hair and cut our nails, and some women didn't like that because they thought the *djabs* was up to bad magic. The *djabs* never bathed and they stank of the garlic they rubbed on their skin to keep mosquitoes away. When one of the *djabs* died he was wrapped in a white funeral sheet, same like in Guinea, and one of

85

their priests said some prayers for him before he was thrown in the ocean. The white *djabs* only fired the big guns for their own dead. The smoke and fire of the guns made some women say that surely the *djabs* must serve Shango who makes lightning. I never heard of Shango before so I didn't know if that was true.

It seemed like we was on the ocean for ever and the nights was the most worst of all. Later, when I learnt some religion of the white *djabs*, I thought they must have shut us down below in their hell. Even if we had candles there wasn't enough air in that room for a flame to burn. What air there was stank of shit and wounds, and it was too hot to sleep. We lay on bare boards and our elbows and hips was chaffed down to the bone. The women cried all the time from pain, from grief, from terror, from every bad thing the white *djabs* could think. All night we heard the gurgling of ancestors from the deep waters below, complaining about how they hungry and cold they was.

One time hundreds of fish jumped from the ocean onto the deck of the ship like it was raining food. The white *djabs* caught plenty fish and the prisoners was happy also because there was enough for everybody, but the *djabs* ate their fill and gave us nothing. Everybody's hair and teeth was loose, and their gums was bleeding because the *djabs'* food was no good. Some of the white *djabs* liked to eat lemons and oranges in front of us and taunt us while they did that.

One day a woman went crazy and tried to jump overboard. She landed in the nets what the white *djabs* strung around the ship, so they tied her up — her arms and legs spread wide open — and two *djabs* whipped her back until it looked like some meat. Her blood was splattered everywhere. The white *djab* what spoke my *langaj* said for that to be a lesson.

When we had been on the ocean for a long time, suddenly it

seemed like we started having more food. The *djabs* even gave to us a lime every day. They made us dance for longer and they wasn't laughing so much while they watched. Seem like they was deciding what parts of us to eat first, a leg or an ass maybe.

One morning the women felt very nervous because there was a bad feeling in the air we didn't like. Suddenly a *djab* shouted from the top of a mast, *Terre*!, and all the white *djabs* gave great shouts of joy. Straight away all the prisoners was ordered below and for the rest of the day we could hear the *djabs* singing and dancing to their dreadful cat music.

Later that night some of the fancy white *djabs* came down to the women's room with lanterns. They laughed as they picked what ones of us they wanted. They was all drunk and stinking of wine and brandy. Captain De la Croix said he wanted to eat me, and I was screaming and fighting as he dragged me to his cabin. He threw me down on his bed and slapped me to shut up. He kept doing that until some of my teeth fell out and blood poured from the broken stumps. Then he tied my wrists to my ankles and raped me from behind.

CHAPTER 7

'I WAS WONDERIN' when the family tree was goin' join up,' Jolie say, as Laura run off to the bathroom crying and retching.

Nobody really sure how to respond, and the only other sound is Floyd's dog panting front of the heater. I know the events in Angélique's journal already, but hearing it from somebody who speak French properly, well everything sound even worse somehow.

'Mama, I heard enough,' Hoover say.

'Okay, baby. It goin' get worse anyhow. Go sleep in my cot tonight,' I tell him.

He don't kiss me goodnight like usual, and he shuffle off to my room, pressing flat against the wall on his way so Laura can pass by. She look like she been chewing on a cane toad.

'You want somethin' take the taste away?' I ask her.

'Please. Anything,' she nod.

'Jolie, fetch the girl a beer out the icebox. Fix that dog up with some water while you at it.'

'You the one needin' the exercise,' Jolie say. 'Get off your lazy wide ass and fix the damn dog some water yourself.'

ANOTHER WOMAN CAME to untie me while Captain De la Croix was still sleeping. She spat on him before she helped me back down to the women's room. There was pain and blood between my legs and she held me close like my mother for the rest of the night while I wept.

In my head, I said to my father, 'Fuck you, too. I hope you are starving. I'll never talk to you again because you don't exist for me no more.'

In the morning, when the white *djabs* finally woke up, they ordered all the women to go up to the deck. The sun was only just rising in the sky and I was surprised to see that we was in the busy harbor of a large town. At first I thought we was back in Guinea, but the houses didn't look like any buildings I'd seen before with their spires and chimneys, fancy balconies and wooden tiles on the roofs. There was maybe one hundred ships and boats around us in the harbor.

The *djabs* told for us to scrub everything. They was suffering from their liquor and they had worse tempers than usual, lashing out for the most small thing. Some of the *djabs* went to the town in boats and come back with some freshly killed pigs and chickens, some spices, fruit, milk, cheeses, breads, butter — enough to make a feast fit for the ancestors. After we had scrubbed the ship all morning, with no food or water, the *djabs* made us clean ourselves also, and then they shaved and clipped everybody very carefully. Afterwards we shined our skins with tallow, and for the first time ever they gave to us some coarse cloths to wear. They ordered everybody back down below and said they would whip anybody what got dirty.

When the *djabs* said to come up to the deck again, this time they was all dressed in fancy clothes, even the low ones what normally went about with bare chests. Captain De la Croix was there also, but he didn't look at me, or even look ashamed. The *djabs* had made some shade with sailcloth, and there was a long table with white cloth laid out with wines, brandy and prepared foods what they had made. Some boats was coming from the town with more white *djabs*, and I saw that they had even finer clothes than the *djabs* on the ship. When they come on board, all the *djabs* shook hands and bowed and was very formal with each other. The *djabs* from town had fine handkerchiefs what they waved around like women, and they sniffed powder from silver boxes. They wore big, white wigs and embroidered vests, but they still stank through their perfumes.

When they had finished eating and drinking to their fill, there was lots of angry shouting and cracking of whips as the *djabs* brought all the most big and strong men forward in chains for the town *djabs* to examine. The prince wasn't among them. The *djabs* picked what men they liked the best, then said they wanted to examine the women. One by one we was taken below and they looked in every secret place of our bodies. When they saw what Captain De la Croix had done, they didn't want me.

After the big shots left in their boats with the prisoners what they picked, the white *djabs* was very happy and told us to eat and drink what was left of the feast before we went back down below for the night.

In the morning a huge commotion started before it was even light. The white *djabs* made all the prisoners get into canoes again and they took us to the shore. Now we really thought we was going to be eaten, and everybody was screaming and fighting with the *djabs*, but there was no point. When we reached land, there was many white *djabs* on big horses what I thought was monsters. They marched us to another prison what held slaves from everywhere. Some was very small and fine-boned, some had plenty scarring, some had filed teeth, some had tattoos, and everybody spoke a different *langaj*. The *djabs* separated the women from the men again so I still didn't know if the prince was alive. The white guards at that prison was worse than the white *djabs* from the ship and they beat anybody just for looking at them. They came round with some buckets of gruel and filthy water, but didn't give us nothing until we made some noises like pigs. The ground was dirty with cockroaches and shit, but the pain in my stomach was terrible and I had to lie down.

The next day we was made to go into a huge wooden hall. The men was there also, and this time all the prisoners was in chains, even the women. I finally saw the prince again, and he looked like they had starved him because he was slumped over like a sick old man, not proud and strong and fierce like when I first saw him. When the big doors to the hall was opened up, hundreds of white *djabs* ran into that room, fighting to be first. There was so much greed in their eyes we thought for sure that they wanted to eat us right away, and everybody was crying and moaning from terror. There was much shouting and arguing while the *djabs* looked us over head to foot. Some *djabs* made me bend over and lifted my cloth, examining me like I was a breeding pig. A fat little white *djab* with an ugly red face and lizard eyes kept coming back to me, and finally he gave De la Croix some gold from his leather purse, and I was led outside. The *djab* took me to a wagon, where the prince and three other Guinea men was tied up. The prince couldn't keep his eyes open he so weak, but the other men was very scared. The *djab* chained me up with them and then ordered his driver to move.

The *djab* rode a giant black horse with plenty of whip scars, and a Guinea man in clothes like the fat *djab* was driving the wagon. As we traveled through the streets of that town with its big fine houses and windows and gardens, nobody even looked once at us. The streets was very busy and they stank of the shit and piss, and the chicken carcasses and vegetable waste what was running through them. The white *djabs* didn't even keep their toilet separate from where they lived. I saw some brown-skinned people, not white, not Guinea, dressed like the fancy white *djabs*. All the brown-skin women wore colorful scarves dyed to complement the different shades of their skins. The most grand carriage went past our wagon and inside was the first white woman I laid eyes on. She had skin like the best ivory, and was dressed in silks and jewels. She looked our way but saw nothing to change her haughty, sulky expression.

When we finally left the gates of that town the fat white *djab* rode ahead. One time the prince raised his head and asked the driver where we was going. I was very pleased to understand his *langaj*.

'Is that white *djab* going to eat us?' the prince asked the driver.

The *djab* heard the prince talking and came back to whip him, shouting until his face was red and wet with sweat. The driver didn't stop the wagon or look back once.

For two days it rained as we traveled along the muddy roads. Many times we had to help the oxen pull the wagon clear of deep mud while the fat *djab* shouted and beat us with his horsewhip. In all that time we saw only countryside and mountains. We didn't pass one other person along the way. During the day nobody talked except for the *djab*. He gave us nothing to eat but some cold yams. At night he chained everybody together on the ground, even his driver, and he drank rum and cursed until he fell asleep in the wagon.

While the *djab* snored and grunted like a little pig, the driver whispered that our fate was even worse than to be eaten, for we was slaves to the French now, and we would never know an end or limit to their cruelty. The fat white *djab* was called Batiste, and he was the overseer for some rich white *djab* in Paris what didn't care about us so long as he got his money.

At nights the prince slept close to protect me, and I was grateful, but I wished that it was Sosú lying with me instead.

On the third day we came to a set of large gates, its two brick columns straddled by a high iron arch. Later I learnt that the words fashioned in the ironwork was the name of the Nancy plantation. On the other side of the gates was fields and fields of sugar cane as far as I could see. Maybe two hundred slaves I saw working in the fields, and they was all miserable, skinny and exhausted under the hot sun. Some looked up as the wagon passed and I saw that their eyes was dead. Some low white *djabs* was whipping anybody what slowed down or stopped. Nobody was singing, just the noise of the white *djabs* shouting, and their whips on Guinea flesh. There was many orchards of oranges, lemons, mangoes, avocados, apricots and some fruit I didn't know, then the most big, fancy white house came into view, and there was brown-skinned domestics everywhere, some in brilliant white dresses and head scarves, some what had green eyes like jewels. They helped Batiste from his horse and took his bags. I didn't understand their *langaj* at all. It wasn't Guinea and it wasn't French but it seemed like both of them. A white woman came from the big house to greet Batiste. She was dumpy like a sack of vegetables and her face was sour like she was drinking old palm wine. She didn't even look at us in the wagon. Some white children came running, *Papa! Papa!*, and Batiste gave to them some gifts of toys and candy. The driver waited until Batiste was inside the house before he drove us across a river to where the slaves lived, some distance away.

There was only some old people and children there at the

quarters, because everybody what could work was in the fields. In the same *langaj* as the brown-skinned domestics at the big house, the driver ordered an old man to take the men away, and for some old woman called Modeste to take me. At first I thought she was older than my mother, but she could speak some of my *langaj* and I learnt she was born in this land, what she called Saint-Domingue, some thirty years before.

'Excuse me,' I interrupt Floyd, who somehow is sharing Laura's blanket, 'but anybody got them a clue where the hell Saint-Domingue is exactly? It ain' any place on a map I can find.'

'You should be looking for Haiti,' Floyd tell me. 'Saint-Domingue was its French name.'

'Haiti? You mean where zombies come from?' Jolie ask him.

'Zombies aren't real,' he say. 'They're just bogeymen, like were-wolves and vampires.'

'Keep readin', shrimp breath. Wouldn't be no stranger than anythin' you read from that journal already.'

Modeste took me to a thatched hut what had no windows, and lay me down on a straw bed there. She brought me some soothing herb tea, and bathed me very gently. Afterwards I slept for two days. I wish I never woke up.

Modeste told me to follow her to the big house. The prince and the other Guinea men was there, as was Batiste, his wife, his children, and some low whites. The most vicious dog was chained to the front of the house, its eyes burning with hate and rage. Later I learnt it was a trained slave hound what Batiste bought from Cuba. Batiste was wearing a white collar around his neck, and all the whites *djabs* thought that was very funny. Modeste whispered to me that under French law the *djabs* must baptize us into their religion, and we was going to get a new name now to show that we was Christians like them. First Batiste called for the three Guinea men and he made a sign like crossroads on their heads with some water. The *djabs* was laughing so much they could hardly stand up. Batiste gave the Guinea men new names of Jupiter, Jasmin and Marmelade, and one of the low white *djabs* fell down he thought the names was so funny. Batiste signaled for the prince to come forward just as a Guinea man arrived in a cart with some firewood. As soon as he saw the prince, the man jumped from the cart and knelt at the prince's feet, kissing and wailing, *My prince, my prince*, until Batiste kicked the Guinea man away.

'It seems I have a problem now,' he said. 'You see my dog is called Prince also, and I'm going to get confused because it is so hard to tell the difference between you already.' Batiste pretended to think for a while, and he said, 'It is all right. I know how to fix the problem.'

First Batiste made the sign of the crossroads on his dog. 'In the name of the Father, the Son and the Holy Ghost,' he said, shaking with laughter, 'I name you, Prince le Chien.'

All the whites was crying and falling down with laughter. Then Batiste did the same with the prince, and said, 'I name you, Prince l'Afrique.'

When everybody finally stopped laughing, Batiste signaled for me to come to him, but I didn't want a new name. Tumé was the only thing I had left from Guinea and I wasn't going to let the *djabs* take that away from me also. Some *djabs* tried to hold me, but I fought with them until Batiste punched me in the face. Then I was too dizzy to fight them no more. Batiste's wife was laughing the most then. Her eyes was excited and round. Batiste gave me the new name, Rose, and after that every time I didn't answer to that name, I was whipped.

Back in her hut Modeste made a poultice for my face what hardly had any teeth left now. 'Do not fight them,' she said to me. 'There are plenty ways to seek revenge. In front of the whites, always smile and look content with what you have. Hide your feelings, act stupid, do not show them anything, be servile, let them think you like them, that you are grateful to them. When they trust you to be a good slave, then you can go out at night and cause mischief they don't like.'

For some weeks Modeste taught me the ways of a slave. She was a kind woman like my mother and I was thankful she was my friend. She started to teach me the *langaj* of Kreyol what got the same rhythm like Guinea, but most of the words I had to learn new. She took me around the plantation and explained to me the crushing mill, the boiling house, the distillery, the cooling house, the trash house and so on. One time I asked where her children was, and she said what ones didn't die from lockjaw when they was babies died working for Batiste. I asked her where the brown-skinned domestics at the big house came from, and she said all their fathers was white *djabs* but their mothers was slaves. The whites didn't like to look at Guinea people, so they had the brown-skinned people to live and work in the big house. 'Don't be envious of them,' she said. 'They have to clean Batiste's fat ass for him, and wash his wife's menstrual rags.'

Near to the slaves was the huts of the carpenters and coopers and sugar makers and masons — what was called the *artisans*. They had pallets to sleep on and old French clothes to wear. They got more food than the field slaves, but sometimes they still got whipped.

I helped Modeste sweep the yard of the slave quarters and look after the children and sick people. There wasn't so many children there as my village. Every day we collected fallen fruit from the orchards what the pigs got to eat. Sometimes Batiste's children spied to make sure we didn't eat some rotting fruit for ourselves. The slaves was never happy when they come home from the fields. They was always too exhausted to cook, so Modeste prepared as much food as she could for them, but if it was raining and nobody could cook outside, they ate their food raw in their huts. Batiste gave the slaves some flour, some herrings and some dry peas on a Monday what had to last all week, but it was never enough for more than three days. Under French law Batiste couldn't make the slaves work on Sundays, but they was so starving hungry by then they had no energy to do anything but sleep. We was always so hungry and tired.

One time Batiste caught a boy stealing an egg, so he invited the boy into the big house and acted like he was going to cook something special with the egg. The boy was very happy while Batiste boiled the eggs and cut some bread, laid some butter out. When the egg had been boiling for some time, Batiste asked, 'You want your egg now, boy? *Oui*? You stick your hand in this pot of boiling water and get it then.' When the boy wouldn't do that, Batiste held the boy's hand in the pot for ten minutes, even though the boy was screaming. The cooks was too frightened to stop working.

One day Modeste said that it was time for me to join the big work gang now, and I was taken with all the most strong slaves to clear some land for planting. I'd been feeling sick for some days and I didn't feel too good. I was glad for once that we didn't have some breakfast yet. Batiste was waiting for us and he ordered us to chop down all the trees to make a new field. The wood was very hard and soon my hands was bleeding, but the white *djabs* wouldn't let me stop. The prince showed me how to wrap some leaves around my palms to protect them. I saw some strength had come back to the prince and I thought that Batiste better watch out if he got any stronger. The next day we went back to the same place, and Batiste and the low white *djabs* made the slaves haul the logs back to the big house by some leather straps attached to our shoulders.

Every morning Batiste blew on a big conch and we knew we had ten minutes to be ready. Everybody hated the sound of that conch, for it meant another day of beatings and hard work and shouting and hunger. I still felt sick and the prince helped me as much as he could even though he was whipped if the *djabs* saw him do that.

It seemed like it was raining for months and the slaves had rotten feet what was crack and sore from the wet mud. Everybody was coughing. Every day there was ploughing, digging, planting. Just work, whippings and never enough food or sleep. One day the *djabs* said we had to carry pots of animal shit to the fields and I never saw as many beatings and whippings as that time. The slaves was very angry and fighting with them because it was the job everybody hated, but the white *djabs* was too strong and had too many whips and guns. The white *djabs* drank lots of rum all the time and they was so cruel and bad-tempered I didn't think they liked the work any more than the slaves did.

Soon I noticed something was different with my body, and every day there was another change. Modeste noticed this also and told me I had a baby coming. Batiste didn't let me stop working though, and he still beat me if I was too slow.

Not long after the rains stopped the white *djabs* started getting excited about some day they called *Noël*. Some old slaves said we didn't have to work that day so we was happy also. On the day of *Noël* all the slaves and *artisans* and domestics was made to gather in front of the big house. Some white priest was visiting there, and I was shocked when Modeste told me he was feeding the white *djabs* the flesh and blood of their god. He talked for a long time in some *langaj* nobody could understand except him. Sometimes the whites prayed with him, but I don't think they knew what they was asking for. Their songs was dull and tuneless. Afterwards, Batiste's wife, so she would seem like a good, kind woman to the priest, gave out some oranges and cakes to the slaves before we went back to our quarters and slept.

Later in the afternoon the prince walked with Modeste and me along the river to sit with our feet in the cold pool by a waterfall, where nobody would find us, although we could still hear the *djabs'* music and feast go on long into the night. The prince told some jokes about Batiste, and that was the first time somebody made me laugh since Guinea. Later Modeste said she was tired and went back to her hut. Afterwards the prince led me through the waterfall, right under the water to a small cave what I never knew about before.

'Don't tell anybody about it,' the prince said. 'You might need to hide here one day.'

Over the next few days it was very busy at the plantation and Modeste said that the sugar season was about to start. 'Rest every second you can,' she advised me, and I wished I listened to her because it was the most hard five months of my life. The white *djabs* split the young, strong slaves into two gangs and we had to work from dawn to dusk, or dusk to dawn. All the slaves still had to do their other plantation work like building and tending the animals, and every day I got weaker as my stomach was growing bigger.

When I could no longer cut the cane, I was made to work in the crushing mill, feeding cane through the press stones to make the juice come out. One day a woman got some fingers caught between the stones and her screaming panicked the mules what was turning the stones. Her whole arm was dragged through to my side, flat like a plank of wood. A white *djab* cut her arm off with one stroke of his axe. The woman was taken back her hut where she died that night.

The white *djabs* was even more angry and cruel because of the extra work and heat, and conditions got even worse for the slaves.

One day was the most hot day I'd ever known and we'd been working for hours with no breaks or water. The slaves was moving about like the dead. Suddenly, with a roar like a lion, the prince threw down his cane knife and started to run down a cane break. The white *djabs* shouted for him to stop and chased him on their horses. They almost caught up with him, but the prince made it to the woods and disappeared between the trees. I hoped the prince was going to get free, but when the *djabs* couldn't find him easily, Batiste let his hound loose from its chain. Soon everybody could hear that the dog had tracked down the prince, because it sounded like it was tearing him to pieces.

When the *djabs* brought the prince back, he couldn't walk properly because the dog had ripped the back of his knee out. Batiste ordered his men to tie the prince to a tree, and then he took his thick cowskin whip that he had made special and gave the prince one hundred fifty lashes. Batiste's *zozo* was standing up while he did that. Nobody was allowed to help the prince, and I thought he must be dead, but when night fell some slaves brought him to Modeste's hut, and I helped her bathe his back with some water steeped with leaves to cool his pain. Some of the lashes was so deep I could lie two fingers in the wounds.

We nursed the prince for many weeks and eventually he was well again, but he wasn't the same man like before. Now he was something hard and dead. He didn't talk with nobody and he didn't look at nobody. Just limp, limp, work, work, his back all scarred and sweating under the hot sun.

You decided you wanted to be born in the middle of the night, my daughter. At first I thought it was cramps because we never had salt with our food and we was used to suffering from the lack of it. But Modeste, when she saw my waters had broke, she told me to relax. My baby was coming and she was going to help me. She called for some other old woman what helped deliver many babies and they made a bed of perfume leaves and a mat for me to lie on. They brewed some tea for me to drink what made the cramps more strong. For many hours I was just pushing and pushing and it seemed like the world was only blood and pain. When the women saw that your head was crowning, *bébé*, they held me up so I was squatting over the mat, and in seconds there you lay. I'd never seen such a fine, delicate, beautiful creature in my whole life. Right away my heart was filled with love for you. The women bathed both of us in some warm water and wrapped us both in some clean blankets. I saw then that you was brown-skinned like the domestics, and you had blue eyes like white babies. They wasn't the color of Guinea honey like your father's eyes yet.

So the ancestors wouldn't know your real name and torment you the same way like me, I asked Modeste to bring me a nail and a little bottle. With the nail I drew three crosses in the dirt floor and added a pinch from the center of each to the bottle. Then I told Modeste and the other woman to cover their ears and look away before I whispered your name into the bottle and sealed it with a cork. I gave the bottle to Modeste to bury someplace what even I did not know. Be thankful, *bébé*, that the ancestors never found out what your real name is or their power to hurt you would be great.

When Modeste came back to the hut I asked her to give you a slave name, and she chose Angélique. Then she said, 'If you don't want Angélique to be a slave, I can kill her for you now so Batiste can't have her.'

I'm sorry, my daughter, if I made the wrong decision for you, but I couldn't do that. I would willingly die for you, but I couldn't let you die for me, just so I wouldn't have to watch you being whipped or raped in front of me some day.

Instead Modeste taught me how to nurse, and I sang to you some songs what my mother sang to me as you drank my milk.

As always the white *djabs* had to ruin every good thing. Batiste's wife arrived in the morning because she heard there was a new baby, and she wanted to take a look. She didn't come as a mother though, she came as a wife, and when she saw that you had brown skin and blue eyes like Batiste, her face went crazy with rage, and she beat us both with her shoe.

CHAPTER 8

SHE MUST HAVE rained fifty blows down on us. I tried to protect you, but her sharp little heel caught your head and there was blood everywhere. Modeste and the other woman was screaming but there wasn't a thing they could do to stop her. Just when I thought the mistress meant to kill us, the prince burst into the hut and grabbed her wrist. He threw the shoe to the floor, then snapped her arm across his knee so it was hanging down like a broken stick. All the white *djabs* came running from the big house, and when they saw what the prince had done to her, they dragged him outside all the way to the whipping post.

Everybody on the plantation was made to go to the post what was always covered in wet blood because it never had time to dry. The prince had gone crazy with rage now and fought the white *djabs* with all of his strength. It took every single *djab* to tie the prince down. Batiste told his most old son to fetch his cowskin whip, and then he whipped the prince until he was just a lump of raw meat on the ground. Some of the prince's flesh landed at my feet, long and thick as a slug. Everybody had to watch the prince's whipping, and the white *djabs* beat anybody what looked away.

It took almost two hours for Batiste to kill the prince that way. Even after the prince was dead, Batiste still whipped and whipped, until he could hardly stand, panting like a dog.

Nobody saw the wagon piled high with bags and cases arriving at Nancy, because in their minds they had gone someplace where they didn't have to watch the whipping, but everybody noticed the fancy white *djab* what came walking slow as you like to where Batiste was.

"*Sieur* Chalmette,' Batiste bowed, like nothing wrong. 'I wasn't expecting you.'

'I can see that,' the white *djab* said, 'or you wouldn't be killing my slaves and stealing from me.'

There was a white lady in the wagon, dressed in a dark velvet traveling cloak, bonnet and gloves. Her face might have been beautiful, but now it was twisted with horror at what she could see. She couldn't stop staring at the prince what didn't even look like a man no more. Chalmette ordered some domestics to help his wife into the house. She sobbed in little bursts as they supported her up the wooden stairs to the veranda. I saw that she had a *bébé* coming herself. Chalmette told his driver and some slaves to take what was left of the prince away and bury him someplace. Then he said for Batiste only to come into the big house with him.

Chalmette's driver helped us carry the prince to Modeste's hut. His name was Boukman and he had been loaned to Chalmette from some other planter in this area. He was a big, giant man like the prince, and he carried the prince all by himself. Boukman was wearing old French clothes like most of the *artisans*, but around his neck hung a small leather pouch tied with tiny bones and some feathers. He lay the prince down on the floor of the hut and ordered us to clean the body like he was the master of us. The prince was nothing more than a skinned animal now, ready for cooking, but I was glad he had escaped back to Guinea where his spirit belonged.

'That driver is a *bokor*,' Modeste whispered to me. 'He's a priest but plays with the left hand also. Be careful of him because he uses powerful magic. He can make people die long enough to be buried, but not so long they don't wake up and run away to the hills at night.'

'MAIS, THERE ARE your zombies,' Floyd say to Jolie. 'Nobody's going to look for an escaped slave they think is already dead and buried.'

Jolie roll her eyes at Mozzie like they collaborating on something. 'Yeah, I got it, Bayou Bob. I ain' stupid.'

WE COULD HEAR the white *djabs* shouting and arguing up at the big house while Modeste and I prepared the prince for burial. After we had finished we went to find Boukman. He was talking quietly to some slaves about something and he shut up when we arrived. Modeste told Boukman that he could take the prince for burial now, but Boukman said he wasn't going to bury the prince like a dog. He hid the prince's body under some straw in his wagon so later, someplace secret, he would conduct a fitting funeral like royalty deserve.

I was surprised that Boukman wasn't too scared of the white *djabs* to disobey their orders.

He said, 'Why I should be scared? I got plenty *lwa* to protect me. Every time the French kill a slave, the slave's spirit is fighting with me, ten times as strong as before. The French should be scared.'

For the rest of the afternoon we heard the white *djabs* fighting. Chalmette and Batiste went to the storage house where the sugar was packed in barrels ready for transportation to the ports of France. Modeste told me that Chalmette was the master of the Nancy plantation, and he had returned to Saint-Domingue after receiving news from the merchants in Nantes that Batiste was cheating everybody by hiding poor sugar in the middle of the Nancy barrels and keeping the extra money for himself.

Later Chalmette came down to the quarters and inspected all of his slaves. He seemed angry that we was so skinny, and that evening he sent Batiste and his family away from the Nancy plantation. He didn't even give them a wagon to travel in. Boukman was nowhere to be found all evening, but he came back in the night and said that Batiste wasn't going to whip a slave ever again.

The conch wasn't blown the next morning and the slaves didn't know what to do. Boukman left for his own plantation, some way from Nancy, just before dawn, and we stayed around the quarters, waiting for some sign what to do from the big house.

In the middle of the morning Chalmette came riding to the quarters on the fine horse he brought with him from France. He dismounted and gave the reins to the groom, then told us to gather around him. In Kreyol he said that things was going to change, and that from now on we was to have the full protection of French law. He picked Ti-Pierre — a slave what was born at Nancy — to be the *commandeur* now, and said we had to obey everything what Ti-Pierre said. Nobody was going to get whipped so long as they followed his orders.

Chalmette still made the slaves work in the fields, but he didn't shout all the time like Batiste. Ti-Pierre knew if a slave really needed a little rest, and gave him that. He didn't make nobody work what was sick. Over some months the *artisans* built new huts for everybody, with windows and shutters, plank flooring, and pallets for beds. Some older slaves and children began cultivating fruit and vegetable just for us, and Chalmette ordered a *tonelle* to be built so it was possible for us to cook outside in the rain. He picked some old women to be slave cooks, and afterwards, even though the slaves was still exhausted from the fields, they always had a hot meal in the evenings. He gave us some meat and salt, and rewarded any slave what learnt a new trade with more food and favors. Slowly the slaves became more friendly with each other, and at nights we sat around the *tonelle*, telling stories and histories, and we started to learn some things about each other.

Chalmette made sure the slaves got plenty water while they was working, and he allowed us rest in the shade for the most hot two hours of the day. He gave everybody cloths to make clothes and finally we had some modesty again. For one month after your birth, *bébé*, he gave me very light duties, but then I had to go back to the fields. I could only nurse you at the end of the cane rows, and in between my breast milk dripped to the ground with my sweat.

The best thing that happened under Chalmette was that once a month he gave the slaves the whole weekend off. Everybody worked in our gardens then, and sometimes a slave would forget and sing some *dókpwê* song what made everybody homesick. In the gardens we grew yams, cassava, millet, limes, peppers, beans, melons, onions, garlic, corn, spices, cabbage, any vegetable what could grow there.

Chalmette permitted dances on these weekends, and when the garden work was done, the children was sent to collect leaves, berries, flowers and fronds to decorate the *tonelle*. The cooks made the most delicious dishes for everybody, and sometime Chalmette or his wife sent some jams or some candy for the children what the domestics made. Some men made drums from logs and rattles from calabashes, the same like in Guinea. The women made jewelry from dried berries and rubbed flower petals on their skins for perfume. From when the night was cool enough for the people to have fun, we sang and danced until dawn. At first everybody had different dances, so we took the best ones and made something new.

Soon the domestics and *artisans* started coming to the dances, and they showed us how the white *djabs* danced at the big house. Everybody laughed because it was so stiff like trees.

On Sundays, even though the dances went on all night, we still had to rise early and clean our huts for Chalmette's inspection, because Cleanliness Is Next To Godliness. After his inspection we gathered at the big house for Mass what everybody thought was very dull and boring. Chalmette said we got to learn to be Catholics like the law said. The priest was a little fat French man like Batiste and he always reeked of brandy. He had some pictures of some Catholic saints, and afterwards when we was back at the quarters, somebody asked, 'Did you see that St Patrick has snakes like Damballa?'

Somebody said, 'Yes, and St Peter has the key to heaven just like Legba has the key to the world of the *lwa*.'

Some woman say, 'The mother of Jesus has a sore heart like Erzulie.'

One man said he didn't know why the whites' god would help them if they killed his son, Jesus. Surely a god would seek revenge for that?

One time I saw a slave pour some soup on the ground, so I asked him, 'What? You have enough food to waste now? Have you forgotten it wasn't so long ago that you was starving all the time?'

The man looked at me as though I was the stupid one. 'It's an offering to the *lwa*,' he said.

That made me very angry, and I shouted at him, 'Where was your ancestors when the slave raiders came to your village? Where was your ancestors when you was on the white *djabs*' ship? Where was they when the French was whipping you in the fields? They don't care about you, stupid man. You're wasting that food. It's better you have it because the ancestors won't help you. They're too feeble.'

'It doesn't work like that,' he said to me. 'First you have to serve the *lwa* well enough so they have the strength to help you. And anyway, we have some Kreyol *lwa* now. They are warriors and plenty strong enough to fight the French.'

Chalmette's wife was always at Mass on Sundays when the priest came along on his mule. Every time I saw her she looked more depressed, like the slaves. I never saw her smile even once. Her stomach was growing bigger, but she was shrinking like she was dying from the inside. Finally she had a baby boy what they called Etienne. After his birth she was too sick to nurse him, and a young domestic girl came and told me to follow her to the big house right away.

I'd never been inside of there before, and at first I was scared of the white *djabs'* likenesses hanging on the walls because I thought they was alive. It was dark and airy in that house and there was plenty of fancy furniture what was fit for a king. It was the first time I'd walked on rugs. They was the most fine quality you can buy, so you can imagine how good they felt to my feet. The domestic led me to where the mistress lay with her son on a high soft bed, her breathing fast and shallow. She didn't open her eyes to me and I thought for sure she was dying. Another domestic pulled on some rope what made a wooden fan go round and stir the air.

Etienne was a greedy little baby and there was never enough of my milk left over for you, *bébé*. Domestics came and fetched me any time day or night that boy wanted some milk, and you was getting skinny and not growing right. I didn't know what to do and I was going crazy with worry. Modeste saw what was happening, so she crushed some *laloi* leaves into a paste and told me to spread it on my nipples. The first time you tried to nurse after that your face was disgusted and you cried like I was trying to poison you. Straight away Modeste mashed some banana what you liked and gave that to you. Next time, same thing, until by the end of the day you never wanted my milk again.

Some weeks later, when I was up at the big house to feed Etienne on the morning of his baptism, some white visitors arrived from the plantations in the area. I was surprised to see that Boukman was driving one of the wagons. It was the first time since the prince was killed that I'd seen him. The mistress was so happy the white *djabs* arrived she jumped out of bed and ordered the domestics around so she was dressed nicely to greet her guests. She said to the women who helped dress her, 'Thank God some French people have come. I'm sick to death of only seeing your miserable black faces.'

When I got back to the quarters that night, Boukman was enjoying a nice meal of chicken and bean stew what the cooks made especially in his honor, and he was doing all the talking there. The Nancy slaves was listening to his every word. I took some stew myself and sat down to listen to him. He was talking about a revolution happening in France because the peasants there wanted equality. They was sick of the nobility what didn't pay taxes but had all of the power and privilege.

Already in Saint-Domingue the French Revolution was having an effect. Some free brown-skinned people in the south was fighting the French for equal rights. Some of them was very rich, with their own plantations and slaves, and they didn't like how some sly *djab* convict sent from Paris was allowed to vote because he was white, while they was denied this right. Mostly they didn't like how the French could take their freedom away at any time for the slightest thing. Boukman had some pamphlets from Paris what he read aloud, calling for an end to the *Ancien régime* there. The words the Nancy slaves heard most clearly was *liberté* and *égalité*. When it was late at night, Boukman took Ti-Pierre and some other slaves deep into the cane fields. They was for gone a long time.

The white visitors stayed at the big house for a week. During that time Boukman disappeared every night with Ti-Pierre and some other slaves, only to return close to dawn, wide awake and sweating with exertion. I began to find animal offerings buried in the ground around the cane fields where the white *djabs* wouldn't find them.

After Boukman had left with his master, some Nancy slaves began to run away and join the bands of rebels in the hills. Chalmette sold the ones he caught, even if they had families, because he didn't like to whip. The slaves he didn't catch came back at night to steal what food and supplies they wanted. I know there was some slaves at Nancy what helped them do that. Sometimes the rebels doused the fields with stolen rum and set fire to them as they was leaving, then everybody had to get up and put out the fires.

The rebels was getting more brave and most nights it was possible to hear their drums what was more hard and fast than Guinea drums. At nights some brown-skinned men what Chalmette hired especially from Le Cap patroled the plantation with guns and dogs to keep the rebels away. However, one night a rebel made it to our quarters with news that the King of France had been killed. The people what worked the fields like us was in charge of France now, and all French citizens had been declared equal.

'The revolution is coming to Saint-Domingue,' he said. 'Get ready.'

The domestics told us what gossip they heard from the whites. The *djabs* didn't think the domestics was smart enough to understand them so they didn't try to hide what they talked about. Lots of white *djabs* in Saint-Domingue's towns had been poisoned and everybody was fighting with everybody. The low *djabs* supported the revolution in France but they only wanted equality for themselves. The rich planters was fighting France's officials because they thought the officials was charging too much in duties, and then they never paid the planters when and what they was supposed to. The planters didn't like what was happening in France, so they didn't want Saint-Domingue to belong to France no more. If Saint-Domingue granted equality to everybody, then the slaves would have to be paid to work the fields and the planters wouldn't be so rich. Everybody was fighting only for himself. There was nobody fighting for the slaves because slavery was in everybody's best interests but ours.

Etienne still wanted my milk, even though he was almost four years old, so still I'd go to the big house any time of day or night to nurse him. His mother and father gave him everything he wanted, including my milk what should have been yours, *bébé*.

It was very dry that year and plenty fires started from the lightning what didn't bring rains. The river was down to a trickle, and the ditches round the cane fields stank of something rotting. The mistress was very unhappy because no visitors had called at Nancy for some time, and she was always shrieking, wanting this, wanting that, but nothing was ever good enough for her.

One day we heard Chalmette shout at her, 'I'm sick of the sound of your voice. It's horrible. You're always complaining or demanding something.'

They had a big fight and the mistress said she was going to stay with their friends at the Lenormand de Mézy plantation. She said Chalmette should go to hell for bringing her to this miserable, Godless country.

First thing the next morning Ti-Pierre and a driver hitched some mules to a wagon and went to the big house where the mistress and Etienne was packed and ready to leave. At the last minute Etienne refused to leave Nancy without me, so Ti-Pierre came and ordered me to the wagon. Modeste promised she would take good care of you, daughter, but I had a bad feeling, and I wasn't happy to leave.

On the road to Lenormand de Mézy it was very hot. Ti-Pierre made some shade over the wagon for the mistress and her boy, but I wasn't allowed to share it with her. The roads was dusty and dry enough to make even the mules choke. Every plant in the fields was brown from the drought. At a crossroads a good distance from Nancy we came upon a black cock what had been sacrificed. I saw that Ti-Pierre and the driver knew its meaning and it pleased them.

The sun was going down when we arrived at Lenorman de Mézy, and the white *djabs* there was very glad to see the mistress and Etienne. They all came out from the big house what was covered in bougainvillaea and honeysuckle to make their guests welcome. Lots of domestics was running round, carrying the many bags of the mistress. Etienne was too busy playing with the other children to bother with me. I was glad to go to the slave quarters and get away from the mistress's scolding voice.

I was very surprised to see Boukman in the *tonelle* there because I didn't know he lived at Lenormand de Mézy. He looked up from where he was talking with some men, and made a small nod to me. He called some woman over and whispered in her ear, then she told me to join her with some other women in a hot meal of stew and yams. Ti-Pierre and the driver joined with Boukman and his men.

Early the next morning, the second he woke up, Etienne demanded I come to his side. It made me sick that he ate candy with one hand and drank from me with the other. The Lenormand de Mézy children saw him do that and mocked him until he was ashamed and sent me away.

All the men was missing from the slave quarters when I got back. I asked the women where they had gone, but they said it wasn't for me to know.

'Come, forget about the men,' a woman said. 'Have some fruit with us.'

With their right hands they give me some pineapple to eat what was delicious, but with their left hands they had sprinkled some powder what made me sleep.

CHAPTER 9

When I woke up it was night, and from far away in the hills came the sound of drumming, very fast and war-like. I was on my own in the *tonelle* except for some old slaves and babies and children what would have to be carried. The women was embroidering some cloths by candlelight, gray heads bent close to the cloth because their eyesight was failing them. The men was drinking clairin and playing a game with some bone dice. My head was heavy and dizzy and I had to lie there for some time before I could sit up. There was lightning flashing in the dark sky above the hills but no rain yet, only some strange wind what made the hairs on my arms stand up.

When the old people and babies went to their beds for the night, I crawled away into the darkness until I was strong enough to stand up and walk. I went in the direction of the hills, following the violent energy and rhythm of the drums from there. For some hours I walked deep into the woods. Thunder rolled like giant boulders down the hills, and the wind made the trees dance as though to the drums. Sometimes the whole woods was lit up by lightning and I saw that many people had already traveled on this path before me, because the leaves and twigs on the ground was trodden flat, and there was many discarded torches what had burnt out.

The path became very steep and my feet was bruised and bleeding from the stones underfoot. Through the wind what brought rain now, hard and sharp like little bush thorns, I could hear many people chanting, *Eh! Eh! Mbumba! Eh! Eh! Mbumba!* The drums was wild now, almost out of control, and the ground was trembling with the stamping of hundreds of feet. *Eh! Eh! Mbumba! Eh! Eh! Mbumba.*

There was some light up ahead so I got down on my stomach and crawled like a snake onto a ledge what looked over a big clearing in the woods. There was maybe three hundred slaves below me, dancing like wild winds, everybody armed with a cane knife or machete, an axe or a gun. *Eh! Eh! Mbumba! Eh! Eh! Mbumba.*

The ground in the clearing was old and bare so I knew it had been used for some time. Most of the people had better clothes than the field slaves so they must have been *commandeurs* and *artisans*. Nobody wore shoes, but still they slammed their feet down frantically on the earth as they whirled around to the drums. *Eh! Eh! Mbumba! Eh! Eh! Mbumba.*

In the middle of the clearing was a huge bonfire and Boukman stood there with some beautiful brown-skinned girl dressed in red like him, her black hair hanging right down to her waist. She had a fine face like the French ladies, but she was strong and graceful like a Guinea woman. Boukman seemed even more like a giant in the firelight. He knelt to draw some fine patterns on the earth with what looked like ashes. They didn't even stir in the wind, and when Boukman put some fire to them they exploded with great bangs and smoke. He did this with his left hand not his right like when you do things for the ancestors. *Eh! Eh! Mbumba! Eh! Eh! Mbumba.*

The rain was falling harder now and the fire was hissing like a thousand snakes. Boukman made some signal to Ti-Pierre, and Ti-Pierre brought forward a little black pig what was screaming and shitting from terror. *Eh! Eh! Mbumba! Eh! Eh! Mbumba.* Boukman lifted the pig to the air, and I thought he going to present it to the points before he called on Legba, but he lifted the pig to the opposite points instead. Right away some other old man spirit what was full of rage came into the beautiful woman's head and ripped the testicles from the pig with his teeth. A huge gust of wind, reeking of death and destruction, came howling down from the sky and blew the fire right over the woman, but she wasn't hurt while that *lwa* was in her head. Her hair didn't even burn. *Eh! Eh! Mbumba! Eh! Eh! Mbumba.* The pig was groaning and shaking with pain and shock.

The drums became even harder and faster, and the people was dancing wild and angry. It was hard to know what was their feet and what was thunder. *Eh! Eh! Mbumba! Eh! Eh! Mbumba.*

Boukman bowed to the beautiful woman. 'Carrefour, my lord. Welcome to Saint-Domingue.'

'Thank you,' Carrefour said, his voice rumbling and slow like some massive, ancient, angry, dead thing. 'It is my pleasure to be here.' Blood from the pig ran down the chin of the beautiful woman while he talked.

'Are you ready?' Boukman asked.

'We are all ready,' Carrefour replied.

Boukman give his knife to Carrefour, and the woman took the pig and made one slash across its throat. While Ti-Pierre held the pig so it couldn't struggle, Boukman caught the blood in a bowl. *Eh! Eh! Mbumba! Eh! Eh! Mbumba.*

One by one all the people broke from dancing to drink some

blood and swear allegiance to the fight against the French.

Carrefour screamed to them, '*Koupe tèt, boule kay.* Cut off their heads, burn their houses.'

Finally only Boukman was left to drink some blood. He held his fist over his heart while he drank, and then he demanded of Carrefour, 'Open the gates of the night, my lord, and allow the slaves what was killed by the French through. Let them come forward and fight with us for freedom and revenge. It's time for war.'

Eh! Eh! Mbumba! Eh! Eh! Mbumba.

Suddenly Boukman was staggering and convulsing around the clearing, his face clenched tight with pain and fear. His body, shuddering and moaning, was writhing like a snake. Then, as suddenly as he started, Boukman stopped and looked very slowly and carefully over everybody what was there. The rain was very heavy now and the wind was bending the trees almost to the ground. Boukman lurched into the bonfire and everybody was roaring, *Eh! Eh! Mbumba! Eh! Eh! Mbumba.* There was something about Boukman's furious, jerking limp what was familiar, and slowly I started to understand what I saw.

Boukman took a log from the middle of the fire, and then he stood there and ate it like it was a cucumber while the wind flayed him with flames. When he finally stepped from the fire, Ti-Pierre dropped to his knees and threw a libation of water at Boukman's feet.

'How dare you insult me with water!' Boukman shouted, and kicked at him. 'Don't you know who I am?' Straight away I recognized the voice what wasn't Boukman's no more. 'Bring me some rum — the good sort like the French drink, not that shit they give the slaves. And some gunpowder. Hurry before I change my mind and kill you!'

Ti-Pierre quickly brought forward a bowl of rum and a pouch

of gunpowder what Boukman mixed together and drank down in one swallow.

'Welcome, Prince l'Afrique,' Ti-Pierre say to him. 'We have been waiting a long time for you.'

Boukman wiped his mouth and grabbed Ti-Pierre's throat, lifting him off the ground like he was no heavier than a little *bébé*.

'The French destroyed Prince l'Afrique and made me instead,' he laughed. 'Prince le Kreyol.'

'Is — was —' Laura start to say. She couldn't look more shock if she met a real-life ghost, which I guess she has, kind of.

'That's him,' I nod. 'One and the same.'

'Who y'all talkin' about?' Jolie ask.

'Prince le Kreyol is my daddy I was tellin' you about last night. Laura met him too. He the one give her that *fleur-de-lis*.'

'Are you tellin' me that my granddaddy is a *lwa*? Get out of here.' Jolie turn to Mozzie and twirl her finger around the side of her head. 'She ain' right in the head,' she mouth to him.

Now I knew why Boukman wanted to bury the prince's body so bad. Not because he thought the prince deserved a fitting funeral, but so Boukman could use his spirit.

Prince le Kreyol staggered and lurched around the clearing, slashing wildly and ferociously at the air with a machete. *Eh! Eh! Mbumba! Eh! Eh! Mbumba.* The drums was almost one continuous frantic beat, and the people was whirling around the clearing almost as fast as the wind, the trees thrashing wildly to and fro above them.

'Don't listen to the lies of the god of the whites,' Prince le Kreyol was screaming. 'He just lives in the clouds and he doesn't care what happens to slaves. He only wants your freedom and your flesh for the French. He only cares about the whites. The *lwa* are your gods. Serve us well and we will fight with you. We will help you destroy all the whites and their children. We will make them pay for destroying our lives. We will murder every last one of them and then we will stand alongside you while you drink their blood. Make them die slowly, torture them, let them know the same terror they give to us every day.'

Eh! Eh! Mbumba! Eh! Eh! Mbumba.

'Don't be afraid. The French can't kill you. If you die, then you will you join the *lwa* and continue the fight for freedom.'

Next a *lwa* came into Ti-Pierre. His mouth was moving but no words came out, because now he was some slave what had swallowed his tongue to die and escape back to Guinea. Ti-Pierre just moaned and stabbed the earth in a vengeful frenzy. Then the beautiful girl in red bent over like an old woman, and she was biting her arms, ripping the flesh on her legs with her fingernails, mad with frustration, screaming obscenities and curses against the French. *Eh! Eh! Mbumba! Eh! Eh! Mbumba.*

One by one more *lwa* came into the people's heads. The *lwa* was filled with rage and thirst for French blood, hacking the trees and ground with knives and axes, swearing revenge. There was a huge streak of lightning overhead what made me scream, and I thought for sure I would be discovered, but everybody was a *lwa* now, howling in fury, slashing, stabbing, hacking, bleeding, chanting, *Eh! Eh! Mbumba! Eh! Eh! Mbumba.*

'MON DIEU,' FLOYD say, looking like he just woke up with a leg missing. 'Do you have any idea what this is?'

'No,' everybody say, except for Jolie, who say, 'Yeah, a bunch of wackos havin' a hell of a party in the woods.'

Floyd holding Angélique's journal like a newborn baby he seeing for the first time. His hands shaking. 'This is a first-hand

119

account of the Bois-Caïman Ceremony, and it's the only one. This is like finding an eyewitness account of King Arthur of Camelot removing his sword from the stone.'

I ARRIVED BACK at the *tonelle* before dawn, well ahead of anybody else, and even though I was exhausted I could only think of you, daughter, and I knew I wouldn't sleep until I got back to Nancy. A few hours later, the slaves from Lenormand de Mézy arrived back in the quarters and I pretended I was still drugged from the powder what they gave me. Some women checked on me before slipping back into their huts for what sleep they could get before the sun rose. For hours I plotted how to get back to Nancy until it seemed obvious that Etienne was my only chance. If he wanted to go back there, then his mother would have no choice but to follow, because he got everything what he wanted.

In the morning I waited for Etienne to demand some of my milk, but I was never summoned, and I cursed the white children for mocking him. The same thing happened in the afternoon and evening, and although I was almost frantic with worry I stayed around the *tonelle* and helped the women prepare the slave food, pretending not to see the gouges and scratches on their arms and throats.

It was over a week before I had an opportunity to speak to Etienne. He came down to the slave quarters with the other white children to pick out some slave children to be their horses.

'Good morning, Etienne,' I said to him. 'You have not called for me in a while. Don't you like me no more?'

He looked at me with such hate in his eyes I was shocked. 'Don't call me by my name, nigger,' he said.

'I'm sorry, young Master. I just thought you might want —'

'I don't want to talk with you. Get away from me,' he said.

'But, Master, wait. Listen to me.' I took his arm to stop him from leaving and he started screaming like I was trying to kill him. 'Stop it,' I said, shaking him. 'I have to tell you something.'

The other children was shouting and crying, but I wouldn't let go of Etienne.

'Listen to me,' I said to him. 'Your papa has bought lots of toys from a French ship in Le Cap. He has them all back at Nancy waiting for you. We should go back there as quickly —'

I was knocked to the ground by the crack of a whip butt across my skull.

'How dare you touch our children, you filthy black bitch!' some white man was shouting at me. He beat me about twenty times, spit flying from his mouth as he screamed curses down on me.

Not once did I hear Etienne tell him to stop, and just when I thought the white man was going to beat me to death, Chalmette's wife shouted for him to stop.

'She's not your slave to kill. Stop it at once.'

The man hit me once more before he obeyed her. 'Never touch any of these children again or I will kill you. Do you hear me?' he demanded.

'Yes, *'Sieur. Je suis navrée.* I'm sorry.'

For a moment I caught the torment in the mistress's eye before it was replaced, in a blink, with the unfeeling wall she withdrew behind in her mind. After the whites had left, some women helped me back to my mat and gave me some bitter tea for the pain, and I slept feverishly for a short time.

On waking, I bided my time until the Lenormand de Mézy slaves had retired for the night. When I was sure everybody was sleeping, though I was bruised and stiff, I crept from the *tonelle*, and walked deep into the tinder-dry cane fields, well away from the dogs, then I started to run, not stopping for two nights until I reached Nancy. I kept to the thickly wooded hills as much as I could, once stumbling on a wide clearing like Boukman's, the ground sticky with fresh gore and black feathers. I was so exhausted and sore, if it wasn't for you, *bébé*, many times I would have just stopped and let myself die.

When I finally reached Nancy, I kept away from the big house and made my way to Modeste's hut. She was frightened to see me, but worse I couldn't see you anywhere, *bébé*, and I thought Chalmette had taken you to punish me.

'Tumé! What are you doing here?' Modeste whispered. 'It's not safe for you. Chalmette knows you ran away from Lenormand de Mézy — they sent a rider ahead of you. He arrived at the big house this morning.'

'Where's Angélique? What's happened to her?'

'Calm down, Tumé. Keep your voice down. Look. She's sleeping on my bed there. See?'

You was such a tiny little thing, daughter, that you hardly made a bump. When I got under the coarse blanket with you, you smiled at my touch even though you didn't wake. I held you close and tried not to think about how I would feel when the time came that I wouldn't be able to protect you from harm. If you didn't die in Prince le Kreyol's war against the French, your beauty meant that eventually you would be used as a white *djab*'s whore. And I wasn't wrong, was I, *bébé*?

'You can't stay here,' Modeste said to me. 'It's too dangerous. Chalmette's looking for you. He'll send somebody back here soon to see if you've returned yet.'

I decided the best place to hide was in the cave behind the waterfall. I didn't tell Modeste about the cave, but I told her to come to that spot and call for me if she had more news. She gave me a cold meal of rice and beans before I left without waking you, daughter, and I went to the cave where I hid for a few days. I didn't dare move in the cave because there wasn't much water to cover me, and the slaves was coming to draw water from the pool there because of the drought. I was terrified somebody would see me. Then early one morning, I heard Modeste calling my name, and I stepped through the feeble waterfall to find Modeste hardly able to breathe.

'They've all gone,' she panted. 'Ti-Pierre, the *artisans*, the women, all of them except for the old people and children.'

'When?'

'Sometime in the night. They was gone before I woke up this morning. The mistress and Etienne have gone also. She came back from Lenormand de Mézy yesterday and packed up all her belongings. She's going to Le Cap with Etienne because she said that she can't stand to live in this in unholy country no more. She's taking the first ship back to Paris before her soul dies here.'

'Lucky for her she has that choice,' I said.

Then suddenly the sun darkened behind a wall of black smoke what was rising across the whole horizon like it was the end of the world, and I knew that Prince le Kreyol's war against the French had begun. Ahead of the smoke was the chanting thunder of a large army, growing closer, thousands and thousands of feet now, not just hundreds. *Eh! Eh! Mbumba! Eh! Eh! Mbumba.*

I told Modeste to fetch you from her hut, *bébé*, and make her way to the big house, then I ran fast as I could to find Chalmette. I found him standing at the top of the stairs leading to the big house, watching the sky of smoke with an expression somewhere between horror and resignation. He aimed his gun at me.

'Master, don't shoot, please. I have come to warn you that the rebels will kill you if you don't leave here right away. You have to go now, quickly, before they get here.'

Eh! Eh! Mbumba! Eh! Eh! Mbumba.

'I'm not leaving everything I own without a fight,' he said, like he could fight them all.

'You have no chance to fight, Master. There are too many of them and they will hack you into pieces as soon as they find you. Please believe me, you have to leave here now.'

Chalmette took one long last look at the smoke what was turning the sky to night, and from his sigh I knew he had decided to flee.

'Help me load a wagon with some valuables,' he said to me.

Eh! Eh! Mbumba! Eh! Eh! Mbumba.

The air was heavy with the choking clouds of smoke, but it was still possible to see the wide glow of fire fueled by the forests and fields it was consuming as Prince le Kreyol's war advanced towards the Nancy plantation.

'There's no time for that, Master. Be grateful you can leave now with your life.'

'I'm not leaving here with nothing,' Chalmette said. 'Go saddle up some horses and bring them here. As fast as you can, Rose.'

For once I didn't care about my slave name and ran to the stables. The horses could smell the smoke also, and was moving about nervously in their stalls. The only horses what would let me come near them was a couple of old mules, so I quickly saddled them up and opened all the stalls before leading the mules to the big house. It was very smoky and hot by the time I got there, and soft ash was raining down from the sky. The ground beneath our feet was rumbling from the advance of Prince le Kreyol's rebel army. *Eh! Eh! Mbumba! Eh! Eh! Mbumba.* It was possible now to hear the howling of the women, fighting alongside the men.

Modeste had arrived at the big house with you, *bébé*, by the time I returned. Chalmette stored several bags of gold in the saddle-bags before he was ready to move.

'Put your girl on one of the mules,' he said to me. 'Modeste, you get on the other one.'

She shook her head. 'I'm not going with you,' she said.

'Don't be stupid, Modeste,' I cried. 'Get on the mule, please. We have to leave at once.'

'No, I am too old,' she said. 'I was born here and I want to die here. I don't know any place else. Quick, you go now, before they get here. Save Angélique while you can.'

'I don't care if she stays here or not,' Chalmette said to me, lifting you onto a mule, *bébé*, 'but you and your girl are coming with me now.'

Eh! Eh! Mbumba! Eh! Eh! Mbumba.

'Please, Modeste,' I tried again. 'You have been like a mother to me. I can't stand to lose another one. Please come.'

'*Na wè pita*, Tumé,' she said to me. Then she placed you on the other mule and kissed you goodbye. '*Au revoir*, little angel.'

I didn't even have time to embrace Modeste before Chalmette pushed me ahead of him and told me to start walking. I called to her, 'Thank you for being such a good friend to me.'

'Be safe, *ma fille*,' was her last words to me.

Our little party picked its way through the smouldering cane fields, barely ahead of the fire racing towards Nancy, the mules stumbling in the hazy dark smoke. You was so sad, daughter, at leaving Modeste behind, but you was brave and didn't cry once. As we neared the entrance to the Nancy plantation and the safety of the hills, we were able to make out two dark shapes, one not much larger than the other, swinging from the iron arch over the gates.

'Oh, dear God, please no,' Chalmette cried, and as many as fifty crows rose cawing from the gutted bodies of his wife and son.

CHAPTER 10

'How could they do that to a woman and child?' Laura ask.

'It's easy,' Floyd say, putting the journal down.

She give him a horrify look. 'Easy?'

'*Mais*, not like that,' he say. 'I mean if you suppress an emotion it's going to eat your insides out until you explode. The slaves had to hide everything — love, anger, grief, hate, fear.' Floyd shrug. 'All those feelings erupted. Lava doesn't think, Oh look, there's a little puppy, I'd better go around, me.'

Chalmette didn't show more emotion as he cut down the bodies of his family. He told me to carry you myself, and then laid his wife and son across the mules before leading them through the gates. The whole countryside was thick with hot smoke and ash.

Eh! Eh! Mbumba! Eh! Eh! Mbumba.

'Master,' I said. 'Stop, please. The rebels are coming along this road. We can't go this way. Come with me. I know a way out of here.'

The master obeyed me like he was the slave. He followed me like a little dog, obedient as you like. I tied some dry cane to the mules' tails to brush away our dusty footprints. There was no sign of Modeste along the way and there was no time to look for her because the rebels couldn't have been more than a mile from Nancy. Some buildings had caught fire now and there was some explosions from the distillery. The mules stumbled under their loads of gold and corpses as we made our way along the trickle of river to the waterfall. They could hardly walk by the time we got there and I knew we had to continue on foot without them. Prince le Kreyol's army would soon catch up with us and I would be butchered alongside Chalmette for helping him.

'Master, we have to leave the mules here. They are slowing us down.'

Eh! Eh! Mbumba! Eh! Eh! Mbumba.

'*D'accord,*' he said, like a rock with no mind of its own.

'That means you have to leave the mistress and young master behind also,' I said.

It seemed like it took him a long time to understand this. '*D'accord,*' he said again.

I told him to put some gold in his pockets, and while he wasn't looking hid some gold in my head rag. Then I helped him to hide the bodies of his wife and child behind the waterfall with the saddles and the rest of the gold. Chalmette obeyed everything what I said.

We heard the sound of some guns from nearby, so I took your hand, daughter, and told Chalmette to follow us into the burning cane fields. *Eh! Eh! Mbumba! Eh! Eh! Mbumba.* Hot cinders rained down on us as we ran as fast as we could. The smoke was so thick I couldn't see what way to run, but I knew to run from the sound of the rebels what was chanting and shouting, until deep, deep into the woods some hours later we dared to stop and draw our breath.

We had been climbing for some time and below us we could see the whole plain was burning — a vast, smoking, blackened waste of countryside. Even from so high in the hills we could hear the chanting of the rebels on the plain, as much a part of the air now as the smoke.

Chalmette looked at what was left of his world, destroyed now, and said, 'What have they done?'

'What have they done?' I asked him. 'This is your fault. You did all this. You created this hell.'

He didn't make a sign he understood me though, and after we had rested for a while I asked him what he wanted to do, because the *djab* you know is better than the *djab* you don't, and I had no chance to escape from Saint-Domingue without him.

'I don't care,' he said. His voice was slow and thick, the words emerging from his mouth like fat sleepy grubs from the ground. 'Do what you want.'

'*Sieur*, if we make it to Le Cap, maybe we can find a ship to take us some place away from here.'

Chalmette looked around himself like a helpless baby. 'And then what?'

'That's not for me to say. You're the master in charge. But we are all going to die if we don't get away from this land, make no mistake about that.'

He closed his eyes and lay down. 'Maybe I want to die,' he said.

I looked at him lying on the ground feeling sorry for himself because he had lost everything except his liberty, and I staggered from the anger that entered my head.

'Get up,' I shouted, and kicked him. 'Get up and start walking before I kill you myself. How dare you take my freedom, my family, my friends, even my name away from me, and now you want to take my daughter's life away from me also. Get up.'

Like a child startled into obedience by the swift wrath of a parent, Chalmette got to his feet and stood waiting for me to lead the way. His eyes was very still and shiny like the mirrors in the big house.

'You owe me this and don't you forget it,' I told him.

For almost two days we traveled on foot towards Le Cap, without sleeping once, taking turns to carry you, *bébé*. If we was lucky we found some berries or fruit to eat. Sometimes we had to hide from bands of rebels searching the hills for whites. Once we came close to the outskirts of a burning plantation and could hear screaming from there. There was hundreds of rebels in looted clothing pouring rum onto crops and buildings to make them burn faster. Some had guns what they had taken from the French, but most had hoes and cane knives for weapons. Some of the rebels wore charms, little bags of enemy teeth and grave dirt to protect them from the weapons of the French.

As we started to come close to Le Cap there was less vegetation and it became harder to hide from Prince le Kreyol's soldiers what was roaming everywhere. Any road we crossed was lined with impaled French heads, faces contorted from the horror of their final moments. Packs of starving, frightened dogs lapped at the blood what was flowing more freely on the roads of Saint-Domingue than the water in her rivers.

Thousands of rebels had set up camp around the Le Cap, their tents and fires visible as far as the eye could see. We crawled between some thorny bushes to wait for the shelter of dark. All day the French fired their cannons at the rebel camps. Sometimes they sent out some soldiers on horseback but those men didn't stand a chance. As soon as they got close to the rebels they was shot from their horses, stripped of their uniforms and guns, and then torn limb from limb. There was also lots of fighting from inside the city as the people panicked and attacked each other like rats. Many buildings went up in flames and there was lots of screaming and shouting like on a slave ship.

In the harbor beyond the city was maybe thirty ships, all preparing to sail as quickly as they could from the horror of Saint-Domingue, but we had no chance to make it to the city in daylight, so we had to wait.

As night fell we could see by the light of the rebels' fires that they was getting ready to attack Le Cap. The rebels was drumming a rapid, angry call to battle, taking up their arms as the Kreyol *lwa* came into their heads. *Eh! Eh! Mbumba! Eh! Eh! Mbumba.* Cut off their heads! Burn their houses!

We knew we had to run for Le Cap before the rebels descended on the city. Chalmette prayed for protection from his god before we ran, but I asked nothing from mine. How we made it to the city alive I do not know. Maybe Chalmette's god did that, because we had to run over the slaughtered bodies of hundreds of French what had been fleeing to Le Cap before us. I wish I could forget some of the things I saw, *bébé*, but those memories will not leave me alone — my punishment for surviving that massacre.

As we came to some big wooden gates of the city, plenty of white soldiers shouted at us from the top of the earthworks to hurry. They held a gate open so we could enter Le Cap, then drew the heavy bolt behind us. A boss soldier stepped forward and wanted to know Chalmette's name and where he had come from.

'My name is Charles Chalmette of the Nancy plantation. The rebels attacked there two days ago. I only just escaped with my life and the clothes on my back.'

The soldiers saw our soot-streaked faces and scorched ragged clothing, and didn't suspect we had gold hidden there. They took Chalmette's gun and gunpowder from him because they was running out of arms, and told us to run for the shore because the whole city would go up in flames if the rebels made it that far.

The streets of Le Cap was a burning, bloody hell, as whites, brown-skinned people, slaves, domestics — everybody there — roamed the streets in murderous packs like animals, fighting each other to the death. The dead hung broken from makeshift gallows, their dripping gore making the streets slippery underfoot. Fires broke out on the dry shingle roofs of the city as the wind fanned clouds of black smoke, heavy with fat embers of fire in from the plains. *Eh! Eh! Mbumba! Eh! Eh! Mbumba.*

Chalmette found a bloody machete what he had to remove from the clenched hand of a dead man, and then he roared and slashed his way blindly down to the harbor where there was thousands of whites trying to buy passage on the few ships left there. On a small beach there was some whites fighting with sailors what was trying to escape in their boat. The sailors had to fight everybody off with their oars and guns to get away. Some white women jumped into the ocean after them and drowned in their heavy dresses trying to reach the little boat. Chalmette shouted for the sailors to wait. He had plenty of gold for them, he said, if they would take us to their ship. The sailors stopped rowing at the mention of gold and said for us to come forward. We waded out to their boat, and the whites on shore was furious when they saw that the sailors was helping a slave woman and her child instead of them. Chalmette had to sever many hands so the boat could get away.

The sailors asked Chalmette to give them the gold he had promised them before they would take us all the way to their ship. But before he could reach for the gold in his pockets, I gave Chalmette a look to say nothing, and gave over the gold tied up in my head rag because it wasn't nearly so much as what he was carrying. What I gave the sailors was enough for them to be happy. When we reached the ship, the sailors pretended to their captain

131

that they had saved our lives from the goodness of their hearts and didn't tell him about the gold we had given them.

'If you would be kind enough to follow me to your cabin, '*Sieur* Chalmette,' the captain said, 'I will have my men secure your slaves below.'

I didn't want to go with the sailors because I already knew what black thing was in their hearts. I fought all I could with them until Chalmette came striding back across the deck and knocked me to the floor.

'Be grateful you are not dying back there with the rest of those savages,' he shouted at me. 'Now do what they say before I have somebody whip you.'

I saw that life had come back into his eyes now we had reached some safety, but it wasn't a good kind of life. It was cold and dark like deep in a well, no warmth there at all.

The sailors took me below to the hold with its cargo of sugar, coffee and rum, and tied me down so I was like a crossroads on the floor. Starting right from then they raped me constantly, day or night, on my stomach, my back, never less than two of them, and never without the utmost shameful ways they could think of. I never once refused or fought with them, because I thought they would do the same to you, *bébé*, if I didn't let them have their way, if I didn't seem like I enjoyed their foul, brutal, stinking attention. There's not enough soap in the world to wash away what they did to me.

I didn't see daylight again until we arrived in New Orleans and the Spanish officials of that city came aboard and found us gagged and trussed behind some barrels where they wasn't supposed to find us. At first they didn't want to let Chalmette take us ashore with him. They had already heard from faster ships than ours that the Saint-Domingue slaves was dangerous and not to be trusted, and the Spanish didn't want me to cause trouble with their slaves. They wanted to put us in some prison, but Chalmette argued with them because we was all the property he had left in the world. When I saw that the Spanish didn't care about this and Chalmette was stupid, I said to him, in Kreyol, 'See if they will look the other way with some gold in their pockets.'

Finally Chalmette understood what I meant and took the Spanish aside to make a bargain with them. They was more smart than Chalmette, because they made him turn out his pockets and took all of the gold he had. The captain was very angry when he saw that Chalmette had not offered to pay for his berth when he could afford to do that. To me it seemed like the captain's men had taken more than enough from me to pay for all of our berths a hundred times over.

When we was finally allowed to leave that ship we was met by many rich French what offered Chalmette their homes. He knew some man there in very fine clothes what he did business with, so we went with that man to his house. Chalmette's friend was called Philippe Gaultier and he was a merchant there in New Orleans. Chalmette rode with Gaultier in a carriage while we was tethered behind like livestock. All along the levee of that mighty river was ships and boats of every kind, some sailing, some docked. Hundreds of slaves was loading and unloading cargo from them. The path was lined with vendors of every kind of fruit and vegetable you could think. It was the most big market I'd seen in my life and everything was for sale there: livestock and poultry, clothes, furs, tools, flowers, simple furniture, shellfish, pickled peppers, biscuits, cheeses, hot soups, cakes, bread, coffee, soap, rope, everything. The smell of spices and cooked meats for sale made my mouth fill with water.

'Buy your Creole eggs here,' a woman was shouting. 'Laid fresh this morning.'

'Buy your Creole oysters here,' another cried. 'Creole shrimp and clams. Caught fresh this morning.'

'Buy your Creole candles here,' some woman with bad teeth was laughing. 'Made fresh this morning.'

There was some people like I'd never seen before selling baskets and woven mats from palmetto leaves on the ground, and later I found out that they was Indians what lived there first before the whites came.

The streets of New Orleans was just as filthy as those of Le Cap. In Guinea we knew to keep our waste and rubbish separate from our houses, but the whites live next their own filth like pigs. They emptied their night-pots out from their front doors, where it lay stinking in the streets with the animal shit. Most of the buildings was wooden with iron balconies along the upper stories. All the windows and doors had shutters to allow what air there was to move in the rooms. There was lots of brown-skinned people about the streets in fine clothes like the rich whites. Some was even riding on grand horses, like they was lords. The women wore pale silky dresses, and they fanned themselves from the shade of the balconies and roofs, surrounded by potted plants and caged songbirds. In satin shoes those women moved about with the sultry languor of cats hiding from the sun, and every one of them made eyes at Chalmette and Gaultier, their smiles inviting and knowing, not ladies at all.

New Orleans was much smaller than Le Cap, but it was noisier by far. It seemed like every second building was an inn, and I was shocked to see women of all colors inside of them, crudely straddling the laps of drunken men with rotten teeth and wandering hands, while they sang bawdy songs about fucking. We traveled down some street what had banks, jewelers, fine furniture, paintings, and tailors to the nobility of France and Spain. The branches of trees what hung over from the hidden gardens and courtyards everywhere was laden with big, lush flowers and fruit, but you couldn't smell their perfumes because of what lay in the streets.

It didn't take us long to come to Gaultier's house. The carriage was driven through some iron gates up an alleyway what opened out into a large brick courtyard. The courtyard had a fountain in the middle and somebody had gone to great trouble to make a beautiful garden all around. Even the balconies what ran all around had lots of flower baskets and potted plants. Here the birds was free of cages and they flew around the courtyard like in the forest. Climbing flowers clung to nearly every surface of the buildings and walls, and away from the streets the flowers smelt strong and sweet. Some slaves came from the quarters what was hidden from view by some fruit trees, and held the horses while Chalmette and Gaultier got out from the carriage. Gaultier's wife came from her house to welcome Chalmette. She took one look at him and her dark eyes filled with pity and tears. She straight away ordered some domestics to draw a bath for Chalmette and to fetch some of her husband's clothing for him. She didn't even so much as glance at us, his slaves what had been through much worse.

'I'll arrange a meal to be prepared for you while you freshen up, you poor man,' she said to him, leading him into the house by his arm. 'I'm so sorry to hear about your wife and son, God rest their souls.'

'I think you're mistaken, Madame Gaultier,' I heard Chalmette say to her. 'I've never been married and I certainly have never experienced the pleasure of my own family.'

A thought came to me then that made my heart beat very fast: if Chalmette had stopped any memories of his butchered family, then maybe he had also stopped his memories of the gold what was hidden with their bodies.

I saw Gaultier frown, puzzled by Chalmette's denial, but he just shrugged to himself and told some young brown-skinned girl to take us to the slave quarters for a meal and somewhere to sleep. Her name was Marie-Catherine and she moved about so quietly you almost didn't notice her.

'*Oui, 'Sieur* Gaultier,' she said, her words soft as a butterfly. '*Bien sûr.*'

She led us to the slave kitchen, and out of sight from Gaultier she became a different person. We didn't speak the same *langaj* but some words I understood well enough to know that Marie-Catherine wore two faces — one for her and one for the whites. While she heated us some chicken stew and green vegetables to eat, she gossiped about the other slaves and domestics, about Gaultier and his mistresses, about the handsome free man of color what called on the mistress when Gaultier was away, about the improper goings-on in neighboring homes. After our meal Marie-Catherine led us to a tiny yard what was enclosed with sacking. She gave us a bucket of water and some soap to wash, and after brought us some faded cotton dresses to wear.

'I'll show you where to sleep now,' she said, and led us up some narrow wooden stairs to a long room above the slave quarters. She opened the shutters to let in some light and I saw that there was a wooden pallet and a blanket on the floor what we had to share. She said to sleep as long as we wanted — she would tell Gaultier we was sick or something — and to come find her when we was ready.

It was wonderful to lie in the private safety of that room, just out of reach of the warm sun what was shimmering on the wall, and know that I would wake up with you in my arms, *bébé*, far from the horror and destruction of Prince le Kreyol's war. For the first time in weeks my muscles and mind unclenched into a deep sleep, and I didn't think of anything until the next morning.

It was Sunday and there wasn't many slaves around because they had gone to the slave market on the outskirts of the city. Marie-Catherine and some other woman was hanging slave laundry on some lines strung between the balconies out of sight from Gaultier's residence.

She gave you a cloth doll to play with, *bébé*, while I helped them hang the clothes.

'Do you have any idea what's going to happen to us?' I asked her.

'Maybe,' she said. 'The mistress said for you to help me with the housework while they think what to do with you, but I heard from Céline, that domestic with the gray eyes what thinks she's special, that Gaultier wants to start up a sugar plantation. He has the money but no skills, and Chalmette has the skills but no money. Seems like they are the perfect solution for each other.'

We stayed at Gaultier's home for some months, during which time both Gaultier and Chalmette went away for some time. It seemed like it hardly ever stopped raining in New Orleans and I began to hate that city and its hot steamy stinking weather. Like Marie-Catherine had said, a handsome brown-skinned man in fine clothes visited the mistress every afternoon while Gaultier was away, never alighting from his drape-drawn carriage until he was in the courtyard and away from the prying eyes of the streets. Marie-Catherine told me the man was a slave once. He made plenty money from selling furniture what he made to invest in some land before anybody wanted it. Now he had his own slaves to take care of his every whim.

'Still,' she said, 'apart from Madame Gaultier, the only favor the whites give him is to borrow his money. He can't even sit at the same table as them to eat.'

While Gaultier's wife was busy in her *chambre* with her lover,

Marie-Catherine sneaked away until the early evenings. One time during a midday meal, just before Marie-Catherine would disappear again, I asked her what business she did when she was gone, because she left me all her work to do and I wanted a good reason for that.

'I lease out my land,' she said.

'What do you mean?' I asked, because I couldn't see that a slave would own land.

'The land between my legs,' she laughed. 'What land did you think I was talking about?'

I was shocked by this news, and didn't try to hide my disgust. 'Don't you have any morals?' I said.

'Morals aren't going to buy my freedom,' she said, and smiled at me like I had just made her a compliment instead. Then she shook her head sadly at me. 'You're a slave like me, Tumé. I'm surprised you haven't realized by now that the whites make any morals impossible. *Non*? You do not believe me? Then think about this: if you don't want to go hungry, you have to steal food. If you don't want to be beaten, you have to make it easy for them to rape you. If you have a sick friend, then you steal some coins for a doctor. Don't you see now how useless morals are to you?'

I understood she was right then, because I had to forget about my morals on that ship from Saint-Domingue to protect my child. I was sorry then for the bad things I thought about Marie-Catherine, because it wasn't for me judge how she lived her life.

Then she spoiled that by saying, 'Your daughter is already very beautiful, Tumé. Give her some years and she could hook a big fish what might buy freedom for both of you. Don't tell me you haven't noticed the way men look at her? If she doesn't sell her land they'll take it for free.'

'Shut your filthy mouth!' I shouted at her, and pushed her away from the table. 'Get away from us.'

Marie-Catherine became angry herself. 'You're jealous because no sane man would want to lease your land,' she shouted back. 'Look at that big sore on your mouth with no teeth,' she said. 'It looks like a wound on a pig's vulva — like you're not ugly enough already.'

From then on I only talked with her if I had to.

Some days later Chalmette and Gaultier arrived back in New Orleans with some big news. They had decided to go into business together, and Gaultier had purchased some land in St Luc Parish, two days' travel from New Orleans. He was starting a new plantation what Chalmette was going to run for him. They spent some weeks organizing building and farming equipment, young cane plants, seeds, supplies, buying what few slaves they could find for sale — mostly runaways and ones what was hard to discipline and nobody wanted.

I was glad when Chalmette took me to work on the new plantation as a field slave because it meant I could keep an eye on him and see if he remembered about the gold.

CHAPTER 11

'WHAT TIME IS it?' Jolie yawn. She look like a zombie herself.

Mozzie check his watch. 'It's just gone three in the morning. Any chance of a feed, mate?' he say to her. 'I'm starving.'

'Sure, baby,' she smile, like she expecting a tip. 'Let me take a look at what we got.'

Ain' nothing in the kitchen worth getting excite about, though, so Jolie and Mozzie take off to the market out by the casino, opposite the gas station. Nobody really in the mood for talking. Floyd say he going get some fresh air and take his dog out for a run.

'You want a beer?' I ask Laura, but she already out cold lengthways on the sofa. I fetch myself a couple of 45s and set back on my La-Z-Boy to study her a while. Hard to believe we relate to each other. Except for her eyes, there ain' a damn similarity I can see between us. She small-bone and cain' be much bigger than five-two. She got a cute, foxy little face, and a hellfire head of red hair with a mind of its own. She got conservative taste in clothes — kind of

Banana Republic — as if to compensate for the color and wildness of her hair. Her jewelry kind of way-out, though — chunky-ass silver and blue-green shell that save her from seeming stick-up-the-ass-repress in that way some white folks got, especially the ones with money.

Mozzie and Jolie come back with some ham and eggs just about to expire, and some more beer. Laura don't want nothing and donate her plate to the dog. She so worn out she look as bad as Jolie, but there ain' much of the journal to go now. After Jolie make some coffee and fetch me another beer — which she practically throw at me — we make ourselves comfortable again before we hear the last few pages.

CANE GREW WELL in St Luc, the soil dark and rich from flooding. Chalmette and Gaultier bought all the latest machinery available, and in five years they was making a fortune from the best sugar in Louisiana. Their barrels, stamped with the *Le Phénix Plantation* brand, was fought over in French ports. Chalmette had a grand, luxurious house built for himself, and he took a Creole wife, Adélaïde, from New Orleans, what he had twin daughters with. He always introduced Adélaïde to people as his first, only, and last wife. I don't think she cared about that because she was happy with all the money Chalmette was making. Soon he made enough money to make an equal partnership with Gaultier and they shared all the profits from that time.

For the first year on this plantation I was very sick. Seemed like every two weeks I had some kind of rash, even on my palms and the soles of my feet. With the rashes came some terrible fevers, and my bones and throat was raw with aching. Sometimes I was so tired I wasn't able to stand. At first I thought it was a sickness from the swamps and dense *siprière* round the plantation what had to be cleared and drained for planting. Then some new slave what arrived at St Luc saw the rash one time. He told me I had the pox from fucking, and I understood those sailors had given me this sickness when they raped me.

Then suddenly for no reason at all the rashes and the fevers stopped. I thought I was well again, and for nearly twelve years I was healthy as you like, not even so much as a headache. But as you can see now, *bébé*, the pox was just biding its time until it could come back more strong and kill me.

When my eyesight began to fail and I didn't even have the beauty of the sky to look at no more, I realized that the ancestors was still punishing me after all this time, just for that one lousy feast in Guinea what wasn't my fault. They had taken my health from me just like Chalmette's god had taken his memory, so now nobody was going to have the gold. I was happy to die so I could make the ancestors' existence a misery for them, but first I had to let you know about the gold, *bébé*, because I wasn't going to let them rob you of it too.

I called for the big Bambara carpenter, Jiffy, what knows some strong magic to come to my hut. When he arrived I told him to close the door.

'What's so important you interrupt my meal, old woman?' he said to me.

'I hear you're a *bokor*. A strong one.'

'So what if I am? It's too late to cure what you've got.'

'I want to die,' I told him. 'I'm ready for that, but that's not why I called you here. No — I want to you to bring the *lwa*, Prince le Kreyol, to me.'

Already Prince le Kreyol was in Louisiana, carried by the few slaves what managed to escape the revolution in Saint-Domingue, and the carpenter understood who I was asking for. He wanted some animal for a sacrifice before he attempted to call on such a powerful *lwa*, so I gave him all the money what you sent to me from time to time, daughter, what you made in New Orleans selling your own land.

'Buy whatever you need,' I told the carpenter. 'Just be quick.'

Some nights later he returned with a goat, what he slaughtered and buried deep in the earth of my hut. After placing a bowl of the goat's blood to one side, the carpenter traced a pattern of ashes on top of the offering. Sacrifice complete, he began to shake his sacred rattle over the ashes and call to Prince le Kreyol. Almost at once Prince le Kreyol came into the carpenter, who seemed distressed by the force of his arrival. His spirit didn't leave without a fight and it seemed like the carpenter struggled for a long time. Finally he stopped convulsing, and in relaxing dropped his *asson* to the ground.

'Your clothes are on that stool,' I told Prince le Kreyol, and watched as he dressed.

'Ah, beautiful, sweet, Tumé,' he said as he knelt at my mat and took my hand. 'You are still an exquisite rare orchid among cabbages.'

I know he was lying to me because of these sores I got all over my body now.

'Finally I can repay your kindness,' he said. 'Please, tell me what I can do for you.'

I couldn't see him clearly, just the red of his clothes and mask, but I thought I could hear some of the kind Guinea prince from all those years ago.

'I want you to bring Angélique back from New Orleans,' I told him. 'There's something she needs to know.'

'Really? Something she needs to know? Let me guess — would that something be about some gold?'

Prince le Kreyol's voice was full of guile and tricks now, and I became wary of him. 'I have no idea what you are talking about,' I said. 'What gold?'

'Come now, Tumé. The Nancy gold you hid in the cave behind the waterfall what I showed you. Remember now?'

'How could you know about that?'

'I know everything. I even saw you hiding on that ledge at Bois-Caïmen. I'm a powerful *lwa* now.'

'Then it will not be a problem for you to fetch my daughter to me, will it?'

'You are forgetting something, I think,' he said.

'Like what?'

Prince le Kreyol reached into his clothing and took out a small piece of gold what glowed like a star in the candlelight.

'My life and freedom are in this gold also,' he said. 'It is not just yours to do with as you wish.'

I thought about this and saw what he said was true. 'So what do you propose we going to do about that?' I asked him.

Prince le Kreyol got up from my mat and helped himself to some food, limping around my hut like he owned it. Not until he had eaten to his fill did he pull a stool over to where I lay and sit down.

'I want a child of ours to have the gold,' he said. 'Your daughter's blood and mine.'

I was so shocked by his idea I almost died right then. 'You want Angélique to have your baby?'

'No, not her. Don't insult me. I want a virgin to bear my child. Don't forget I really am a prince. I deserve the best, not some prostitute what willingly sells herself to the whites. That gold is dirty enough already.'

'Be careful how you talk about my daughter,' I said to him. 'Even if Angélique is not good enough for you, although you should

144

be so lucky, you should walk a mile along her path before you sit in judgment. You men think you got it tough as slaves, but at least the whites don't rape you every chance they get. Better Angélique gets paid for it than they just take it. At least she is free now.'

'What kind of freedom is that?'

'Shut your mouth,' I told him. 'I didn't call you here to insult my family. I might be sick and weak now, but as soon as I die I will come and find you, and make you bleed those words through your ass.'

Prince le Kreyol laughed at me. 'You're very scary when angered, Tumé, but you're wasting that energy. Save it for later. Even if Angélique was still as pure as the day she was born, the time isn't right yet to go back for the gold.'

'What if Chalmette remembers first?' I asked.

'Chalmette will never remember because he doesn't want to. He refuses to think about what's in that cave, that he once had a family in Saint-Domingue. Don't worry about him. It's not his gold to claim.'

'So when will be the right time?'

Prince le Kreyol lit a cigar from somewhere, and took his time smoking it. Finally he tapped some ash on the floor, and said, 'When some daughter of Captain De la Croix comes to New Orleans during Carnival. I'll mark her shoulder with his *fleur-de-lis*, the same place we have ours so you'll know her. Both she and our future daughter got plenty work to do before the ancestors going to leave them alone. This story starts with us, Tumé, but it's going to end with them.'

'You better go to New Orleans quick and find Angélique while I still have time.'

Prince le Kreyol chuckled to himself. 'Oh, that won't be necessary. Angélique will be back here with her pretty tail tucked between her legs soon enough. Then I want you to tell her everything. Make her write down all the story of the gold right away and hide it some place safe, until it's meant to be found.'

'But what if I die before she gets here?' I asked him, because I didn't have much strength left in this world.

Prince le Kreyol gave a small laugh that had no humor. 'I think you're going to live long enough,' he said, dropping something into my palm what felt dreadfully familiar. 'Because if you die,' he told me as I slowly realized what I was holding in my hand, 'then I will remove the cork and let the ancestors know Angélique's true name.'

THESE ARE NOW my own words, no longer those of my mother. She died a few days after I came back here to *Le Phénix*, carrying André Messemé's bastard baby what he does not care about. His wife cares plenty though. It's true about a woman scorned in some way. She attacked me like the barren hag she is, cutting my long hair off with a knife. She smashed my furniture and set my house alight, and not one person tried to stop her because they didn't like the fact André took care of me so well that I ate off best French china, wearing pearls and gems around my neck.

From luxury and a generous lover who adored me, suddenly I was out in the street, my scalp bleeding where André's wife had cut me, my home in flames. Everything André had given to me, his wife was destroying. Some neighbors watched this and they laughed and jeered at me until I ran away. At first I was numb and wandered the streets in shock until eventually I found myself standing outside of André's house. It was a very fine building with many chimneys and new paint on the shutters. The arched glass windows on every story was hung with lace. Without thinking about anything other than a friendly face what would help me, I knocked on his door and waited.

When André answered the door himself, the expression on his face was worse than anything his wife had done to me. I was used to seeing lust and affection in his eyes, but now there was only horror and disgust. André — the man who swore he loved me more than anything in the world — reached into his fancy coat and withdrew a purse full of money. Then, because he couldn't bear to touch me, he just threw the purse at me and slammed the door in my face before I could say a word.

For a while I remained on his doorstep, unable to believe that the same man who had kissed every inch of my body because it tasted delicious to him, the same man who taught me writing and sums, the same man who gave me jewelry hidden in flowers, now thought I was a monster. He didn't even care that his baby was already there in my womb for the world to see. Then, screaming loudly from a balcony above me, André's wife timed it perfectly so that when I looked to see where the terrible noise was coming from, the contents of the night pot she tipped over the railing hit me full in the face.

No cab driver wanted my money because I was covered in shit and seemed crazy. Finally some little hairy man agreed to take me in his wagon if I stayed at the back. He wanted all of André's money to take me to St Luc. It rained most of the way, but I was glad because it washed away the filth and cooled my raw mood.

The slaves at *Le Phénix* thought I was some kind of witch and they kept well away from my path as I made my way to my mother's hut. I found her lying on a mat, barely clinging to life, her weeping sores filling the dimly lit air with the stench of death. I thanked God she was almost blind and unable to see how far I had fallen since leaving St Luc armed only with my youth and beauty and freedom what André had paid for.

Chalmette turned up to see who this witch was, and opened

the door of the hut without knocking. He recognized me right away and stopped in the doorway to cross himself. His hair was white now and his body stiff with age. He saw that my mother's breathing wasn't good, and asked, 'How is she?'

'She's dying.'

'She was a good slave,' he said to me, 'I'll be sorry to lose her.'

My mother slapped her hand against her mat suddenly, surprising us with her strength. 'I haven't gone yet, Chalmette,' she said. 'There's life left in me yet no thanks to you. Bring my daughter some paper and ink, quick, then leave us alone. That's my dying wish what you should fulfill or I'm going to haunt you and yours for eternity.'

Chalmette obeyed my mother at once, bringing me an empty journal and something to write with, then he closed the door behind him after he left, like my mother ordered him to.

'Sit down,' she said to me. 'Light some more candles if you want. Are you hungry? Let me know when you are ready to begin writing what I have to say.'

At first I didn't believe what she told me because I thought the pox had eaten her mind away the same as her body. I thought her words came from fever dreams. But my mother must have sensed my doubt because she told me to open my hand, and lying in my palm, gleaming unnaturally in the gloom of her hut, was a gold coin. My mother smiled at my gasp of surprise.

'Now open your mind, Angélique,' she said, beginning her story again, all of which I have now told to you.

I hope for your sake, whoever you are what shares our blood, reading about my mother's story, that you have read her words carefully. Finding the gold is not possible without the daughter of Captain De la Croix. You are meant to take the journey with her because it's not just about distance. She'll come to Carnival bearing his mark so that you will know her.

All that remains to be revealed to you now is the whereabouts of the gold. My mother thought that the Nancy plantation was perhaps as many as sixty miles southwest from Le Cap and twenty —

FLOYD, FROWNING, FLICKS through the last few pages in silence.

'Hey,' Jolie says. 'What you stop readin' for? You just get to the most important part.'

'*Mais*, there is no more to read. Look — the rest of the journal is completely ruined.' He shows her the journal to prove it. The pages are crumbling away in his hand. Floyd's voice is hoarse from hours of reading aloud, and he sighs as he finally closes the journal and hands it back to Renée. 'You ought to take better care of this, Ma'am. It's a very important historical document, this. I don't think you could put a price on it.'

Renée drops a crushed can into a plastic wastebasket by the side of her La-Z-Boy, rattling the dozen or so empty cans and bottles already in it, before she takes it from him and wraps it again in the soft cloth it was hidden with. 'It ain' goin' no place but this trailer until I found the gold.' Shaking her head, she says, 'All them damn pages and it had to be the ones with the whereabouts of the gold nobody can read. I wish Prince le Kreyol told me about the journal sooner — like twenty years ago. Still, least we got a idea where to start lookin'.'

'Who's we exactly?' I ask her.

Outside the day is dawning hot and fast, the sun dazzling despite thick, ghostly billows of steam rising from Renée's yard.

'You're kidding me?' Mozzie says.

'Me, too,' Floyd agrees.

Jolie raises a hand. 'I'm goin'.'

'The hell you is,' Renée says. 'Nuh-uh, baby. You stayin' behind and takin' care of your kids.'

'I'll go wherever I damn well please,' Jolie mutters, glaring back.

Renée snorts. 'You ain't goin' on no adventures to Haiti this side of fifteen years, darlin'. Get use to it.'

Floyd turns to face me. He hasn't shaved or slept in the last thirty-six hours. His eyes look like a couple of beached jellyfish, and his stubble is bordering on *Lentil Growers' Monthly*. 'Seems to me like you haven't got a choice, Laura.'

'Bullshit I don't.'

'It's your destiny,' he shrugs. 'I wouldn't fight it if I was you.'

'It's not like you've got anything to rush home for,' Mozzie points out. 'Why don't you call someone and ask them to tape it for you?'

'Why don't you tape your mouth shut?'

'*And* it'll make a nice change from the usual crap you take pictures of,' he adds.

'I won't be taking pictures of anything. My camera was stolen, remember? Well, lost maybe,' I concede.

'Hell, that ain' a problem,' Renée butts in. 'Jolie take care of that for you. Just tell her the make and model you lookin' for.'

'I ain' stealin' no camera for nobody if I ain' comin',' Jolie says.

Renée rolls her eyes and gets up out of the La-Z-Boy to fetch another beer. A sudden, pounding on the door of the trailer makes her drop the open can and its contents gush everywhere. Genius goes berserk, and barks ferociously at the door until Floyd quietens him without once smacking or shouting.

'Damn, look at that,' Renée says, standing flustered in a fizzing puddle of beer. 'What the hell goin' happen next?'

The twins, frightened by all the commotion, start screaming hysterically from Jolie's room. 'You got anythin' need flush down the toilet?' Renée hisses at Jolie. 'Only one thing knock on the door like that I know of — and that trouble.'

Hoover runs from Renée's bedroom in his boxer shorts, slamming down hard on the kitchen floor when he skids in the beer.

'You okay, baby?' Renée shrieks, dropping to her knees. 'You broke anythin'? You hurt?'

'Aw, Jesus,' Jolie says. 'Mama, just calm down and answer the damn door. The police never goin' be able to find anythin' I got hidden. Go on — see who it is. And somebody get that mess clean up while I check on the babies.'

A further hammering threatens to knock the door off its hinges, so Renée throws a dazed Hoover a roll of kitchen towel and unlocks the door.

'Yeah?' she says to an overweight man with sweat stains under his arms and a gun holster around his waist. 'What you want?'

'Renée Poupet?' he asks, mopping his face with a handkerchief. The act of beating on the door has left him almost breathless.

'So what?'

He hands her a brown envelope but doesn't let go when she takes it.

'Let go, fool, if you want me to open it.'

The man has fat, showy gold rings on every finger. 'Let me save you the bother, Ma'am. That there's your final eviction notice unless you got thirteen hundred and eighty dollars in rent arrears to give me.'

'Might as well let go,' she tells him, tugging on the envelope. 'I ain' got that kind of money.'

'Well, see, it's in my best financial interests to get my clients their money back. Maybe I could take a look around and see how you might raise —'

Floyd snatches the envelope from both of them. 'Here,' he

says to the man. 'Take it back, you. I'll write you a check.'

The fat man doesn't even look grateful. 'Make sure and add twenty bucks so it clears by the morning.'

Shaking his head like he's been dismayed once again by the dark side of human nature, Floyd goes out to his truck to search through the glovebox for chequebook and pen. He writes out a cheque on the bonnet, then asks the man for a receipt before handing it over. 'Make it out, you, for eighteen hundred and eighty dollars — five hundred extra to cover the rent for a while.'

The man leaves in a very low car he has difficulty getting into, and Floyd hands the receipt over to Renée.

'Sugar, I don't know how to begin thankin' you,' she says, crushing the wind from him with a bear hug. 'I swear I goin' pay you every single cent back when we find that gold.'

CHAPTER 12

AFTER THAT REPO man haul his fat ass off my yard and Floyd convince me he don't want my first-born, not that I want her sometimes, it occur to me that taking off to Haiti ain' going be free. We standing around in the sunshine, Mozzie and Floyd discussing the best way to get there — whether we better off flying or driving to Miami first — and the dog sniffing and pissing on every tree in the yard.

'Where's all the money coming from?' Laura yawn. She sure don't look like Louisiana been too kind on her over the last couple days. 'It's going to cost thousands.'

'How much have you got?' Mozzie ask her.

'Five, six, maybe.'

'Thousand?'

'Hundred.'

'Jesus. What do you spend it on?'

'We're not all trust-fund babies,' she say.

'What about you, mate?' he ask Floyd. 'What's your wedge like?'

'*Mais*, I've just sold a boat, me. I've got a good wedge. Maybe twelve thousand I don't need right away.'

Mozzie position himself front of Floyd in such a way as to shut Laura and me out they conversation. 'How much do you reckon we'll need for Haiti, bearing in mind those two lovelies have barely got a brass wazonga to rub between them?'

'Ten, maybe a little more,' Floyd shrug. '*Mais*, I don't know. It depends how long we're down there. What's your wedge like?'

'Healthy enough to be thinking about buying a boat. Why don't we make it five grand each and play it by ear after that?'

Floyd think it over for about three seconds, then offer his hand to Mozzie for shaking. 'Okay, that sounds fair. You've got a deal, you.'

'That mean the four us is goin'?' I ask, not quite believing things is working out so well, and if my luck carry on like this I going be rich in just a little while.

Floyd shrug, and we all turn to look at Laura slump on the steps of my porch with her head between her knees. 'Laura?' Floyd say.

'What?' she ask, without lifting up her head.

'Are you going to join us?'

'You have to be kidding,' she say through a fifteen-second yawn. 'The only place I'm going is to bed.'

AFTER ANOTHER COFFEE and some pills Jolie slips Mozzie on the quiet, we head back to New Orleans to finish the assignment for Elizabeth. Mardi Gras is officially over tonight: the festivities apparently cease abruptly on the stroke of midnight until next year. We stop by Floyd's house in Bywater — a shotgun cottage saved from sparsely furnished, expensive electronics, wooden-floor austerity by the colourful crazy art on the walls — so he can shower and change clothes. He tells us to help ourselves to anything that takes our fancy.

Mozzie looks through Floyd's CD and DVD collections, pulling out whatever captures his interest for closer inspection. As neither of us is in the mood for talking — or hectoring, in his case — I unlock the back door and follow Genius into an overgrown yard, immediately heading for the hammock strung between the overhanging branches of neighbours' trees. Genius sniffs his favourite spots, making sure everything is right with his six square metres of world before he lies beside me and goes to sleep. I'm dog-tired myself, but with all the caffeine and whatever Jolie gave us I couldn't sleep if I was breathing a general anaesthetic. Instead, jumpy with sleep deprivation and misfiring synapses, I lie with my eyes closed in the shady banana-leafed end of the hammock.

Genius seems perfectly happy to be dropped off with friends of Floyd, a couple of screaming queens who live in the bottom-floor apartment of a slightly run-down, skinny boho place in a rough-looking block off Magazine Street. Most of the houses have bars and razor wire. We leave the guys throwing M&Ms into the shrubbery of their garden for Genius to find. We make one last stop at a pawnshop where I successfully transact a second-hand X-series Minolta for three hundred and sixty dollars on Visa — the money, I reason, I've saved in *per diems* by being abducted.

Back in the luxury and comfort of the Monteleone, I want more than anything to crawl into my pyjamas and sleep for a week, but Floyd, who looks absolutely knackered himself, must be reading my mind. He pushes me firmly into my bedroom, and smiles sympathetically, 'Quick, you. Take a shower. Don't even look at the bed. The devil's just trying to tempt you, making it look all soft and plump and inviting and —'

Laughing, I shove him back into the lounge, close the bedroom door, then wearily force myself to take a shower and blow-dry my hair properly, even going so far as to dab on some make-up. Below my window, the streets of the Quarter are choked with people, many of them puking drunk already.

On the coffee table back out in the lounge, Floyd has lined up all the bottles from the mini-bar and is staring at them glumly. Mozzie, reeking of aftershave, is slumped on the opposite sofa and looking as enthusiastic as me about the prospect of tonight.

'Do I have to?' I sigh, as Floyd hands me a miniature bottle of vodka.

'Trust me,' he says. 'You don't want to go out there sober.'

FLOYD KNOWS SOME guy — a New York Jewish dentist with Crohn's disease — with a condo right on St Charles Avenue, and we watch the huge, elaborate floats pass within metres of the private-box vantage point of his balcony. Mardi Gras is more of a family affair in the Garden District, but the crowd still goes berserk every time a krewe passes, surging into the barricades for free carnival throws. The floats, some almost as big as cruise liners, are fantastic, extravagant depictions of dragons and legends, castles and pirate ships, fairy tales and Disney: shimmering, twinkling, million-dollar fibre-optic light shows.

Floyd's friend Dave, who takes only hot tea and honey himself, continuously and generously blends rum-based fruit drinks, and barbecues marinated shrimp for the entire duration of our stay.

We leave around nine and head into the Quarter, Floyd dragging us around the hard-core gay and strip clubs — in some instances I'm not entirely sure couples are only simulating sex — so we can get Elizabeth the kind of shots she wants. Even in the regular bars people have become insane from drinking, and it turns into a long, ugly couple of hours. The toilets are blocked with vomit and tampons, and the alleyways are blocked with people engaged in indiscreet blow jobs, drug deals, and other things tourists will regret in the morning. Flushed of inhibitions by too much alcohol, girls too young to be legally drunk and women old enough to know better flash their breasts at strangers and squat in doorways to pee. The noise is astounding.

I get absolutely soaked in alcohol and urine when I fall down in a gutter while holding a full Go Cup of frozen mint julep, then covered in grease when some man dressed as Tarzan, or perhaps Fred Flintstone, slings me over his shoulder and tries unsuccessfully to climb a pole coated with a Vaseline-like substance to deter idiots like him from falling and killing themselves. By the time Mozzie and I have what we need to knock a lurid-enough feature together, I've drunk myself sober and my brain is short-circuiting.

Back at the Monteleone, Mozzie — who has been very low-key all evening — makes a beeline for his bedroom.

'Not that I care about anyone else's sleeping arrangements, but keep it professional, guys,' he says, closing his door.

I find Floyd a couple of blankets and extra pillows so he can sleep on a sofa, then with a great deal of relief close my own bedroom door on the world.

IN THE MORNING, drained and bruised, I decide to get the hell out of New Orleans before something else happens. Within three days I've been burnt, robbed, in a fight, arrested, drugged, abducted twice, exposed as the descendant of the slave-trading rapist De la Croix/Delacross, and become personally acquainted with a *lwa*. So, in the cold light of day: bugger going to Haiti.

Floyd interrupts Mozzie's badgering of me to tell him, 'Relax. She won't get very far.'

'Ha. Try ten thousand miles,' I correct him, continuing to pack.

By ten the following evening I still haven't made it any further than the airport. Taxis break down, buses don't turn up; I'm thrown off the passenger list at the last moment due to other people's family emergencies; storms followed by severe fog force flights to be cancelled; and once my bags burst apart at check-in. I miss the one possible flight I think I'm going to make because my obvious anxiety makes Security nervous and they decide to give me the full rubber-glove treatment.

Mozzie and Floyd, feet on the coffee table, are watching *The Osbournes*, drinking wine and snacking on club sandwiches when I arrive back at the Monteleone.

'Mate,' Mozzie smirks. 'I thought you'd be back in New Zealand by now.'

'Would you like a glass of Bordeaux, Laura?' Floyd asks me. 'It's very nice.'

'No, I wouldn't,' I say, kicking my bedroom door shut.

I just starting to worry about them going back on their word, or sneaking off to Haiti without me, when the three of them call by the trailer a few days later. They bring a cardboard tray of coffees and po'boys in with them that we eat at my wobbly-ass table. Mozzie start making a list of stuff need arranging before we can go.

Turn out I need a passport before I can leave the damn country, and the fastest the office down in New Orleans can process my application is fourteen days. Floyd tell the others his *maison* is their *maison* long as they need it, but Mozzie decide he going visit a friend in Whistler, Canada, go snowboarding for a while. Money-wise, Laura ain' got none. She got a ticket back to New Zealand, but no way of buying a ticket back to Louisiana, so she has to stick around here. Besides, even if she had the money, she say she ain' prepare to suffer the long flights involve in going home and coming back again. She arrange to move into Floyd's place the following day. We head down to the passport agency later that morning to lodge my application, and after we done that, all there is to do is wait. It a long slow two weeks.

FLOYD PICKS US up from the Monteleone early the following morning, and we drop Mozzie off at the airport just in time to make his flight to Vancouver. Once we're sure his plane has taken off safely, we head to the American Airlines counter and make bookings for flights to Miami and Port-au-Prince, allowing sixteen days for Renée's passport to be processed. Then we head back to Floyd's place.

His spare room, painted a mellow pastel mustard, is small but light, and as free of junk as the rest of his home. Below a huge modern painting of a woman staring at a fort-like building she's either going to or come from is an antique dresser that has been stripped back and trendily restored with stain and Art Deco handles. On it there's a framed photograph of Floyd and Genius, side by side on a sand dune somewhere. They are both grinning easily and happily into the lens, and there's an extra something in Floyd's smile that makes me wonder about the woman who captured the moment with such fondness, and who was regarded with the same fondness in return. A depression lined with dog hair at the foot of the bed suggests Genius sleeps there sometimes.

'Make yourself at home,' Floyd tells me. 'Put your stuff away, watch a movie, take a bath, have some wine, play some music, read a book, do some laundry, sleep if you —'

'I'd love a coffee,' I say.

'*Mais*,' he smiles, 'I've got some Jamaican Blue Mountain beans, me, just for special occasions like this.'

NEW ORLEANS IS lovely after the majority of tourists have left, and for the first week the weather is soft and balmy, barely a cloud in the sky, gardens and courtyards fragrant with lush spring blooms, trees celebratory bright with new blossom. Floyd lets me tag along on his tours around the Quarter and crumbling cemeteries, and I learn about great fires and plagues, ghosts and slavery, St Joe bricks and Romeo spikes, quadroon balls and wild slave dances in Congo Square, Baroness Pontalba and Marie Laveau. He introduces me to his largely American tour groups as a photographer from New Zealand, which is a great icebreaker because they give me their cameras and ask me to take photos of them. Floyd is always polite and kind to people, regardless of attitude problems or stupid questions, and he keeps his tours to the pace of the slowest walker, abridging or augmenting facts and historical anecdotes at will.

After a couple of days I start bumping into people from past tours, and stop to talk in the street. It makes me feel like a local. Floyd seems to know everyone, from the proprietors of Voodoo botanicals to the street cleaners, and it can take an hour to walk down Royal or Bourbon.

On his days off we head into the country and visit old plantations, walking the length and breadth of carriageways dark with huge, wizened two-century oaks, their branches as top-heavy with Spanish moss as the oaks along St Charles are with beads. Hoop-skirted guides with Seiko watches offer scripted genteel monologues of facts and figures as they steer one shuffling bunch of tourists after another through the museum homes of former slave owners. I try crawfish bisque in a Cajun restaurant overlooking a bayou outside Thibodaux, and get my feet wet taking Genius for a walk along Lake Pontchartrain. One afternoon, after endless miles of cane fields, Floyd turns off the highway and shortly afterwards pulls over by a cluster of sad, rotting, derelict shacks and outhouses, paradoxically fenced off with barbed wire to prevent trespassers. Dachau-like, they emanate an atmosphere of something terrible.

'That's where the slaves lived,' he says.

I'm surprised by the extent of obvious backwater poverty in Louisiana — the number of people living in trailers and sagging shack-like houses not much better than those in the abandoned slave row, the middle-aged and elderly begging for change at inter-sections. There are Stars and Stripes everywhere I look — on houses, offices, yards, cars, businesses, windows, railings and even a couple of pushchairs. I ask Floyd, 'What would happen if you hung out an Iraqi flag?'

'*Mais*,' he laughs, 'ninety-nine percent of people wouldn't know what it was, but the other one percent would shoot you.'

Floyd knows some clubs tucked away from common knowledge in Algiers, and at nights we catch the ferry across the Mississippi to sit in tiny garden bars strung with lacy Mexican fairy lights and listen to local musicians jamming.

Interestingly, he's sensitive to my taste in his clothes, and after a few days the alligator-teeth necklace is gone, and he asks me to go shopping with him for a second opinion. The unexpected flipside of his new look is that women and gays start flirting with him even when I'm standing right there next to him — and, just as interest-ingly, it bothers me.

The following week it never stops raining, and being cooped up with a constantly wet, stinking Genius starts to wear thin. I put on half a stone from eating delivered junk food and watching Floyd's DVD collection with him — every martial arts movie ever made, seemingly — until we start talking in stupid Asian accents that drive Genius so demented with excitement that he barks and jumps at us until we stop.

'Hah, so, Laura. You won lass piss of piza?'

'No flankyou, glasshopper,' I'd reply, the top button of my jeans discreetly undone. 'Be my gess.'

Not until Day 15 does Renée call to confirm receipt of her passport, and then it's all on. Floyd says he'll pick her up around lunchtime tomorrow for an evening flight to Miami. He tells her what she'll have to pack, and couriers three hundred dollars over so she can buy what she needs. Then, in the following order, he calls American Airlines to confirm our flights, a travel agent friend for a hotel recommendation in Miami, the hotel his friend recommends, and finally Mozzie to tell him where and when in Miami to meet us.

'Well, Laura,' he says, hanging up, 'now that everything's finalised, why don't we go out for dinner, us, and celebrate a little?'

BECAUSE IT'S A Tuesday night and *still* raining, Floyd doesn't bother making a reservation at Alfredo's, an old wooden locals' place on Frenchmen, a block or so out of the Quarter. Floyd opens the door to a rickety staircase leading to a tiny, bustling restaurant dense and warm with the rich smells of garlic, wines and spices. Candles and fairy lights give the restaurant a soft-focus glow.

'Hey, Floyd,' a chef calls from the cramped kitchen. 'Why don't you have a few drinks downstairs until we got a table free?'

'Okay, the one in the corner, over there by the window,' Floyd says.

'The romantic one, huh?' the chef winks, resuming the chopping of herbs. 'Sure, no problem.'

The equally tiny downstairs bar is packed with a mixed patronage of obvious in-for-the-long-haul alcoholics, and kids with face jewellery and dangerous-dog-breed puppies tied to chair legs. The bartender, Eddie, is a good friend of Floyd's, and we are able to wangle a few bottles of Bordeaux down from the restaurant. We spend a couple of hours propped up at the bar, being entertained by the hilariously funny Eddie, until our table is free.

Before we've even sat down in the restaurant upstairs there's an open bottle of wine and basket of warm garlic bread on the table. The chef, a large knife in his hand, waves at me from the kitchen and blows me a kiss when I wave back. The waitress calls Floyd *darlin'* and *baby*, and recommends the mumbo gumbo, the chef's special, which we order.

'I thought you said this was an Italian restaurant,' I say to Floyd, after the waitress has gone.

'It is,' he laughs. 'That gumbo is going to taste exactly like risotto.'

'And what's mumbo?'

'*Mais*, stuff that should have been cooked yesterday.'

Outside, the rain is streaming down the window, fat rivulets obscuring all but lights from view. Floyd has been charming, funny company all night, and looks sharp in a casual, tousled way in his new clothes, not to mention flushed and handsome from candle-light and wine. At one point, loose on Bordeaux, and finding his combination of tropical-seas eyes and easy lopsided smile increasingly attractive, I realise that not only am I twiddling strands of hair around but I'm also toying with the stem of my wineglass. After I reveal that my parents are nudists and I will only meet them in public places where they have to wear clothes, he laughs and squeezes my hand, lingering way longer than he has to. For an instant I visualise him naked, and then, realising that he's picturing the same thing about me, take my hand back on the pretext of tucking some hair behind my ear.

Over a dessert of something made in heaven involving choco-late liqueur and preserved autumn fruits, the jokes and anecdotes continue as though nothing has happened. Floyd comes from a large, chaotic family of keen fishermen, hunters, cooks and horsemen, and he tells one side-splitting yarn after another about the little place on Catahoula Lake he grew up in, sometimes mimicking the thick, back-country dialect of friends, family and neighbours.

'Stop it,' I tell him, finally. 'I can't laugh any more. My cheeks are killing me.'

Mainly because Floyd would go to prison if he were caught driving tonight, we catch a taxi back to Bywater, getting soaked again in the few metres from the kerb to his front door.

'Does it ever stop raining?' I complain, dripping all over the floor of his narrow hallway in the dark. 'I'm sick of being wet. I might as well be living in Auckland.'

Floyd gently pushes the front door shut with his foot, but doesn't switch the light on right away.

'What?' I say. 'Has the bulb gone?'

'Follow me,' he says, and takes my hand, leading me through the darkness of his home. Stopping abruptly by the back door, which takes all of a couple of strides, Floyd unlocks it and throws it wide open to the elements. 'I'm going to make you love the rain, me.'

'What's to love?' I ask dubiously.

'This,' he says, and suddenly we're out in the torrential wet, kissing and undoing buttons, and, yes, there is a lot to be said for rain.

IN THE MORNING Floyd's side of the bed is empty, as is the rest of his house. There are plenty of signs of activity, like his bags are packed and stacked by the front door, and wet clothes have been picked up from the floor and laundered, but there is absolutely no sign of Floyd. Just as I come to the conclusion that he's gone out to buy something special for breakfast, I find the note taped to the coffee machine.

164

Laura,

I thought you'd like to sleep in, so I've gone to pick Renée up alone. We should be back here around 5.30 p.m. We'll need to leave for the airport right away so please make sure you're ready.

I hope you have a nice relaxing day.

Floyd.

Nice relaxing day, my arse. What am I, his grandmother?

FLOYD TURN UP just gone two in the afternoon. Got himself a new look from someplace I say Laura probably had a hand in. The man is looking hot for a white boy.

'Where you hidin' Laura at?' I ask him, my heart skipping a beat in case she change her mind about going down to Haiti with the rest of us.

'We're picking her up on the way to the airport. Nice luggage by the way,' he whistle, eyeing the set of genuine ponyskin cases I got for five bucks at the charity shop. He stroke them for a while, before he pick them up and stow them in his truck. '*Mais*, I almost want to saddle them up and ride them, me.'

Jolie still sore she ain' coming and she refuse to say goodbye. She set at the table with her Walkman on, reading a magazine and ignoring everybody, showing her butt crack in those Britney pants she only just wearing.

Just before I leave I drop in front of her the hundred and forty-three dollars I got left over from Floyd, and pull one side of the headset away from her ear. 'You in charge, that money for groceries, and if my trailer and everybody in it ain' alive when I get back, you in big trouble, baby.'

She pop gum while she tuck the money in her push-up cleavage, then go back to reading her magazine, acting like she ain' heard a word.

Hoover and the twins come out in the yard for goodbye kisses, making me swear to bring them back a gift each. Then they stand in the middle of the road and wave us off until we cain' see them no more.

I AIN' NEVER been aboard a aeroplane before. The take-off scare the hell out of me. Floyd pat my hand, and later when the air hostesses come by with they trolley, he buy me some four-dollar beers to relax my nerves. The flight is half-empty, and Laura take a seat all the way at the back of the cabin by herself, not talking to nobody. She pissy on the way to the airport too, and if you ask me those two had themselves some kind of a fight, although I ain' sure Floyd know what the fight is about. There time to catch a in-flight movie before we land in Miami, which in the dark and from the air seem like a whole bunch of lights going on forever.

We catch a cab to a hotel no more than ten minutes from the airport. Mozzie already check himself into the room he going be sharing with Floyd, and the desk man say we got a table reserve for dinner in twenty minutes.Up in our room Laura still got a face like a weekend of bad luck at the casino, so while I look through the contents of the mini-bar I ask her what the trouble is.

'Nothing,' she say, brushing her hair like she trying to kill it.

'You and Floyd fall out over somethin'?'

It like watching a horror movie the speed she turn her head my direction. 'What makes you think that? Has he said something to you?'

'No, but you mad at him for somethin'. What he do?'

From the color her face turn I know it got something to do with hurt feelings.

'Make sure and put some lipstick on, baby,' I say, tossing her a beer. 'The best revenge is to look hot.'

WE FIND FLOYD and Mozzie having a few beers at the bar, watching *The Anna Nicole Show*, laughing their heads off.

'What the hell?' Mozzie says when he spots me.

Floyd looks startled but doesn't say anything.

I regret following Renée's advice about making an effort to look nice. It now feels like complete overkill.

'What the hell is right,' Renée says. 'Now put your eyes back in your heads and lead the way to our table.'

The food at the hotel is horrible. My steak is bleeding though I ask for it well done, and the salad looks like something you'd scrape off a burger. Dinner would be silent and awkward if it weren't for Mozzie regaling us with his feats of athletic prowess on the ski slopes. He's practically glowing with the health and vitality normally associated with pet-food ads.

I avoid eye contact with Floyd, provide him with one-word responses if absolutely required to, don't thank him when he refills my wineglass, and don't laugh at funny things he says, even though the others do. Bugger him if he thinks he can leave me a note that has all the intimacy of instructions for the cleaning lady, then waltz back later like nothing special has happened — no secret smiles, no looks, nothing.

Finally the monologue grinds to a halt. 'Okay,' Mozzie sighs. 'What's the lovers' tiff about?'

My head jerks up from staring glumly at my meal, Floyd splutters wine all over the table and Renée just about pokes herself in the eye with her fork.

'Who are you talking about?' Floyd coughs, glancing guiltily at Renée.

'Don't mind me,' she snorts. 'Hell, it so freakin' obvious even the waitresses can tell.'

'Laura,' Mozzie says, dabbing at the wine stains on his shirt, 'seeing as the whole restaurant is aware of your little tryst gone bad, why don't you tell Floyd what the problem is, then you two can kiss and make up and make the great big atmosphere problem go away.'

'Get lost,' I tell him, my face burning.

Mozzie turns his attention to Floyd. 'Mate? Have you got *any* idea what you're supposed to have done?'

Floyd laughs briefly and humourlessly. 'Don't know, don't care, me,' he says, with a dismissive shrug that sends my heart plummeting.

'I thought I told you to keep it professional,' Mozzie says. Receiving no response, he continues, 'Listen, if you two don't call a truce right now, one of you isn't going to Haiti tomorrow.'

Floyd and I refuse to look at one another.

'I mean it,' Mozzie insists. 'Shake hands before I shake them for you.'

Reluctantly, and without eye contact, Floyd and I reach across the table and submit to a limp truce.

'Pathetic,' Mozzie says.

CHAPTER 13

FROM THE AIR Port-au-Prince could be Los Angeles with its scrubby mountains and urban sprawl, but on approach the rusty tin roofs, the grey, overcrowded, unplanned construction, banana trees, and dust and smoke from cooking fires signal a much less affluent destination. It takes forever to get off the plane because the mostly Haitian passengers have stretched the hand-luggage allowance to capacity with gifts for family and friends.

It's immediately obvious from the mercilessly stifling blanket of oven-air baking the ground and airport buildings that Port-au-Prince is way hotter than New Orleans. Customs is a misleadingly civilised affair because the arrivals hall is pandemonium, the noise comparable to the last fifty metres of the Melbourne Cup. The snaking carousel is ten deep in people attempting to retrieve huge identical black suitcases, made marginally distinguishable only by the coloured ribbons tied to the handles, and piled so high it takes thirty minutes to collect our entire luggage.

'Where we stayin' at?' Renée asks, lowering her sunglasses against the glaring concrete outside when we finally escape.

Except for about a dozen French missionaries, and a couple of white guys in Hawaiian shirts who never took their sunglasses off the entire flight, Floyd, Mozzie and I are the only *blans* to arrive in Port-au-Prince, and we attract a curiosity bordering on scary.

'The Oloffson,' Mozzie says, dumping his bags in a space by a crumbling wall. 'Floyd, mate? Can you help me organise a taxi?'

While we're waiting for them, Renée and I watch in disbelief as a young man with threadbare, filthy clothing shares a cigarette with a friend via a metal hole in his throat. Seconds later, for no obvious reason, he takes off in furious pursuit of a small boy, stopping to hurl a rock when outrun.

'Bet that ain' in no freakin' tourist brochure,' Renée mutters.

The sun is frying us by the time Mozzie and Floyd show up in a beat-up Lincoln with four completely bald tyres, one noticeably smaller than the others. The driver, on the malnourished side of skinny but wearing plenty of gold, makes a drama out of stowing our luggage, securing some bags to the roof of his taxi with rope even though there's plenty of room in the boot. Finally we drive away from the airport, with Floyd — whose French and scanty Creole vocabularies are our only means of communication — sitting up front with the driver.

EVERY VEHICLE THAT go by is a inch-away tragedy. In the whole time to the hotel we only pass one set of traffic lights and they out. There ain' no traffic laws to speak of and it just a matter of horn-blowing and swerving to get anyplace.

I seen travel shows about the Caribbean — places like the Bahamas and Cancun — and I expecting Haiti going be all palm trees and sandy beaches, but it look like CNN footage of Kabul after we went over and kick some al Qaeda ass.

The traffic get even crazier nearer we get to the hotel, big piles of trash and rubble blocking the streets, manhole covers missing — and suddenly we driving through some big iron gates up the driveway of the Addams Family retreat, a big old frilly white place with turrets and balconies.

WHILE FLOYD DEALS with reception and Mozzie reads old articles about the hotel stuck to the door of the office, Renée and I inspect the sequinned Voodoo paraphernalia and ironwork on sale in the glass display-cases of an adjacent foyer. We're sweating profusely in the steadily increasing heat. Except for hotel staff there's hardly another soul around. Anyone with an ounce of common sense is presumably seeking the relief of AC.

'You can kiss an early night *au revoir*,' Floyd calls out. 'RAM are playing tonight — this place will get crazy later on.'

'Who are RAM?' Renée and I ask together.

'RAM?' Floyd says to Renée, not even looking at me though I'm standing right beside her while she fans herself with hotel postcards. '*Mais*, they're one of the biggest bands in Haiti. I'm surprised, me, that you haven't heard of them. They play in Miami and New York all the time.'

Mozzie and Floyd are staying in the 'Graham Greene' bungalow set slightly apart from the main building where Renée and I are staying. The Oloffson must have had some glorious heyday once, because the flowery hand-painted nameplates mounted outside each room — Mick Jagger, Marlon Brando, Truman Capote, Anne Bancroft, Noel Coward, to name just a few — are testimony to a legendary A-list period in her history.

A porter leads the way to our room — the 'Jonathan Demme' — via a gloomy, spongey staircase that winds above a row of three currently unoccupied guest computers. The stairs shift and creak dangerously as we make our way past bizarre, spooky paintings to a narrow landing on the first floor. He shows us into a long, dim, L-shaped room, its sagging floorboards loudly protesting our presence. Two sets of French doors on the far wall lead out to a huge private balcony at eye level with the lush, tropical canopy of the garden below, where pairs of birds flirt and coo, framed beautifully by the *Arabian Nights*-like gingerbread carpentry of the hotel.

'AC?' Renée asks the porter, pointing at the inert wall unit. 'Fan?'

He shakes his head and some says something unencouraging in Kreyol.

She looks devastated.

After he leaves, I open the French doors for some air. Renée kicks off her shoes and collapses onto one of the brass beds with a groan. 'It like a oven in here,' she says. 'I sweat so much since I got off the plane it feel like there a damn cheese grater between my thighs.'

I win the coin toss for first shower, and the water pressure — an oxymoron if ever there was one — is barely enough to rinse off the soap. Several times it stops all together, only to spit violently back to life for a few seconds. Stupidly I didn't check for towels first, and have to coerce Renée into organising some.

THE DINING AREA locate outside on the ground-floor veranda, over-looking the garden and fountain. Most of the tables occupy with local business lunches. There a smell of cigar smoke but I cain' see nobody smoking. Floyd and Mozzie save us some seats at a table cover with a nice white tablecloth, and they already drunk some beers by the time we get there. Floyd get up from the table and hold our chairs out for us.

'What the menu say it got for lunch?' I ask.

'Goat,' Mozzie say.

'Give that menu here,' I say, snatching one off him. 'I ain' eatin' no goat.'

The menu wrote in French, but it easy enough to understand it got fries and burgers on it.

There a bunch of sequin flags hung up around us, and a painting of the Last Supper down one end of the veranda, except all the disciples is color. Floyd see me looking and laugh. 'You don't like the art here, Renée?'

There a kind of relax'ness about Floyd make it easy to have him around. He ain' looking for a fight all the time, and he a real gentleman to everybody. He ain' nobody's dog though, and Laura a damn fool for expecting him not to bite if she going kick him all the time.

'Like hell I do,' I say. 'Some of it just downright creepy.'

'*Mais*, that's because a lot of it was painted by *lwa* while they possessed an artist. It's spirit art, not human art.'

'I wish you didn't have to tell me that. Already seem like the paintings in my room is staring at me.'

'Has anybody come up with a plan yet?' Laura ask, moving a vase of flowers to one side so the waiter can put down a loaf of warm crusty bread.

Mozzie too busy giving the eye to a couple of blonde girls just sat down the next table over, and not listening to a word. Floyd fill in so as not to let things get awkward. 'We're going to stay here for a few days and find out what we can about the Nancy plantation. Maybe the Bibliothèque Nationale has some records of its where-abouts, I don't know. *Mais*, in the meantime,' he say, raising his beer to her, 'you can do whatever you want.'

'Thanks,' she say back, just as pissy. 'I'll try to have a nice relaxing time.'

AFTER LUNCH WE find the AC in our room has been fixed, so Renée has a post-four-beers nap while I go out onto the balcony from where, on the hazy, distant horizon of the Caribbean, I can see huge storm clouds piling up, forcing muggier air ahead of them.

I collapse onto one of the fainting couches with the nagging sense that maybe I over-reacted to Floyd's note, and that his impartial behaviour towards me yesterday was the gentlemanly thing under the circumstances. However, I'm feeling so hot and lethargic, I can't even muster up the energy to get off my arse and find him.

Finally, laughter from the hotel pool below draws me to my feet, and I spot Mozzie and Floyd standing chest deep in the shady end of the water. They're both holding beers and wearing sunglasses. Floyd looks particularly gorgeous now I've messed things up.

Keeping them company, bikini-clad on the sides of the pool, feet dangling in the water, are the two blonde girls from the table next to us at lunchtime: Belinda and Michelle from the Peace Corps. Everyone seems to be getting on just grand, especially Floyd and Belinda, deep in exclusive conversation. Belinda, her long fair hair restrained in plaits, keeps smiling and reaching out to lay a hand on Floyd's bare shoulder.

WE MEET UP for dinner at seven as arranged. Distant lightning flashes in the steaming-hot night sky. There's a lot of sound-checking activity in the back area of the bar where RAM will play, and out on the veranda the dining tables are full. A table of eight next to us, foreign sailors and local girls, drink expensive European liqueurs as if money is no object. Two husky-like dogs with thick, matted coats, one black, one brown, circle the driveway and bark at arriving vehicles. The fountain has been lit up for the evening and looks stunning, the surrounding royal palms magnificent in the borrowed illumination. We order what are talked up by Mozzie to be the world's best rum punches while we check out the menu.

A large white Jeep with completely blackened windows pulls up in the driveway below, and the same two white guys from the Miami flight get out, still wearing shades but sporting fresh, loud shirts. One is dark and angular, a little like Charlie Sheen, and the other is kind of beefy and Germanic. They bound up the stairs with ease, and although they glance at our table as they make their way inside the hotel they make no sign of recognising us.

'So, what you get up to for the rest of the day?' Renée asks Floyd.

I pretend not to be interested, but my ears prick up.

Floyd shrugs. '*Mais*, I went for a little walk with Mozzie to find a bank, I had a swim, a few beers, I talked to some people — by the way, if anybody asks, we're researching the plantation history of the Cap-Haïtien area. They don't need to know why we're here.'

The rum punches are absolutely delicious pink-tangerine concoctions served in tall glasses with ice and straws, and we're on our third, suffering heartburn, by the time dinner arrives. Mozzie and Renée both have conch, Floyd tries goat, but I stick with the safe option of chicken, only to be presented with a leg the size of a turkey's even though I have yet to see a chicken larger than a quail.

The Oloffson is packed with mainly Haitians, the men flashing gold jewellery and teeth, the women in skimpy J-Lo clothes, and, when RAM goes off, the crowd does likewise, launching as a single entity into MTV-class dancing. It's impossible either to hear yourself think or to get inside the bar-lounge area, now cleared of rattan furniture for a dance floor. The Haitians are sensational dancers, possessed of faultless perfect rhythm, hot moves and no easily discernible inhibitions. Couples gyrate suggestively against each other, fast and lewd, in a juicy yee-hah celebration of the music, then, dripping with sweat, come out to the veranda during breaks to drink bottles of five-star Barbancourt rum neat with ice.

Suddenly there's a noise like war starting, and the walls and floors of the Oloffson seem set to splinter as the storm breaks overhead. Rainwater gushes down the exposed rock wall behind where the band is playing and threaten immediate electrocution. Staff drop towels and buckets under leaks, and after a spectacularly ferocious crack of lightning the power goes out. It takes five minutes for staff to get the generator going. For a while the Oloffson sounds hollow, like a pub after last orders when the landlord pulls the plug on the jukebox, and my ears are ringing. Renée leans over and whispers, 'Keep a eye on your purse. They all drug dealers and prostitutes.'

The Oloffson goes crazy again as soon as the generator kicks in, enough for the police to start cruising the driveway with semi-automatics and menacing attitudes. As the ladies' room in the bar is impossible to reach and my bladder is now the size of a child's head, I head back to my room to use the toilet there. The noise on the upstairs landing, separated from RAM only by a roof of two-millimetre tin, is phenomenal. In our room, directly above the dance floor, the furniture is beyond vibrating. The beds have shifted half a foot away from the wall.

As I reach inside the bathroom for the light switch, at first my brain refuses to comprehend the violent rustle of the shower curtain and someone's sudden, painful grip on my wrist. Then a hand clamps over my mouth before I can scream.

From the intruder's heavy grunts as he tries to wrestle a pillow-case down over my head, I know he's a man. The fear of suffocation brings a burst of blind strength, and I heave backwards into him, ramming him into the shower taps. Kidney-punched, the intruder relaxes his grip on me for a second and, seizing the opportunity, screaming and mindless with terror, I trip out of the shower stall into the shelves, causing shampoo and toiletries to come crashing down.

I hear, '*FUCKING BITCH. I'M GOING TO KILL YOU*', and, like the cornered animal I am, start scrabbling blindly and uselessly against the wall to get away. Under normal circumstances, the noise would attract the cops out patrolling the grounds within seconds, but with RAM playing they couldn't hear a gang war in here.

'Hey. What's going on in there?' a man shouts, hammering on the glass of the front door. 'Open up!' He rattles the door aggressively. '*OPEN UP BEFORE I KICK IT DOWN.*'

A sharp plastic eyelet on the intruder's shoe cuts my lip as he makes a run for it, and I hear him sprinting out onto the balcony and the hooks of the french doors clattering against the glass as I frantically tear the pillowcase from my head.

'*OPEN UP!*' the man outside shouts again. He just about kicks the door off its hinges.

'*I'M COMING,*' I shout back, staggering to my feet, keeping one eye on the French doors in case the intruder comes back. I fling the door open to find the dark-haired Hawaiian-shirt guy from the plane poised in a Kung Fu-y position for a second kick to the door.

'Are you okay, honey?' he says, lowering his foot to the floor again. 'Are you hurt?'

When I shake my head he moves me gently out of his way, then runs out onto the balcony, leaning dangerously out over the balustrade to see where the intruder might have disappeared to. Thankfully RAM choose that moment to wind up for the night and the relative silence — enthusiastic cheering and whistling — almost caresses my eardrums.

'Did he jump?' I ask, stepping out onto the balcony, heart still pounding.

The man shakes his head and motions for me to join him at the balustrade. 'Not unless he had a death wish. Take a look at how big the drop is — we'd be looking at a big old Humpty-Dumpty omelette if he had. He must have climbed over into your neighbour's balcony.'

I join him in contemplating what the huge drop to the concrete steps below would do to a human body. Up close he really does bear close resemblance to Charlie Sheen — good-looking in a bad-boy way, the same irresistible-to-women, amused and bemused air about him. Then, glancing further afield to the Oloffson's illuminated fountain, I'm severely bummed to see Floyd and Belinda sitting cosily together on its low surrounding wall.

'Look, you're bleeding,' the man says, frowning as he notices the gash on my lip. 'Sit down while I take a look at it. I'm Donny, by the way.'

'Laura,' I smile, as best I can, taking a seat on one of the rattan chairs.

Donny tilts my chin up towards the light and takes a closer look at my injury. 'Have you got a first-aid kit?'

'Try in the bathroom somewhere.'

'Sit tight. I won't be long.'

Donny ruffles my hair before he goes looking. My spirits plunge as I watch Floyd and Belinda stroll back to the hotel, not quite holding hands, but brushing together as they walk. Belinda laughs a lot.

'Is that an accent I can hear?' Donny asks, returning with the first-aid kit.

'New Zealand,' I say morosely.

Donny dabs at my lip with a round gauze pad soaked with hydrogen peroxide. 'New Zealand, huh? I've never met anybody from New Zealand before. Are all the girls as pretty as you?'

He's about as original as buying your granddad socks for Christmas, but I allow a small smile, which hurts when the hydrogen peroxide gets in the cut. 'Where are you from?'

'Southern California. Is this your first time in Haiti?'

'And the last.'

'Yeah, I bet it's not every day you get attacked, is it?'

'No, just once a week,' I say, absolutely deadpan.

'Sorry,' he says when I wince. 'I'm trying not to hurt you.'

'It's okay,' I tell him, even though my lip feels like a bee sting.

'Did you get a look at the guy who attacked you?'

I grit my teeth as Donny loads up another pad with fresh hydrogen peroxide. 'Too dark.'

'Probably someone local,' he says. 'Who's going to hear a robbery with RAM playing?'

Fucking bitch. I'm going to kill you.

'No,' I disagree, remembering. 'He had an American accent.'

'Maybe someone ended up in the wrong room and you scared the shit out of him when you came back.'

'Maybe,' I shrug.

Finally, Donny throws the bloody pads into the ashtray on the table, and screws the lid back on the hydrogen peroxide. I notice for the first time that his left index finger is missing about a quarter of its length.

'Are you okay on your own here for a while? I'm going to go downstairs to see if I can find your friends.'

'Sure,' I smile. 'Thanks for your help. I dread to think what would have happened if you hadn't come along.'

'You've got beautiful eyes,' he tells me, out of the blue. 'Unusual.'

'Thanks,' I say, wishing it was a compliment from Floyd instead.

DONNY CAN ONLY find Renée among the dispersing RAM crowd, and once he's escorted her back to our room and secured our

French doors shut with rope, he bids us farewell for the night.

'That Donny sure is a nice man,' she says, before she can't stay awake any longer and topples into bed.

I've picked up the mess in the bathroom and am cleaning my teeth when I hear an urgent rapping on the front door and Floyd calling my name. I almost choke on my toothbrush, making my lip bleed again. The sight of it clearly shocks him.

'What happened to your face?' he says with genuine concern. He looks rumpled and tired, unshaven and sexy. 'Did you hurt yourself?'

'Actually, no,' I tell him, suddenly and massively irritated that I could have been murdered while he was flirting with Belinda before two nights ago is even cold in its grave. 'I didn't hurt myself. What happened is, while you were off gallivanting with that girl, yet another wacko went and jumped me.'

It takes a couple of seconds for Floyd to let this pass. 'But you're okay now?' he says, almost all sympathy gone.

'Just.'

'That's good.'

Neither of us says anything for so long the silence gets strained to twanging-point.

'So, is there anything else?' I ask, moving to close the door.

'*Mais*, is there ever.' He sighs strangely, his warm breath stirring my hair. 'Follow me. You should see this.'

Rattled in all sorts of ways, I grab the key and follow him back towards the stairs, where he takes a left along a climbing path, sheltered by a roof low enough to make us stoop, that leads away from the hotel. In the vegetation below the path, roosters have started cock-a-doodling already, though there is absolutely no sign of dawn. Floyd stops about halfway down a row of rooms that share a common veranda. It's furnished with rattan rocking chairs and potted plants, somewhat backpacker-like in appearance. He knocks on a door.

'Look at that, you,' he says, pointing to a painting in Belinda's room, 'and tell me what you see.'

What I see, apart from Floyd's badly and undoubtedly hurried buttoned shirt, is an oil depiction of lush, hilly vegetation and a small waterfall cascading into a shady pool in the foreground,

'I see a nice landscape,' I shrug, backing the hell out of Belinda's room. What's he trying to do, torture me?

'*Mais*, you're not looking properly,' he says, impatiently tapping the painting. 'It's a very big deal. Look there, behind the waterfall. Closely this time.'

'It's really cool,' Belinda says. She's sitting barefoot and cross-legged on her bed.

Suddenly what Floyd finds so startling about the picture becomes apparent, because staring despondently from behind the waterfall, almost transparently pale, are the ghostly figures of a colonial woman and small boy.

'You see them now?' Floyd says, when I gasp.

CHAPTER 14

IT STILL DARK when I wake up and only got about two seconds to make it to the bathroom. It a choice between what end I point at the bowl first, because whatever I ate for dinner coming out any place it can. Laura, God bless her, hear all the noise I making losing a quarter of my body weight in one go, and she come clean up all the mess on the floor. Then she help me to shower and put me to bed, with the wastepaper bin beside me to vomit in. Ain' never felt this bad my entire life before and it a relief to finally sleep.

IN THE MORNING, when the roosters are quiet again, the bathroom still stinks of whatever *Exorcist*-like gastric entity Renée managed to pick up, so after mixing her up some Gastrolyte, and rinsing out the bin, I decide to have a dip in the pool instead of a shower.

Downstairs the tables haven't been cleared from last night, and empty glasses and bottles lie everywhere. The few staff on duty this early are still trying to wake up. The pool is full of leaves and fuchsia-coloured bougainvillaea petals blown down in the storm, and the only clear patch of water is under the cement-fish fountain at the deep end. Dog-paddling through the debris — I am in water as a fish is on dry land — in body-temperature water, I realise there is so much chlorine in the pool I'm in danger of chemical poisoning. The water doesn't offer much refreshment, and only seconds after climbing out I feel just as seedy as I did before I went in.

Heading back to my room, I bump into Floyd at reception. He's in the same clothes as he was when I left him with Belinda last night.

'How did you sleep?' he asks, covering up a yawn.

'Not well,' I reply, annoyed that he doesn't look even slightly guilty. 'Renée was sick as a dog.'

Floyd rubs sleep from his eyes. 'Mozzie too. *Mais*, when I got back to the bungalow just before, it smelled like a sewage pipe had burst in there. I asked the girl on reception to send some cleaners over, but it's going to be a while.'

His shameless allusion of having spent the night elsewhere sends a twisting, jealous surge to my guts. He couldn't rub my face in his jollies more if he produced Polaroids.

'You and I need to talk,' he says, frowning. 'Let's get some coffee and find somewhere private.'

Momentarily buoyed, and rapidly formulating both an apology and an acceptance speech, I follow him out to the front veranda. A table by the kitchen door has been set up with a silver urn of coffee, crockery, toast, butter, fruit juice, sugar, jams, and a jug of milk sitting in ice. Floyd and I are the only guests up, and we take the table right at the far end of the veranda, which among other things still has a dirty ashtray on it.

'So, it looks like Mozzie and Renée will be out of action for a day or two,' Floyd says all businesslike, brushing crumbs from the table. 'It's going to be up to us to do all the investigation. I was thinking, me, that a good place to start would be with the artist who painted that picture. The owner of the Oloffson will probably know something about its history. What a lucky clue to find.' He pauses mid-sip of his coffee. 'What, you? What do you keep looking at me like that for?'

'Because you're a complete prick.'

He recoils with surprise. '*I'm* a prick? *Mais*, you're the one with the problem. You're the one who —'

'I'm the one who what?' I interrupt him. 'Fucked Belinda?'

'Since you went and turned into Kathy Bates overnight,' he says with deliberate, slow coldness, 'who I fuck is none of your business.'

'See you back here in half an hour,' I tell him.

FLOYD IS IN the office talking to the Oloffson's owner, a tall handsome man with curly, greying hair, when I cut through reception to the front veranda. Floyd briefly glances my way, but goes back to his conversation without so much as a flicker of recognition.

I say good morning to the few guests up for breakfast, each and every one of them looking slightly shell-shocked from RAM night, and help myself to another coffee while I wait for Floyd.

He doesn't appear until a taxi pulls up in the driveway. He casually waves an acknowledgment to the driver, then bounds down the stairs. I drain what's left of my coffee and take my time getting into an empty back seat.

'*Bonjour*,' the driver smiles, eyeing me up in the rear-view mirror.

'*Bonjour*,' I reply, nodding.

As we're leaving, the same white Jeep that dropped off Donny and his companion last night is waiting to pull in. I wave, but because of the Jeep's black windows can't tell if Donny's in there or not. The taxi driver gets directions from Floyd, then switches the radio on. The station seems to be a mixture of news and part-Mexican, part-Cuban-sounding Haitian music.

The streets are choked with traffic; everything from vehicles that look car-bombed to huge, swank, European luxury imports — although why anyone would want to risk sixty thousand dollars-plus driving those around Port-au-Prince is beyond me. Colourful, ornately decorated *taptap* buses, their painted names for the most part an indication of the driver's faith in God, the Virgin Mary, Jesus and *lwa* rather than collective adherence to the highway code, seem to be the main form of public transport apart from bicycles. We drive through a crowded open-air market that also serves as a bus terminal — although there isn't an actual building, just a gridlock of *taptaps* and people. Young boys selling plastic bags of drinking water knock on the taxi windows as we crawl along in the choked traffic. *Dlo! Dlo!* Market women carrying on their heads loads that would kill a donkey risk life and limb in the streets to avoid the stinking heaps of garbage piled high on the sidewalks.

At some point we begin heading along a wide busy road, the sparkling Port-au-Prince Bay to one side of us. The beaches are marred by slum dwellings and huge mounds of discarded corn husks or tyres. During a traffic snarl-up, I watch three men — their arms and bare feet peppered with shiny old burn-scars — pour car-battery acid into a bucket in a hut not much better than an animal's lean-to shelter.

The area has been completely deluged by a slurry of garbage and wet mud washed down from the mountainsides in last night's storm, like so much urban diarrhoea. A dead bloated dog, no more than an hour away from exploding, lies partially covered by scraps of plastic, rags and mud.

Gradually the population and traffic become less dense, and the cab is alternately filled with the smells of struggling *taptap* fumes, delicious roadside cooking and pungently exotic garbage fires — exactly what I would imagine a gypsy to smell like. We stop outside a wooden shack-like structure and Floyd hands the driver some money to buy a bottle of Barbancourt. Hungry and not sure how far away lunch is, I check my watch, only to find that the face has steamed up and the hands have ground to a halt. Sighing loudly, I throw the watch in my bag.

'What?' Floyd snaps, sweaty and tired and grumpy.

'Where are we going, for a start?' I snap back. 'I'm not your bloody dog in the back seat here.'

'To meet the artist,' he says at last. Then, more politely, 'St Louis St Brice — he's originally from the Chaine du Borgne area. *Mais*, the driver says that's within sixty miles of Cap-Haïten.'

AFTER A COUPLE of hours, during which time we can't have gone more than fifty, sixty kilometres, the driver stops in a small town consisting of a gas station and an impromptu market of spindly-twig stalls to fill up and ask for directions. After we've tanked up, Floyd goes with the driver into the almost bare shop to pay.

An albino kid in a T-shirt as long as a dress and man-size sneakers on his feet knocks on my window and waves. His grey-milky skin is raw and damaged, with deep wrinkles and melanomas like the surface of something crammed into a jar at a hospital museum. My first reaction is to flinch, but when I smile and wave back, he breaks into a wide, delighted laugh and runs back to his friends.

The contrast between the marsupial-looking albino boy and the other kids — the fact that he will be the normal one in the negative — is too good a photo opportunity to miss, so I get out of the taxi

186

with my camera and snap off a couple of shots. Suddenly some women start shouting, and one starts hitting me with a stick. There's some jostling, and a man with dark-black skin and blood-shot, mistreated-animal eyes snatches my camera from me. He runs off down a narrow path between ramshackle houses, dogs and kids in pursuit.

'Hey!' I shout. 'That's my camera! Come back!'

The woman with the stick hits me again, so I run back to the taxi and lock myself in until Floyd and the driver get back. They have to sweet-talk the hostile gathering into calming down and allowing us to drive off safely.

'What did you have to upset all those people for, you?' Floyd says. 'Someone could have been killed. *Mais,* it can happen so quickly in a place like this.'

'Gee. Thanks for leaving me *unattended* then,' I say, killing any further blame.

The houses in the country are simply made from wattle and daub, and every dirt yard boasts its share of roosters and guinea fowl, barefoot kids, poodle-size goats, mangy dogs, and laundry hanging out to dry on nearby scrawny fences and cacti hedges.

At last the driver turns off the highway up a dusty, rocky winding road that climbs steadily for a couple of kilometres, then he pulls over in front of a high-walled enclosure, its spiked security system along the top concealed by bougainvillaea. Three Doberman pinschers bark dementedly from behind the bars of ornate double gates. An old man, silver hair contrasting sharply with his dark aubergine skin, approaches with a rifle and calls out to the driver. The driver shrugs and shouts something back, gesticulating to Floyd and me. The only words I recognise are *Oloffson* and *Oui.* By now I've come to realise that most Haitian conversations sound like arguments so I can't tell if the old man with the gun is quite as hostile as he seems. Eventually, after Floyd makes a gift of the rum, he chains his dogs up and — with a wonderful smile — invites us into his compound.

The driver stays with his taxi while Floyd and I enter the gates, the old man warmly shaking our hands before leading the way. He speaks to us in French, quickly concentrating on Floyd when he realises I don't understand a word he's saying, but he considerately graces me with a light touch and a smile occasionally.

His home is a crumbling two-storey colonial relic of brick and overgrown vines, peeling wooden shutters painted a pastel aquamarine, with bars instead of glass to allow breezes to pass. He leads us into a courtyard, shady under the wide orange spread of a royal poinciana, its rampant roots now ruining the fancy brick paving, cracking the arid fountain and fish pond.

St Louis St Brice has paint under his fingernails, and art stacked everywhere. He indicates that we're to sit at an outdoor table, and addresses Floyd.

'He wants to know what you'd like to drink,' Floyd tells me. 'He's got his own well here, so the water is safe.'

'Whatever you're having,' I say, not really caring.

While the old man goes to fetch whatever Floyd has asked for, I sit in the sweltering heat of the yard, drooping like a bunch of old flowers on a grave. Floyd moves around and flicks through stacks of strange Australian-Aboriginal-like paintings of black angels and crosses, hooded fish-faced figures and gigantic ravens, candles and drums, pulling a couple to one side. They couldn't be more unlike the waterfall painting at the Oloffson if Rolf Harris had painted them.

St Brice brings out a tray of glasses and ice, cups, a pot of coffee, a bowl of white sugar and a plate of sliced limes. Floyd returns with the paintings he's picked out, and negotiates a price, handing over what looks like about six hundred US. St Brice is a charming old man, eyes warm and sharp, and he's happy to drink rum and chat away with Floyd for the rest of the afternoon. I wake up only when the ground is dark with shadows lengthened by the sun's descent, and the taxi driver is tooting his horn.

AFTER MY LONG siesta in St Brice's courtyard I'm wide awake all the way back to Port-au-Prince, but Floyd sleeps from the second he gets in the taxi until I shake him awake outside the Oloffson to pay the driver. He veers off to his bungalow, telling me he'll meet me for dinner in an hour.

Early evening, the dining area is almost deserted. Only a solitary white couple, diplomats or journalists, are eating already. Behind the mahogany bar in the lounge the rattan barstools are unoccupied, and the barmaid is watching a movie on the TV bolted to the wall. Because I left the one room-key behind with Renée, I have to get her out of bed to let me in. She looks a little healthier and has managed to dress herself. She's watching the same movie as the one showing downstairs.

I take a seat on the end of her bed. 'How are you feeling?' I ask.

'I been pukin' on the hour and I damn grateful Haiti got soft toilet paper,' she says, propping herself up with all the pillows in the room. I notice she's turned the paintings around to face the walls.

'Mozzie's got the same thing,' I tell her.

'Damn. Now I cain' hope it serious if I got it too,' she winks.

'You could always hope he's got something else. I do.'

'You got that right, baby,' she says. 'So, you find anything out today?'

Turning the TV down, I tell her everything about St Brice's painting in Belinda's room, about the eerie coincidence of the waterfall and the woman and boy behind it, and about our visit to St Brice to ascertain the painting's significance.

189

'And what St Brice have to say about it?' she says.

'I don't know — he doesn't speak English and I can't speak French. And then Floyd fell asleep in the taxi on the way home, and — I'm meeting him downstairs in a bit — why don't you join us and we can find out at the same time?'

'You two made up? I thought he was payin' that Peace Corps girl a bunch of attention last night.'

'He was,' it pains me to admit. 'All night as it happens.'

'That just plain rude if you ask me,' Renée says supportively. 'No matter what y'all fall out over.'

'So, will you come?'

'Sorry, darlin',' she says, patting my hand. 'I ain' up to goin' no place.'

'BRING ME A sandwich back with you,' she calls through the bathroom door. 'And find out from Floyd how I can call Jolie.'

'Okay,' I yell back, taking the key as I go.

Downstairs at the high mahogany bar I sit at the row of empty barstools, stub out a smouldering cigar butt and push away the ashtray. The barmaid watches the last five minutes of the movie she was watching earlier before she acknowledges my presence with a pretend surprised smile, and then takes ten minutes to make a rum punch. Afterwards she turns her back on the bar to watch a repeat of *That '70s Show*, making an extravagant show of wiping something if another staff member appears.

The dimly lit lounge area, reflected in the huge baroque gilt mirror mounted behind the bar, is somewhere between antiquated and dilapidated, decadent and *Alice in Wonderland*. The walls are crowded with mad, tobacco-stained Haitian art that's probably worth millions. The barmaid spots Floyd approaching the bar at the same time I do, and flirtatiously enquires what *M'sieur* would like to drink. *M'sieur* wants a rum punch too, and after getting served — more quickly this time — we head out to the veranda to eat.

'How's Renée doing?' Floyd asks, making for a table near the head of the stairs. The waitresses hanging around by the kitchen with nothing better to do look over briefly, then continue their conversation.

'On the mend. She wants me to take a sandwich back for her. What about Mozzie?'

Floyd snorts. 'I left him drinking beer to replace electrolytes. I think he's going to live, him.'

One of the waitresses finally shuffles over at the speed of necrotising fasciitis, and we both order shrimp, plus a couple of cheese sandwiches for Renée and Mozzie. As soon as she's out of earshot, I ask Floyd, 'So what did St Brice have to say about his painting? Does it mean something?'

Floyd takes a sip of his drink, then shakes his head. When he looks at me now, the tenderness and attraction that were there just a few days ago are completely absent. 'He said he didn't paint it.'

'Damn.'

'No, you don't understand. St Brice held the paintbrush, but it's not his art.'

Goose bumps rise swiftly and painfully on my arms, despite the ninety-plus-something-percent humidity. 'A *lwa* painted it?'

Floyd nods. 'Guess which one?'

'No — is St Brice sure?'

'It was definitely Prince le Kreyol, no question about it — there were plenty of witnesses. It happened during a Voodoo ceremony in the Chaine du Borgne.'

'I keep hearing Chaine du Borgne.'

'*Mais*, that's not all,' Floyd tells me, evidently getting ready for the big one. 'St Brice knew all about the woman and boy behind the waterfall. He said every child in his village grew up knowing not to swim in the pool, or the ghosts of a French mother and son there would drown them. He's given me directions to the exact location. We can leave as soon as Mozzie and Renée are well enough.'

'Wow,' I whistle. 'Who'd have thought it was going to be so easy?'

SOME OF THE Oloffson guests start drifting back from wherever they went for dinner, smiling hi or *bonsoir* depending on nationality. Floyd keeps glancing at the driveway, obviously keeping an eye out for someone.

'Why don't you just go down to the gates and wag your tail until she comes back?' I ask, more insulted than annoyed.

Just when I think he's pretending not to hear me, because he doesn't turn around for ages, he sighs deeply. 'Wag my tail? You need to get some help, you.'

'*Help?*' I splutter. '*Me?*'

'Yes, you. I've never met such a —'

Floyd doesn't get a chance to finish his insult because Donny appears at our table as suddenly as if he'd been beamed there.

'Hey, Laura,' he grins. 'How you doing, babe?' He kisses me on the lips in a proprietary manner and, uninvited, takes a seat and lights a cigar. 'And friend,' he says meaningfully to Floyd, puffing smoke in his face.

Floyd smiles wryly to himself and rises. 'Don't mind me. I'm done here, ' he says, picking up a sandwich for Mozzie. 'Don't wag your tail too hard,' he tells me.

DONNY WATCHES FLOYD leave, then, turning back to me, he smiles. 'That cut on your lip looks good.'

I respond half-heartedly, irritated by his overfamiliarity. But the guy did save me, and etiquette demands I be nice to him. 'Thanks to you.'

'Well, I won't say no if you want to buy me a drink.'

Donny's confidence is not that of a man used to being refused anything by a woman. Tonight he's wearing a red, short-sleeved shirt with a repetitive hula-dancer pattern. Raven-black hair and a Blarney-Stone twinkle in his amused blue eyes suggest an element of Irish ancestry. When the waitress comes back with the drinks order, he insists on paying and gives the waitress two hundred gourdes for a tip. I notice Donny's friend — or rather his friend's equally lurid shirt — at the bar. He's drinking a bottle of the local Prestige beer while he chats with the barmaid.

I ask Donny, 'What's your mate's name?'

'Bobby,' he says, glancing briefly in his direction.

'What are you doing in Haiti?'

'Just taking a vacation,' he shrugs. 'Chilling.'

'Wouldn't you have been less conspicuous in Hawaii?'

'You'd think so,' he says, 'but we went there last year and got caught up in an armed robbery. Bobby took three slugs in the butt — one half of his ass is a prosthesis now.' Donny seems delighted when I laugh properly. 'You just got ten times more beautiful,' he says, smiling at me.

Tapping his cigar in the ashtray, Donny turns to greet the returning Peace Corps girls, Belinda and Michelle, coming up the stairs in pretty dresses. 'Good evening, ladies. How's your night been?'

They say hello and fine, but grudgingly. Belinda looks around the bar and lounge, then approaches our table while Michelle buys a bottle of wine.

'Hi, uh —'

'Hi, Belinda,' I say.

'Is Floyd around?' she asks, not even embarrassed, somewhat impatient even.

'He's in his bungalow — the Graham Greene one over there.'

'Yeah, I know where it is,' she says, making her way back to her friend without any further conversation.

'You're welcome,' Donny calls as they pass us on their way down the stairs again, but they act like they don't hear.

He turns back to me with a shrug. 'Have you got time for another rum punch?'

'See if they serve them pint glasses.'

CHAPTER 15

ALL THE NOISE of Laura carrying on in the pool with Donny wake me up. Probably woke the whole Oloffson up, yelling and singing at the top of they voices like that. She finally turn up around three in the morning after the security guard kick them out, soak head to toe, clutching what left of my sandwich in her fist. She ain' in the door two seconds when she pass out, face down on her bed, and it one hell of a job removing her wet clothes and wrestling that sandwich out her hand.

Ain' no chance of sleeping again afterward, especially now the damn roosters have start up already, so I watch TV until it light enough to make me think there a chance of finding something to eat.

'Laura,' I say, shaking her awake. 'How about some breakfast? You comin' down?'

She open eyeballs look they been in a fight with wasps, and groan almost right away at remembering some things, no doubt.

'You got that right, darlin'. I be ashame, too, turnin' up drunk in the middle of the night after wakin' half the hotel up. How you end up in the pool with Donny? I thought you was meetin' with Floyd.'

She groan again and curl up into the smallest ball she can make.

MOZZIE SITTING AT breakfast already and he get up when I come along, and kiss me on my cheek. 'You look like you've lost some weight there, mate,' he say, as charming as can be. His niceness is disturbing — it just ain' a natural part of his nature. He pull my chair out and pour me a glass of water from the jug. 'Another couple of meals like that and watch out Tyra Banks,' he smile. 'Renée Poupet is in the building.'

'When did you get yourself a personality change?' I ask suspiciously, raising my eyebrows at Floyd, who looking a bit blue if you ask me. 'Although I ain' complainin'.'

'He woke up like this,' Floyd shrug. 'Enjoy it while you can.'

'I can't wait for Laura to get here,' Mozzie say all gleeful, grinning and rubbing his hands together like he just won a million dollars. 'What was she *thinking* of, fucking that guy in the pool? *Donny, Donny, catch me,*' he mimic, sounding just like her last night.

I notice Floyd flinch some.

'She a grown woman,' I sniff. 'She can do whatever she want, where she want, with whoever she damn well please. Besides, you two ain' exactly Doris freakin' Day.'

Floyd look at me, hurt, but Mozzie look like he trying to decide what to spend the million on. 'So, is Laura dressed yet?'

'Sorry to ruin your fun,' I tell him, 'but I be surprise as hell if she make it out of bed this side of twenty-four hours. If you want some kicks you goin' have to go down in the yard and pull wings off bugs instead.'

FLOYD BUY ME a calling card at some place not far from the

Oloffson, then he take off with Mozzie some place to negotiate a price with a possible driver. The maid's trying to clean up around Laura when I get back to the room. She still sleeping, the bed-cover pull right up over her head. I wait out on the balcony until the maid's done, then it take me a few minutes figuring out how the card works.

Hoover answer on the first ring.

'Hi baby. Can you hear me okay?'

'Mama?' he say like I come to save him from a bad dream, and right away I know something ain' right.

RENÉE NEARLY GIVES me a stroke, shouting down the telephone. I lurch into panicky self-loathing, remembering my final moments in the deep end of the pool where, blindingly illuminated by the security guard's torch, Donny had me pinned against the side, his hands on my arse, my legs around his waist, my hand down his pants. *Yeah, that's good, baby. Harder.*

And, oh Jesus, the business with the cigar.

'HOOVER — WHAT GOIN' on? Where Jolie? Put Jolie on the line.'

He start to bawl like he was only holding it together long enough till somebody else took over. 'She ain' here, Mama.'

I don't think my heart ever going to start again because he ain' just talking about her being out at the store. That much I know. 'Where she gone? Where the twins?'

'She took off to Texas with them. A couple white guys turn up here,' he sob, hysterical like a girl, 'just after you left. Jolie sold the journal to them, Mama. Then she call some guy Alfie to come pick her up, and she —'

'What white guys, sweetie? What guys came by the trailer? What they look like?'

'One of them look like that guy from *Spin City*,' he say.

'You mean Michael J. Fox?'

'No,' he sniff. 'The new one.'

'Charlie Sheen?'

Laura sit bolt up right in bed like somebody throw a bucket of ice over her.

'I told her it was wrong, Mama,' Hoover cry. 'I try to stop —'

'Okay, baby. Calm down. It ain' your fault. I ain' blamin' you.'

YOU LIKE THIS, *huh, Laura? Does it feel good?*

Yes. Giggle.

It feels like fucking heaven to me, baby. God, you're so beautiful — I think I'm falling in love with you already. Don't leave Port-au-Prince. Stay here with me.

I have to go.

Jesus. You're so hot. Where?

Some village up north. In the Chaine du Borgne.

You've got great tits, Laura. I'm so turned on right now I feel like I'm going to explode any second. Why there?

Because of the waterfall.

'SHIT,' LAURA SAY, running for the bathroom.

'Wait up for a second, baby,' I tell Hoover. I walk to the bathroom and hold Laura's hair away from her face while it just about in the bowl. 'You okay, darlin'?'

She give me the thumbs-up while retching up a whole bunch of rum punches.

'You got enough to eat, baby?' I ask Hoover when I get back to the phone. 'How you doin' for money?'

'Okay. Jolie left me a hundred forty-three dollars. I still got seventy-somethin' left over.'

'Well, you make sure and buy some vitamins with that, baby. You got to eat right while you still growin'. I don't want to come home and find you with a deficiency.'

'Why cain' you come home now, Mama? Let them others find the gold. I don't like bein' the only one here. It sound like there somethin' prowlin' around at night.'

'Hoover, baby, listen to me — just a couple more days. I promise. We just about there then I comin' home on the first plane out of here. Why don't you call a friend, see if you cain' stay over until I get back? What about Eugene Junior? Why don't you give him a call?'

'Because Jolie sold him some pot and his mama found out and I ain' allow to go over there no more.'

'Jolie been sellin' pot to school kids?'

'Only to eighth grade and up.'

LAURA GET UP off the floor and wash her face in the sink.

'It was Donny,' she say, after she rinse her mouth out.

'It was Donny who do what?'

'Donny was at your trailer.'

'What make you so sure? Did he tell you he was?'

She step into the shower and turn it on full blast, which ain' much, and start soaping herself clean.

'Renée, trust me on this — Donny was at your trailer. I bet Hoover said the other guy was blond, didn't he? Now that I think about it — *Jesus.*' Her sentence come to a abrupt stop and she look depress as hell.

'What?'

'I bet it was the blond one who attacked me that night.'

'Do you think he was lookin' for somethin'?'

'No,' she sigh. 'I think I got had. The whole thing was orchestrated.'

She wait for me to disagree, but I don't.

'Start packing,' she say. 'They've got a head start on us.'

'You — uh — you know — with him?' I say, handing her a towel.

She think about it for a bit, and shrug. 'Would you believe me if I said I did not have sexual relations with that man?'

'Not really, darlin'. And you better grow yourself a bunch of thick skin before Mozzie track you down. He was just about comin' in his pants at breakfast thinkin' about it.'

'No,' she whine, pausing in the middle of drying off. 'How did he find out? Does Floyd know?'

'Baby, ain' nobody alive in this hotel didn't hear your show last night.'

'Unbelievable,' she say. 'Floyd spends the night corrupting a Peace Corps girl but I'm Monica Lewinsky.'

'Least he was quiet about it.'

'Mais, how much did you tell him?' Floyd ask Laura.

'Pillow talk, mate,' Mozzie butt in. He hopping from one foot to the other with the excitement of it all. 'She would have blabbed everything faster than Donny could pay her compliments.'

'Why don't you be quiet, you?' Floyd say to him. 'You're not helping any.'

'Don't take your PMS out on me, mate,' Mozzie snap back. 'Jesus, have the waitress make you a camomile tea or some —'

'Hey — everybody!' I holler. 'My grandbabies is missin' in case y'all forgot. Now quit fightin' and start gettin' along, because the sooner we find the gold before Donny and Bobby do, the sooner I can get home and start lookin' for them.'

'Sorry,' Laura the first to say.

'Renée, please,' Floyd apologize, taking my hand. 'Forgive me.

You're right. Are you okay? Should we call the police or something?'

'No. Jolie take good care of them — until the money run out, at least.'

'Sorry, Renée,' Mozzie mumble.

'*Mais*, there's one thing in our favor,' Floyd say. 'I didn't tell Laura the exact location of the waterfall.'

'Ergo,' Mozzie smirk, perking right up again, 'Mata Hari over there couldn't have passed it on.'

MOZZIE AND FLOYD come back with transport and a driver around two, by which time Renée and I have done all the bag-packing and are waiting in the driveway. The sky is pearlescent and hazy with a thin cover of cloud, humidity crushing the life out of every molecule of air around us. Surges of remorse and self-reproach make me dizzy and sick, as does standing up, and I practically collapse into the back of the 4WD after Renée.

She gets comfortable between Mozzie and me, then offers me a mint. 'Here you go, baby. Take one of these.'

'Thanks,' I smile, dolefully grateful someone is being nice to me even though I don't deserve it.

'It ain' the end of the world,' she says, patting my knee. 'I bet there a million waterfalls in the Chaine du Borgne. Donny and Bobby goin' be runnin' all over the place for weeks probably, and we goin' to the exact right spot. Why, I bet we is on our way home tomorrow with the gold.'

North of Port-au-Prince, Route Nationale 1 is fairly straight and flat, although I wouldn't go so far as to call it smooth. The motion of the 4WD as it weaves to avoid the potholes makes me travel-sick, and the driver has to keep pulling over so I can vomit bile into dusty cacti, snagged scraps of plastic fluttering from their spines.

The eighty-kilometre-long mountain range that follows the

highway to the right is not much greener in places than sand dunes and, if it weren't for the Gulf of La Gonâve to our left, drained to the colour of washing-up water by a hot aluminium sky, it could be Arizona. The driver is as tidily dressed as if he were going to church, and is obviously a family man if the sun-bleached photographs of children stuck to his dashboard are any indication. He talks incessantly — Floyd translating — drawing our attention to sites of local interest along the way, such as the cement factory where a succession of ex-presidential megalomaniacs had people disposed of.

We stop in a little beachside village that's trying hard to be a resort, to eat a late lunch of black *djon djon* rice in a covered outdoor restaurant that the driver recommends. Although it's delicious — the others are *mmm mmm*-ing like a tree full of doves — the gas from the local *kola aysien* I wash it down with makes me queasy and bloated. Floyd is absolutely neutral if he has to talk to me directly, coolly keeping me at arm's length. Some kids have gathered to stare, and after a discussion among themselves, a little skinny barefoot boy with a cheeky smile is pushed forward. He says something to the driver and shows him a metal cigar container. The driver responds in a tone of voice I interpret as, 'Get lost,' but Floyd calls the kid back and questions him for a while. From the kid's hand gestures, little is required in the way of a working Kreyol vocabulary to get the gist of what's being discussed. Finally Floyd gives the kid a fifty-gourde note and turns back to the table, rubbing his temples, flashing me a strange look that's probably blame.

'What was that all about?' Renée asks him.

Floyd takes the deepest breath before replying. 'He says the two *blans* who stopped here earlier today gave it to him. They turned up in a white SUV with black windows, and a Haitian driver. One of the *blans* was missing the tip of a finger. Laura? Do you know anything about that?'

'It's them,' I nod, not looking at anyone.

Everyone is quiet for the rest of the journey to St-Marc, our pit stop for the night because the driver won't go further in the dark, and when we arrive there the power is either out or they just don't have any. Lamps and cooking fires glow beacon-like in the gloom of a pre-storm dusk. The place is part construction-site, part Africa's interpretation of the Wild West. Fat raindrops start exploding like water bombs against the windscreen as we pull up outside a four-storey structure that's about as architecturally alluring as somewhere unwanted dogs get put down.

THE DRIVER TAKE off some place else to stay with a cousin, and Floyd tell him to come back at six in the morning to pick us up. Rain falling like the sky crack apart and we all wet through by the time our bags unload and we make reception. Seem like there only this one kid working at the hotel I seen nicer prisons than. He lead us up three flights of stairs, then down a narrow hallway, a bunch of roaches scurrying away from his flashlight. The kid smell like he ain' taken a bath for a month, and he leave a trail of body odor behind him make my eyes water.

Suddenly Laura start screaming, 'Get it out, get it out!' and she brushing frantically at her hair, leaping all over the place like her head on fire.

Floyd take her by the scruff of her neck and bend her over so she cain' jump around none, then fish a bug out her hair, stamping it flat when it hit the floor. 'It's okay, it's gone now,' he tell her, letting her up again.

'Thanks,' she say, twitching and jerking, hair all mess up like a crazy woman.

The kid stop and open a couple of doors side by side, the two rooms completely dark until he light some candles, then they

spooky and depressing instead. The room I sharing with Laura ain'
got no plaster, just cinder blocks, and the shower and toilet separate
by bricks ain' even cement together. The toilet seat crack and
missing half, and the carpet cover on the lid stink of urine. There a
ten-inch turd floating unflush for God knows how long, and the
soap on the sink already been use by somebody. There ain' no
running water, just a filthy-ass bucket with a quarter inch of
mosquito eggs floating on the top.

'I'd give this place *minus* five stars,' Laura say, standing in the
middle of the bathroom looking like she don't want to touch
nothing. 'Jesus, what is that smell? It's horrible.'

'Nobody empty the waste bin in about a year,' I tell her. 'It full
of use paper and sanitary towels.'

'Oh, that's just foul,' she say, steering the waste bin out into the
hallway with her foot, just as Floyd show up from next door.

He look at the contents of the bin and shudder. 'Not that I feel
like eating any more, but I thought maybe after everyone had fresh-
ened up we could find somewhere nearby for an early dinner. *Mais*,
I don't know about anyone else but I need to sleep, me. The
concierge,' he say through a yawn, 'is bringing some towels.'

'He wastin' his time bringin' me a towel,' I snort, 'unless he
plannin' on holding a gun to my head.'

I WIPE MYSELF down with some perfumed refresher towels and
throw Renée the rest of the pack. The walls in our room have
already started absorbing rainwater, and are sweating and stained
with damp. Renée gives me a couple of Dramamine to take the edge
off things, and I decide to have a lie-down while she modestly gets
changed in the bathroom.

I pull back the bedcover — greasy to the touch and reeking of
something rankly organic — to find a yellowish stain about the size

of a dinner plate in the middle of the one rumpled bed sheet. My pillow is bloodstained and, when lifted, reveals six or seven used condoms lying crumpled underneath.

Someone knocks on the door. 'Are you decent, ladies?' Mozzie asks, opening the door a crack.

'Come in,' I tell him.

Behind Mozzie an enormous coloured woman in six-inch wedge sandals, a towel and curlers, swings her hips in an exaggerated parody of sexy as she passes. She raises her eyebrows suggestively at Mozzie, saying something softly, almost a whisper, in Kreyol.

'Lady, whatever you said, I don't think so,' he says, smiling just as suggestively back at her. 'But, thank you.'

She laughs derisively as she sashays off, and a door opens and slams shuts further down the corridor. 'Special,' he nods, spotting the condoms under my pillow. 'But no less than you deser —'

The rest of his sentence is lost in the cinder-block-trembling thunder of a generator firing up.

'Is that us?' Renée calls from the bathroom. 'Is the power comin' back on?'

Music, about as loud as it's possible to go, starts blaring from the nightclub next door, and whoops and cheers reach us from various rooms throughout the hotel.

'Joy,' Mozzie sighs wearily. 'Saturday night just kicked off in St-Marc.'

THERE AIN' NO point trying to sleep through the racket unless you deaf or in a coma. It too wet to go wandering around outside, so we decide we might as well join them seeing as they right next door and we ain' got a show in hell of sleeping through them. Some big dude dress like a pimp check us for guns on the way in. The basket next to him pile up with about twenty of them already, check in like coats.

The place pack with women in low-cut tops, miniskirts right up to they asses, and shoes with thick soles like folks with one leg shorter than the other have to wear. The men eyeing up Mozzie and Floyd, who both smart enough not to go square off with nobody. There a DJ wearing all the latest MTV gear wouldn't look out of place in New York. He got shades he never remove even though it hard to see a thing in here. Some fool grab my ass but they lucky because I don't see who it is. We find a little table back in a corner out the way, and then Floyd take an age buying some drinks. He come back with a bottle of Barbancourt, Cokes and a Prestige.

The music too loud to hold any kind of conversation and nobody got the energy to shout, so we sip our drinks and watch the dancing, thinking our own thoughts to ourselves. Laura still down on herself and I glad Floyd ain' been making things worse by being mean to her because Mozzie enough for one person to bear, although Floyd ain' exactly overly warm considering he did spend the night with that Peace Corps girl right under her nose.

Floyd offer to fetch me another beer but the place twice as busy as when we first arrive, so I make it easy on him and say I think I going switch to rum instead. At first it make my mouth numb and everything on the way down contract, but then the glow feel kind of nice and it ain' too bad at all.

After about a hour, because I ain' use to drinking hard liquor never mind on a empty stomach, when the DJ announce the next track over his mike and everybody cheering and whistling and on the dance floor *moving*, making me proud to be color because white folks cain' dance like that, I get up out my seat and let everybody know what moves this grandmammy from St Luc, Louisiana, got.

RENÉE KIND OF faints to sleep in her underwear. I spray her with bug repellent and cover up everything but her face with hotel towels. I've moved way beyond exhaustion to a permanent, disorienting sense of *déjà vu*; peripheral hallucinations and mosquitoes make me jumpy and unable to sleep. It sounds like the devil is humping someone with a swallowing problem next door, and outside in the pre-dawn hours, during which most people eventually die, the freaking roosters have started up already. I sit on my suitcases and cry.

AT FIRST THERE *just blackness and silence, but then — whoosh — there a whole bunch of folks calling my name, invisible hands grabbing at me like they all drowning in a swamp or something.*

We are hungry.

We are cold.

We are weak.

I try escaping but I cain' get no place fast because it like running through syrup with all they hands on me. There hundreds of them pulling and tugging at me. They start clawing, ripping my clothes, yelling accusations at me.

The harder I try fighting against them, the harder they smother me with their arms and bodies.

You must serve us.

You must feed us.

You must warm us.

Because I cain' breathe with them asphyxiating me, I stop struggling. One whispers in my ear, thin and feeble as a voice on the brink of death, You have no choice, Renée.

They breath make the inside of my eardrum moist.

We demand that you serve us.

CHAPTER 16

LAURA SHAKE ME awake from some kind of nightmare leave a bad taste in my mouth. It disappear like ice cream left unattend in my trailer for two seconds, but whatever it was about I ain' got no mind to chase after it.

'Hey, Renée, are you okay?' Laura ask, though she the one look like she could use a month in a Betty Ford Clinic.

Almost immediately I open my eyes it feel like somebody trying to drive a fork into the top of my skull, twisting and digging with all they might. Every muscle in my body aching, especially my heart when I remember Jolie and the twins missing, that Hoover home alone and afraid of the dark, and then that the smart money on Donny and Bobby reaching the gold first. The whole world feel like it compressing down on me, squeezing every inch of the will to go on.

'I'm not surprised,' Laura say, offering me a bottle of water and some Tylenol. 'There was hardly a man in St-Marc that didn't shout you a drink last night. You were the belle of the disco, girlfriend.' *Girlfriend* in my accent. 'Thanks for taking the heat off me. Mozzie is going to have a field day.'

My skin itchy as hell, and when I pull the towels up to take a look, I cover in some kind of rash. 'Jesus, what the hell that?' I shriek, getting them the hell off me.

'God knows,' she shriek herself, flicking the towels off the bed in case she catch whatever I got.

Somebody bang on a wall and yell something pissy-sounding at us.

'*YOU'VE GOT A CHEEK, BEELZEBUB!*' Laura yell back, finally showing the temper to go with the hair. '*FUCK OFF!*'

I stand up and the room spin like crazy for a while, make me think I going pass out. Then my equilibrium return and I take a close inspection of the rash: millions of red, tiny hives spread over almost my entire body. 'The hell? That look like scabies to you?'

'I don't know,' she frown, peering up close to my belly. 'I've got some antibiotic talc somewhere. Maybe that'll work.' She go searching through her bags and find me a tin of something say it going cure everything from jock itch to diaper rash.

IT MUST BE a hundred-something in the shade by noon and the driver ain' shown up yet. Everybody sick of waiting round for him all morning, especially when we tense about Donny having at least a day on us. Mozzie been riding me all morning, waving his butt in my face, lisping, '*I see you baby, shaking that bootylicious ass, shaking that bootylicious ass*', and in the end I have to threaten him with eating his own manhood through his own broken teeth to shut him up. So then he go start on Laura again instead, and don't that end in tears?

'There was a young doxy called Mata Hari,' he say.

'Stop talking, Mozzie,' she warn him. 'I'm not in the mood.'

'Who took people's beans and spilled them.'

'Shut —'

'Sometimes it was Heinz, spasmodically Wattie's —'

'— *up, you irritating cock-sucker*,' she yell, kicking the hell out his bag like it the one doing the rhyming.

Mozzie just about wet himself laughing and then Laura burst into tears, running off back into the hotel some place. Mozzie turn to Floyd and myself, acting as surprise as a innocent bystander caught up in events. 'Jesus. What a tantrum. Has Laura the Luggage Slayer got her monthly or something?'

Floyd sigh and shake his head. 'Why?' he ask Mozzie.

'What?' Mozzie say, fighting not to grin. He enjoy rattling folks so much I think he either he got bully a whole bunch as a kid or his mama was mean to him. 'It's not my fault she's unstable.'

'You a asshole the size of the Superdome,' I tell him, before I go after Laura.

I find her on the stairwell two gloomy, stinking-of-urine flights up, crying like somebody just died. Even in the dark I can see she just as upset as Jolie the time told me she got herself knock up and she thought her life going to end. Laura don't hear me coming, even though I puffing like a asthmatic, and she jump when I take a seat on the step and put my arm round her.

'Just me, sugar,' I say.

Her face all puffy and her eyes swollen to slits. 'I'm sorry, Renée,' she sniff.

'Don't be sorry, darlin'. Hell, we all made mistakes like Donny.' I hand over some tissues and stroke her hair that need a good combing.

'If it makes you feel any better,' she say, blowing, 'you couldn't hate me any more than I hate myself right now.'

'Listen, baby, I don't hate you. The only thing I hate is celery.

Sure, you put the squeeze on things, but you just got to deal with the consequences now. Cryin' about shit ain' going help — especially when there ain' no consequences yet that we aware of for sure.'

'But what if Donny does get to the gold first?'

Some bells start up from some church nearby, and if I close my eyes and ignore the smell I could be sitting back home in La Salle Square under the shade of a tree with my mama, listening to the bells ring out for Mass.

'Then that the way it is,' I tell her, keeping my eyes shut for comfort, because now ain' the time to elaborate on how much I need that gold. Hell, I would probably cry myself.

THE DRIVER FINALLY decides to turn up ten minutes after we order lunch. Reeking of booze and with eyes like organ transplants, he staggers and weaves all over the place as he secures our luggage to the roof. We try cancelling the food, but it's too late and we have to pay for it. Mozzie knows he's pushed everyone too far and is quiet for once, although he may just be recharging his batteries for later. Floyd, very withdrawn, sits next to the driver again and winds his window down for fresh air, hot and pungent as it is.

St-Marc is fairly busy for a Sunday, as residents, as well dressed as their means allow in pristine dresses and shirts, polished shoes and hats, meander between church and calling on family and friends. The sun is broiling down on the town, making it hard to breathe, but ahead in the north — the direction we're heading — cloud is rising from behind the mountains in a solid black sheet of menace.

Breathing becomes more of a problem shortly after leaving St-Marc because of road dust, so faced with suffocation we opt for the driver's breath circulating through the AC. Every now and again Floyd shakes the driver and shouts, '*HEY, YOU, WAKE UP!*' and the driver swerves back on the road again.

'Jesus,' Renée whistles, after a close call with a cement truck, 'if closin' my eyes didn't make me feel nauseous, I be too scare to look.'

'Nausea-*ted*,' Mozzie corrects her. 'Nause-*ous* means to make someone else feel sick.'

'Is that so?' she says. 'Well I guess that would make you the one doin' the nausea-*ting* then, don't it?'

Mozzie snorts. 'Nauseating is an adjective, not a verb.'

'Whatever. You still makin' me sick. Verb that up your ass.'

On the way to Gonaïves we traverse the furthest edges of the Artibonite Valley, a vast, green plain of rice. The only maintenance the road has seen in the last twenty years is the rocks that naked local kids, hopeful of donations from grateful motorists, use to fill the potholes. Closer to Gonaïves, out of the irrigated cultivation of the valley, the land is ravaged, stripped of vegetation by the ravenous appetite of the chronically poor, baked to arid dust and sand and cacti by the hot Haitian sun, with barely a thing left to offer.

We pass an open-sided, tin-roofed structure tucked away behind a fence of spindly sticks, rafters strung with miles of coloured plastic bunting. A painted caber-thick pole in the centre runs from dirt floor to roof, a flat foot-high cement doughnut circling its base. Close by is a thatched, three-door building, its exterior walls adorned with pastel murals of mermaids and saints and intricate lacy symbols. A few thin trees on the well kept, peaceful grounds offer dappled shade from the fierce sun.

'What's that?' I ask nobody in particular.

Floyd points the place out to the driver and asks him about it.

'It's a *peristyle*,' he explains afterwards. 'A Voodoo temple. He says the mambo there is famous because she can walk on water.'

'Now *that* I would like to see,' I whistle.

Floyd turns to me, laughing, the first time he's smiled at me in days. 'Apparently it doesn't work if there are any *blans* around.'

The last ten minutes into Gonaïves are the bumpiest and roughest of the whole trip, and the wall of storm that has been moving toward us all afternoon finally and completely blocks the sun, throwing the town into an eerie twilight just as we arrive. I suspect Gonaïves isn't what you'd call a nice relaxing stopover at the best of times — a dusty, neglected, coastal slum — but in premature shadow it's positively *Tales of the Unexpected*.

Young males bristling with the lethal cocktail of too much time and not enough money hang in intimidating malcontented gangs on the streets as we pass. Anti-Aristide slogans are plastered across walls and gates, leaving no doubt as to this crumbling, ramshackle town's resentment of its government. A splay-footed kid in a pair of filthy shorts starts to run alongside our vehicle, banging on Mozzie's window, becoming even more aggressive when we don't stop. 'Give me dollar, give me dollar,' he demands. He spits a wad of phlegm onto the glass.

'*HEY*!' Mozzie shouts, rolling down his window. '*PACK IT IN, KID. YOU'RE STARTING TO PISS ME OFF*!'

If it's not enough that Renée's luggage stands out like stallion bollocks, marking us as *blans* as surely as we'd been flying US and NZ flags from the roof instead, Mozzie screaming English from an expensive 4WD-import while traversing the town's main thorough-fare kind of clinches it. Hundreds of hostile pairs of eyes stop to watch our progress, glaring their disapproval.

'What you have to shout at that kid for?' Renée scolds Mozzie. 'Now look what you done, pissin' them all like that.'

'Mate, if you're so keen on catching TB, you sit by the fucking window,' he snaps back.

The driver is sweating buckets, his knuckles tight on the steering wheel. He's no longer drowsy with hangover, and his eyes are wide and alarmed.

213

Everyone screams when a rock hits the windscreen, a sharp crack splintering violently across the glass, my own alarm a shrill, gut-wrenching soprano. The driver hits the horn, clearing bicycles and pedestrians from our path, gunning it as we're chased by upwards of fifty locals and dogs the last few kilometres out of town. Gunshots ricochet in our ears.

'You better pull over so I can change my underwear,' Renée sighs, once it's a fairly safe bet we've escaped.

I THOUGHT LOUISIANA could rain something biblical, but it a pleasant drizzle compare to what beating down on the roof of the vehicle now. The headlights on full beam and the wipers going like crazy, only just clearing a view of the road through the crack windscreen. The driver swerving round all the potholes, skidding some when he spot them late. The damn traffic ain' going any slower on account of the conditions, and I swear to God I ain' never been so scare in my life.

We in some kind of valley look like the Garden of Eden compare to round Gonaïves, but it ain' too long before we climbing up over a mountain, on a hairy-ass string of switchbacks that require sounding the horn to let folks know we coming round the bends.

The AC don't work uphill so the inside of the vehicle get steam up so bad nobody can see out and the driver ask us to crack the windows a inch. Everybody in the back seat soon wet through from the rain hitting us like it was fire-hose in through the windows, and we shivering from the cold of being this high. My skin start coming up in weals from itching at my rash, and Laura vomiting in a plastic bag Floyd find her in the glovebox. The driver having trouble staying awake again, and even though everybody just as famish as he is, Mozzie acting like we deliberately trying to starve

214

him to death. There enough water falling out the sky to bring the whole mountain down in a landslide.

The driver tell Floyd there a police stop coming up, but although the lights of they building is on, the rain hard enough to knock a man off his feet and we drive right on by without nobody stopping us. The road start to head back down to earth soon after, and the driver tell us to wind the windows back up so he can turn the heater on.

Unfortunately the heat make him even drowsier and I praising the Lord by the time we safely pull up outside the gas station of a long, sloping town. The driver fall asleep almost immediately we come to a halt.

'Somebody better buy the man somethin' with a bunch of caffeine in it,' I say.

WHEN I FINISH what I got to do in the filthy bathroom — the toilet might as well be a bucket because it ain' even connect up to no plumbing — I find Laura outside, leaning against the wall under the narrow overhang of the roof, trying to light a cigarette from a book of matches. Gusts of wet wind keep blowing them out. Finally she get the damn cigarette lit and throw the burning match away.

'When you take up smokin'?' I cringe, waiting for the explosion.

She exhale smoke in rings like a pro. 'Since the back wheel of that Jeep went over the edge of the road and I thought we were going to plummet a thousand metres and die.'

'Well, you keep tossin' lit matches out in the forecourt of a gas station, honey,' I say, 'and we still might.'

IT TURNS OUT Donny refuelled here early yesterday, and was asking questions about waterfalls. In our favour he was directed about sixty kilometres from where he needs to be, but it's only a matter of time before he stumbles on the Nancy waterfall, if only by sheer luck. So far I've been more of a hindrance than a help in Renée's quest to claim the gold, and I can't see how I'm supposed to be an advantage to her, seeing as I may well have cost her the future Prince le Kreyol wants her to have. The gas-station attendant has also warned us about travelling any further in these conditions, as we have several rivers to ford and levels will have risen quite considerably by now, with worse to come. A freak storm from the Atlantic is tracking southwest over the country, and Haiti looks like taking a pounding over the next six hours or so. The driver has to be bribed with a two-hundred-dollar bonus to continue on to Nancy.

As soon as the paving of town runs out, the road turns to a river of mud and topsoil. Mozzie and Renée both fall asleep, athough how anyone could do so while being shaken to death is their guess. The driver gives staying on the road everything he's got. I keep my fingers crossed, and Floyd braces his feet against the dashboard as we begin descending carefully through a valley of lush vegetation and quarter-acre farms, our headlights picking out the eyes of domestic animals sheltering under trees and crude shelters of tin for warmth.

'*Mais*, what a night,' Floyd says, wiping the breath-mist from his window. 'The weather couldn't be worse if it tried.'

The driver doesn't speak English, so he has to be talking to me.

'I thought you liked rain,' I say.

Floyd doesn't respond for ages, then he turns just enough to present his profile. 'I thought you did too,' he says. 'But it seems you prefer pool water.'

'What's not to prefer?' I snort just to get the last bitch in, though I instantly regret it. Why the hell did I even start a conversation that was bound to go nowhere pleasant.

The first few rivers we come to have bridges, and although

submerged are easily traversed with big 4WD tyres. The driver seems unperturbed about the one we're approaching, despite the chocolate torrent of stormwater raging down off the mountainsides. I'm so busy seething about Floyd's snide comment, and my unerring capacity to make things worse, that I don't even have my fingers crossed.

We almost make it too — a split second was all it would have taken to reach safety — but a roaring two-metre wall of flash-flooding slams into the bridge, smashing it apart as though it were woven from straw and carrying us away as easily as a bath toy.

WE HAVEN'T EATEN *for over two hundred years, Renée.*
Feel how cold we are from so long under the waters.
Feel how weak our limbs are from neglect.
We are your people, Renée.
Serve us.

My first thought is a damn train hit us. The noise is unbelievable — screaming, roaring, heads cracking, horn blaring. I ain' even work out we in a river yet when we slam into something big and the wind-screen give way and a tidal wave pour through, snapping my neck so far back I think it going break off. For the briefest second we lodge in the mud of the bank we hit, but then half of it fall to pieces on us, pinning us underwater until the current rip us free again, ramming us into a fallen tree instead. The screech of branches on metal loud enough to hear above all the noise of the river as a tree come crashing through what left of the windows and pin me to my seat.

Feed us, heat us, serve us.
Help us and we can help you.
Without us you have nothing.
We are your family.
We are your ancestors.
A tree can't grow without watering its roots.

'Get off me!' I yell at them. 'Leave me alone. You suffocatin' me.'

THE SECOND I release my seat belt the current wrenches me from the back seat and propels me through a lacerating tangle of branches, only to jam me up against the tree trunk. The horrifying force of the water makes my limbs as useless as wet rags. Unable even to lift my head above the water, there is nothing I can do to save Renée or the others, all drowning in the 4WD behind me.

All that is left is to tolerate the terror and grief until the river decides, Enough.

'GET OUT MY damn face,' I yell at them. 'I cain' breathe.'

It's a disgrace how we've been treated.

Ignored, neglected, abandoned.

Some of us haven't even had proper funerals.

It's your duty to serve us, Renée.

Don't fail or we will continue to punish you with what strength we have left.

I claw back at them, fighting for my life. 'Leave me alone. Get off!'

You must serve us. You must.

'Okay, I promise, I promise,' I yell. 'Just let me breathe and I'll serve you.'

STRONG HANDS SNAP the thick branches away from me like they was twigs. My seat belt rip apart as easy as tissue and I drag out from the vehicle into the full thundering force of the river. Somebody carry me ashore, hauling me up to safety some ways off, laying me on my stomach with my head to one side when I start vomiting up half the river. The rain hammering down on my back and face,

218

making it almost as hard to breathe as when I was trap out in the river.

I grab hold of the bare bleeding leg in front of me like I was grabbing onto a lifebelt, and trickles of blood dilute to pink in the rain run down over my hand.

'Where the others? What happenin' to them?'

Don't worry about them. Have some rest, daughter.

'They still trap out in the river. They drownin' —'

A firm hand stop me from rising to my hands and knees until I give up.

Wait here. Don't move.

After all that fight it take every last ounce of energy I got in me to lift and turn my head toward the river where I ain' sure which of two things disturb me the most: my left foot going a different direction to my knee, or Laura heading back into the river.

There a mighty crack like a cannon going off, and the tree trapping our vehicle snap clean in two, headlights whirling and dipping as the vehicle get snatch up by the current and flung back into its cauldron — the most scary-ass show of nature I ever been a witness to.

CHAPTER 17

It's hunger more than anything else that rouses me, grumbling and demanding and punishing with stomach acidity. Opening my eyes, it takes a while to focus on the plastered wall in front of me, yellow paint burnished the colour of flame by sunset pouring through the windows of a thatched hut decorated with complex, vaguely Masonic symbols and bottles decorated like Vegas showgirls suspended from the ceiling.

Then, remembering what I assumed were my final moments in the flood, I sit up too fast, and the multiple lacerations across my body split where they've scabbed over so far. The pain is excruciating.

'*GOD DAMN*,' someone else screams.

Recoiling from the noise, I twist awkwardly to find Renée on the mattress beside me, her face swollen and criss-crossed with scratches, her raised left foot swaddled with aniseed-smelling bandaging.

I'm so delighted to see her alive, I lunge across the mattress to hug her. 'Renée! Thank God.'

'*STOP MAKING THE BED SHAKE!*' she yells, screaming herself flat as a board.

'Sorry,' I grimace, trying not to move any more.

Panting until she gets the pain under control, she takes a deep breath and sighs. 'No more sudden movements, okay, darlin'?'

'Okay. I promise. I'm sorry.'

'Jesus Christ. My foot,' she groans. 'What the hell is up with it?'

'I think it's broken,' I tell her. 'Someone's made you a cast. Probably whoever rescued us and brought us here.'

Renée frowns at me. 'I don't know who brung us to this — this, what is it?' She looks around dubiously. 'Some kind of Voodoo hospital?' Then she looks me directly in the eye and at least twenty emotions undulate across her face, all of which scare the hell out of me. 'You the one that rescue us, honey.'

'What do you mean?'

'I mean you save my life, is what I mean. You was heading back for the others, too, cutting right through the river like a Olympic champion, but they got swept away before you got to them.'

'I was doing *what*?'

'Believe it, baby. I saw you with my own eyes.'

'Don't be ridiculous. There's no way it was me. I can barely swim. Someone else must have saved us — which means there's a good chance they saved the others as well.'

Renée shrieks at the top of her lungs as I start shuffling my way off the mattress and over her foot in the process.

'Hey! Come back,' she demands, as I limp stiffly towards the door. 'Don't leave me in this creepy-ass hut on my own. Hey! Where you goin'?'

'Where do you think? To find the others.'

Her expression changes to exactly that of the young man who once turned up on my doorstep to tell me he'd just run over my cat. 'Well, be prepare for some bad news, sugar,' she says. 'That river was the devil last night, and I know what I saw. I doubt they stood a chance between them.'

'Shut up,' I snap, not willing to face any truth other than what I want it to be. 'Shut up unless you've got something positive to say.'

Indignation inflates Renée three dress sizes up. 'Positive to say? Did you just say, *positive* to say? Oh, that rich comin' from you, darlin'. Because there ain' no positive since you went and blab your fool mouth off to —'

'*Bonsoir*, ladies,' calls a melodious voice. As one we turn to the doorway to see a tall, coal-black Haitian woman of indeterminable age holding two cups of steaming herbal tea. 'I thought I heard your voices. It's nice to meet both of you, finally. *Ça va?*' There's a strong hint of USA in her soft accent, as though she's spent quite a bit of time there.

Renée takes in the woman's gloriously bouffy red flamenco dress, the matching silk headscarf, the steady, cat-like, almost turquoise eyes and matching eyeshadow, the gold lamé sandals and scarlet lipstick, and says, 'That some outfit you got on there, Carmen Miranda.'

The woman smiles tolerantly, revealing perfectly even white teeth and supermodel cheekbones. 'Actually my name is Mambo Miranda. You're in the healing room of my *peristyle*.'

'*WHAT THE HELL?*' Renée suddenly shrieks, the fright causing me to bite my tongue.

'Jesus Christ, Renée. What?'

'When you find the time to have yourself a damn manicure?' she demands. Then she shrieks again when she looks at her own hands.

'*What?* Stop shrieking.'

She starts combing frantically through her hair. 'Look at that — a big patch of my hair is missin'. Mambo freakin' Miranda been helpin' herself to bits of —'

'Why don't you allow me to put your minds at rest?' Mambo Miranda says. The skirts of her dress waft a breeze of herbs and spices around us as she crosses the hut and removes two strange little double-joker-hat objects, wrapped in satin ribbon and topped off with feathers and sequins, from an altar covered in gold cloth. 'I used the clippings to make these *pakèt kongo* for you. One each.'

'Why?' I ask warily.

'To make you heal faster,' Mambo Miranda says, handing me my *pakèt* — red and green ribbons as opposed to Renée's one of white and gold. 'And bring you luck.'

MAMBO MIRANDA GIVE some orders to folks waiting outside the hut, then she kneel on the mattress to help Laura prop me up, the pain involve making me wish I gone and drown with the others.

'Your ankle's broken,' Mambo Miranda tell me. 'But don't worry — it was a clean break and easy to set. Here, drink this tea. It'll help with the pain.'

'Are you the one that found us?' Laura ask, accepting a cup of Voodoo tea, probably.

'Yes, I was,' Mambo Miranda nod. 'I went out first thing this morning to inspect the flood damage and my dogs found you. You were lucky — the river had come up almost right to where you were lying during the night. Another foot and it could have swept you away. You've both had a very narrow escape. Your vehicle was smashed to bits — the debris is all over the river. On both sides.'

Laura drop her cup and yell some when the hot tea hit her bare feet. 'Did you find anyone else? Three men?' she ask, jumping round, looking like she might have a stroke any moment. 'There were five of us. We all got washed away when a bridge collapsed. Please, help me look for them,' she beg, when she can tell from Mambo Miranda's face that only the two of us was found this morning.

MAMBO MIRANDA TELLS us there's been no word about the guys on any of the local radio stations, which is good news for being no news, I suppose. She takes immediate charge, and organises a twenty-strong search party.

'Okay,' she says to me when they're ready to head off, 'I guess I don't need to ask you to wish us luck. We'll be back as soon as we know something. Try and get some sleep while we're gone.'

'Sleep, my arse,' I tell her. 'I'm coming with you.'

'But —'

'But nothing. I'm coming — barefoot if I have to. I'm not kidding.'

Mambo Miranda reluctantly submits to finding me some shoes, and I join the search party, heading downstream from where Renée and I were found, spreading out for wider coverage. Flood damage extends three paddocks wide each side of the river. The remaining crops and trees are flattened and tangled with flood debris, and massive landslides have cut raw swathes through the lush hills and mountains of the valley around us. As locals on the other side of the river hear our shouts and whistles, they literally come out of the woodwork to help in the search, swelling our number to over a hundred. We come across the flipped, body-mangling wreckage of the 4WD and roll it over using sheer manpower. I shake and cry for a while after we find empty.

A couple of intense hours later, on the brink of night, no news now harder to bear than bad news, a violent commotion breaks out up ahead as Mambo Miranda's dogs start pack fighting over something, ignoring her threats and whistles to come back.

'Oh, Jesus,' I gag, as my eyes adjust to the dimness and distance, to the hellish savage hierarchy of the dogs hoeing into lifeless, silent bodies, ripping guts from bellies, tearing skin from muscle, breaking bones with audible snaps. Screaming and stumbling over the river-bank to reach them, my heart never spasming below 200 bpm, I haul the dogs off and fling them away, hurling rocks and swinging driftwood half my size, guarding the bodies until Mambo Miranda arrives and gets her dogs under control.

'Laura, look', she says. 'It's okay. It's okay. They're just pigs. They were staked to the ground and drowned.'

WHEN WE ARRIVE back in the *peristyle*, Mambo Miranda's dogs giving me a baleful wide berth the whole silent trudge back, two chestnut-skinned women with orangey afro hair who have to be twins almost fight each other in their rush to give Mambo Miranda the news first. From their rapid, urgent exchange and the pointed look Mambo Miranda flashes me, it's obvious the women are talking about something to do with me.

'What they sayin'?' Renée calls from our hut. 'They been in here for hours babblin' Kreyol at me like Lassie tryin' to let me know somebody fall in the well.'

'What's going on?' I ask Mambo Miranda. 'Do they know what's happened to the guys?'

Mambo Miranda blocks further questioning from me with her palm while she finishes listening to what the women have to say. I have to resist the urge to shake her. Finally she thanks and dismisses them.

'Is it good news?' I ask, and she breaks into one of the most beautiful smiles I've ever seen. It's like watching a flower blossom.

'Yanik and Anaïs were trapped overnight by the floods in Nancy — that's seven miles from here — and they said some *blans* stopped them in the street this afternoon and asked directions to the water-fall. Two of them — with a Haitian.'

'*All right*,' Renée whistles. 'Halle-freakin'-lujah. The boys are alive and takin' care of business. *OW, MY FOOT, GODDAMMIT!*'

'What's the matter, Laura?' Mambo Miranda asks, frowning. 'Why isn't that good news to you? It means your friends are alive.'

'Yeah,' Renée shouts. 'What part of alive ain' good news exactly, huh?'

Mambo Miranda takes my elbow. 'Yes, Laura? What's the problem?'

My problem is that I can believe Mozzie would try to find the gold before making sure Renée and I are still alive, but not Floyd. 'Can you ask Yanik and Anaïs what the *blans* were wearing?'

'Sure,' she says. 'Wait here and I'll ask them.'

'*LAURA*,' Renée roars. '*GET YOUR ASS THE HELL IN HERE AND HELP ME UP!*'

Ignoring her increasingly irate demands for attention, I watch as Mambo Miranda questions the twins again, though nothing about anyone's body language — like the hand gestures I would expect from someone miming a partially missing finger — gives me a clue. Finally Mambo Miranda comes back to where I'm standing and lays a hand on my shoulder.

'I hope this is what you want to hear. Yanik says you couldn't miss them. They were wearing Hawaiian — hey, are you okay?'

'Not really,' I say, running around in circles like a decapitated chicken. 'I've got to get to Nancy. Has anyone got a car?'

IT WOULD BE faster to have gone on donkeys. A shrunken wiry man of about ninety with milky, watery eyes insists on driving us to Nancy in his Land Rover that it takes him half an hour just to fetch. Whether he thinks he's driving an automatic or it's his only option, the old man never changes out of first gear. It sounds like the engine is going to scream itself to death during the aeon it takes to reach Nancy.

Mambo Miranda, wedged tight between the old man and myself, maintains her serene, unruffled composure, singing and humming to herself despite being jostled quite violently by the state of the road. She doesn't ask a single question about why I need to get to Nancy in such a hurry, although at one point she says, 'It takes as long as it takes, Laura. You're going to give yourself a heart attack if you don't relax a bit.'

Close to midnight, after curbing the constant urge to hijack the Land Rover and drive it myself, we finally arrive in Nancy, a lush prosperous little town of decoratively painted homes and orchards extending up into the foothills of the Chaine du Borgne. The area obviously gets plenty of rainfall, and the neat, well-tended gardens are blessed with vegetables and flowering tropical shrubbery.

Mambo Miranda directs the old man to pull over by a lantern-lit bar the size of a garden shed, where a group of eight young men dressed like an LA street gang are playing dice for money around a plastic table and listening to a transistor radio. Mambo Miranda calls out to them in Kreyol and they eyeball us with blank-faced hostility.

Authoritatively, used to being obeyed, she calls to them again. A man with a gap in his front teeth big enough to fit another tooth into responds with something insulting. His sneer drops instantly when whatever he's said unleashes a ferocious, bruising Kreyol diatribe from Mambo Miranda. His friends stop laughing abruptly, even reducing the volume on the radio when commanded. The gap-toothed man shuffles reluctantly but respectfully over to the Land Rover, meekly agreeing, '*Oui*, Mambo Miranda,' to everything she says. Finally she starts questioning him instead, and his friends come over to join the discussion at the window, all rum fumes and shoving and help that sounds like arguing. Mambo Miranda at last dismisses them with a gesture somewhat like brushing flour from her hands, and they return to the picnic table, topping up glasses, resetting the radio to full-blast, arguing over whose turn it is to play with the dice next.

'Laura, I'm sorry,' Mambo Miranda says. 'I've got bad news. We've missed the *blans* by a couple of hours. They stopped here and bought rum and cigars before they left — to celebrate something big, they said — then drove off with their horn blaring. I guess they were very happy with whatever they found.'

Our driver nods off in the time it takes me to respond.

'Mambo Miranda,' I say, after I've considered all my options, 'at the risk of sounding culturally insensitive, is there any way you could, like, well, uh, engage your religion? Nothing bad — just enough to stop them leaving the country. They've got something really valuable that belongs to Renée, and if it wasn't for me —'

'You want me to use *Vodou*?' Mambo Miranda whispers, eyes large and glinting in the night.

'Yes,' I whisper back.

'Now?'

'If that's okay.'

She snorts something in Kreyol — which the driver wakes and sniggers at — while rifling through her small beaded bag, and withdraws something small and hard to see in the dark.

'What's that?' I ask, imagining it to be made of bone and hair and umbilical cord.

'Do you think we're living in the Dark Ages down here?' she says a tad sarcastically, selecting a number from the address function on her mobile phone.

MAMBO MIRANDA CALLS a fellow mambo in Pétionville who has a cousin who is married to a baggage handler at Port-au-Prince

Airport, and arranges to have Donny and Bobby's bags disappear so they won't have a clue until they're back in Miami and have spent an increasingly desperate best part of an hour beside a carousel.

'I'm sorry for asking you to use Voodoo,' I apologise, after she's filled me in on her telephone conversation. 'I live in the PC capital of the universe. I should know better.'

'Be quiet,' she snaps, index finger to her lips. She calls out to the men at the picnic table again and the gap-toothed man brings the radio over. She snatches it from him and listens intently to the tinny Kreyol, her ear to the speaker so as not to miss a word. Finally, when the station resumes playing music, she gives the man back his radio. Lacking her usual composure, she chews on a thumbnail as she mulls over whatever she just heard.

'What's up?' I ask, prompted by her weird expression.

'Don't get your hopes up, Laura,' she warns, 'but two *blans* have just been airlifted out of the Holy Cross Clinic in Pilate. The river that runs by my *peristyle* eventually joins up downriver with the one that runs through Pilate.'

For the first time since I wanted a pony I clasp my hands together in prayer. 'Oh, please, God, let it be Floyd and Mozzie.'

'Laura,' she says, 'I mean what I said about not getting your hopes up. The *blans* who left Nancy earlier would have had to pass through Pilate whether they were heading for Cap-Haïtien or straight to Port-au-Prince. Anything could have happened to them between here and there. They might have crashed, or been ambushed by bandits, or stopped by the police, or —'

'What about the driver? The Haitian. Was he mentioned?'

Mambo Miranda shakes her head. 'Or they might have been robbed by their own driver. Especially if what they found in Nancy was very valuable. You shouldn't be too optimistic.'

229

ALL MORNING SINCE they got back, Mambo Miranda ain' been receiving nothing but Chinese whispers about DEA and CIA plots in the area, trying to work out who it was got airlift out of Pilate. While we eating lunch together in the healing room, Laura and Mambo Miranda setting on stools they brung in, Mambo Miranda receive a call from Port-au-Prince to say Donny and Bobby ain' turn up at the airport yet, meaning it looking more and more like it might be them that got airlift out of Pilate.

'It's no good,' Laura say, lowering the fork she ain' eaten a damn thing with so far. 'I'm going to have an aneurysm if we don't leave for Port-au-Prince soon. The not knowing is —' She start crying, great heaving sobs like a new widow.

'Hey,' Mambo Miranda soothe, taking Laura's plate away. She set it uneaten on the mattress and put her arm round Laura's shoulders. 'Hey, come on. It's not a problem. We can leave for Cap-Haïtien in twenty minutes. You can be in Port-au-Prince by this evening. And we have to go through Pilate — maybe we'll receive good news there.'

MAMBO MIRANDA LOAN us a couple thousand dollars and some crutches to get home despite neither of us with a clue how or when we can pay her back. She decide she going accompany us as far as Cap-Haïtien in a antique-ass old Jeep that Laura said I should be grateful the owner's son is driving instead. Laura sit up front with Mambo Miranda and the driver so I got the whole back to myself with a foam mattress and some pillows.

Everybody holding they breath for the best when we pull up outside at the Holy Cross Clinic in Pilate. Laura turn to look at me before she go inside with Mambo Miranda, and show me her fingers is cross on both hands.

'I hear you, sugar,' I say, crossing mine back.

The damn driver decide to go off some place and leave me unattend, and folks is three-deep staring at me by the time Mambo Miranda arrive arrive back with a mean-temper, baggy-eye Cuban doctor from the clinic. Laura trailing behind with bad news on her face.

'*NEVER MIND MY ANKLE*,' I yell, as the doctor manhandling the cast like he was thinking of buying it. 'Hey! Somebody get this third-world quack the hell off of me and tell me who got airlift out of here last night.'

'The *doctor*,' Mambo Miranda answer, holding my leg still so he can take a proper look, 'doesn't know anything about an airlift. He was here all night delivering a baby and he says if there was an air rescue he'd have known about it. He thinks there's been some confusion because the medics of the Holy Cross are running a vaccination program in this area from a mobile health unit. He's going to find out what he can and then he'll call me.'

Finally the doctor seem like he please with the cast, and he have a long conversation with Mambo Miranda before the driver haul his ass back and we ready to hit the road again, nobody saying a word. Laura's sniffing soon turn to tears and she ain' consolable until the driver stop so she can buy cigarettes.

'You mind?' I complain. 'There a sick person back here breathin' in your filthy-ass smoke.'

APPROACHING A POTHOLE as we leaving Pilate and the road turn back to dirt, the driver is suddenly face with the option of driving into a bunch of women selling produce along the roadside or a head-on collision with a *taptap*. He decide to drive right over the pothole and the ten-foot jolt feel like it broke my ankle again.

Mambo Miranda finally realize I ain' capable of taking much more, and toss me a unlabel bottle of pills from her bag. 'They're not

231

candy,' she say. 'Don't be a pig. No more than one every six hours.'

'Aw, that nice,' I sigh when a couple kick in, making the edges soft and fuzzy and giving me a break.

'I thought you'd like that.'

'Yes, I do. This is some mercy-ass medication.' My eyelids drooping and the pain in my foot subsiding to a tolerable level I cain' hardly feel no more. 'What you got that hurt so bad you need shit like this?'

The last thing I know, until I wake up and somebody wheeling me across the runway tarmac in a wheelchair, is Mambo Miranda winking at Laura like she got a joke to share. 'Carpal tunnel syndrome from wringing chicken necks,' she say, and Laura still belly-laughing when I pass out cold.

RENÉE, WHO YELLS at the pilots to '*do some loop-de-loops, you chicken-ass fairies*' for the entire flight, is still wacko-ed by the time we arrive back in Port-au-Prince, and it's a hell of a job just to get her off the plane. It takes four men to carry her down the stairs in the airline wheelchair, manhandling her somewhat contemptuously because they assume she's roaring drunk.

I give the go-ahead for a porter to organise a taxi for us, and wheel Renée outside the terminal so I can have a cigarette while we're waiting. Everyone is rubbernecking at us, as morbidly and ghoulishly curious about our battered appearances as if we were lying dead and mutilated by the wreckage of a high-speed car crash. Blanking them out, I don't notice the middle-aged white man with a Southern accent and a grey crewcut until he's standing right in front of me, asking, '— Laura Delacross?'

'What?'

He smiles reassuringly. 'Ma'am, are y'all Renée Poupet and Laura Delacross?'

Renée has the mental resources to respond before I do. 'That right,' she grins. 'Renée Poupet and Laura Delacross. And who might you be, handsome?' Her head lolls back in a grotesque wink, her mouth gaping wide until I push her upright and she can close it again.

The man regards Renée for a few moments, then chuckles knowingly to himself. 'Yeah, sometimes Haiti can do that to a person.' He reaches over her head and offers me his hand.

'Officer Kneale from the consulate,' he explains. 'Mambo Miranda told us to expect you.'

THE NICE MAN from the consulate finally get us on a plane the hell out of Haiti the following morning, by which time we know that Floyd and Mozzie hospitalize up in Jackson Memorial in Miami. Some kids found all three of the guys tangle up together in some bushes about ten miles away from Mambo Miranda's *peristyle*. Thinking they was dead, the kids strip the clothes right off they backs and was playing dress-up until somebody's mama had the sense to find out where they got designer clothes from. Finally the world got reason to be glad Mozzie so hot on himself he never leave the house with less than a thousand bucks' worth on his back. Floyd and Mozzie both in a pretty bad way by all accounts, although nobody letting on how bad except for they was lucky to escape from the wreckage, because the driver wasn't. The consulate trying to track down his widow so they can return his body to her.

Donny and Bobby turn out to be smarter than we thought and they fly to the Dominican Republic from Cap-Haïtien instead. Immigration got a record of them arriving in Miami on a flight from Santo Domingo yesterday afternoon, but that was a good three hours before they got the call from the consulate saying to watch out for them. Where the hell they is now is anybody's guess.

I try calling my trailer before we leave to give Hoover the good news I on my way home, but the phone been disconnect, probably for not paying the bill, and I worry sick about how he doing on his own. On the plane, going back to God knows what trouble without the gold I set out for, and people hurt and drown because of it, I wish I never found that damn journal. I thought it was going make my life better, but it turn out to be rotten and make things a whole bunch worse. Because I cain' cope with my thoughts at the moment, they all too much to endure right now, I take a couple of Mambo Miranda's magic pills and adjust my seat back. Laura just have to take care of things for a little while longer.

AT MIAMI AIRPORT we're met by medics and Immigration officials who whisk us through all the Customs palaver, and then transport us straight to Jackson Memorial by ambulance. Renée is in La-La-Land and flirts outrageously with the paramedics on the way to the hospital. They have a great time: nobody's dying and they dig the Miss Scarlett act.

'Do you know what's she taken?' a nurse asks as she wheels Renée through the automatic door to the emergency department.

'I dread to think,' I say, collapsing into another wheelchair brought out by an orderly.

Renée gets taken to X-ray, while a young black doctor examines me in a curtained-off cubicle. She swabs my cuts and abrasions with something clear that stings, and asks, 'Is there any reason why you can't take antibiotics?'

'No,' I say.

'You're not allergic to penicillin?'

Why is it that doctors never believe you? 'No.'

'Is there any possibility you might be pregnant?'

'Ah,' I say, after a pause. 'Now that you mention it.'

ONLY HIS EYES turn my way as I'm wheeled into his room. The rest of him is strapped down with restraints and machinery and plastic tubing.

'G'day, mate,' he says. 'I'd tell you to pull up a chair but I can see you brought your own. Wheel yourself over.'

'Hey, Mozzie,' I smile back, trying to mask the overwhelming pity I feel for him. His doctor had warned me there'd be some heavy-duty apparatus, but he looks like some animal completely immobilised for an experiment, some poor lab monkey with parts of its brain exposed so scientists can stick wires in. 'How are you feeling?'

'To be honest, Laura,' he says, 'I'm not feeling much of anything. Below the waist, at least.'

Tears I have no hope of stopping stream down my face. 'I'm sorry, Mozzie. I wish I could —'

'There's no way of knowing until the swelling goes down,' he interrupts, putting on a brave face. 'You need to worry about Floyd. Now *he's* hurt.'

THE ICU NURSE tells me to talk to Floyd, who's hooked up to half a tonne of medical hardware, heavily bandaged and breathing with the help of a ventilator, about anything that comes into my head. I stare at a plastic concertina thing rising and falling in a glass tube with artificial breaths, unable to think of anything to say, because what is there to say to someone in a coma when you're the reason they're so badly hurt? If I hadn't blabbed everything to Donny we'd all be celebrating by now, instead of trying to deal with consequences.

The nurse gives me an old *People* magazine, and says, 'It's okay, honey. Just read to him instead. They like hearing a familiar voice. It's comforting.'

I'm just telling Floyd about the genuine leather shocking-pink wallpaper in P. Diddy's mansion in the Hamptons when the doctor who examined me in the emergency department shows up.

'Do you want the results in here?' she asks, her tone and face unreadable.

I put the magazine down and nod. 'Okay.'

'You're pregnant,' she says, and the luminous green line monitoring Floyd's well-being might as well be flat-lining for all the reaction he shows.

CHAPTER 18

SOMEBODY MUST HAVE put a curse on me while I was in Haiti. I arrive home, rushing in the door quick as I can on crutches to let my boy know his mama home, only to find Hoover been taken into custody by Child Welfare and I got some abandonment of a minor charge against me. My trailer been ransack by junkies, too, and what they couldn't carry they smash up. I ain' even pick up the mess yet when Sheriff Girouard call by to say Jolie been arrest for arm robbery of a liquor store in Amarillo, looking at twelve to fifteen years. She swear blind she didn't know her boyfriend was going to pull a gun on nobody, but the cashier say he think she did. The twins split up into different foster-care homes, and I ain' getting no place fast with Legal Aid.

It less than a week to Christmas and only Hoover allow to come stay the day with me if he want to, but he ain' talking to me since he was taken into care. He so mad at me for messing up everybody's lives, he won't even let me visit. I couldn't care less about the gold now. I wish I never heard of it. The only thing I want is my family back with me where they belong, and things back to normal.

I give up liquor all together after Haiti in case the social workers or whoever drop by unannounced and consider me to be a unfit guardian. Instead I got to take anti-depressants to get through the days and sleeping tablets so I can get through the nights.

Floyd medi-vac back to Charity Hospital on Tulane in April so his family and friends can visit, but he ain' even breathing on his own, let alone woke up yet. I been down to New Orleans, visiting once a month, timing it for early in the morning so there less chance of Floyd's family there blaming me for his coma. His bandages and bruising long gone and he look like he just sleeping, but he don't even flinch if you stick something sharp in him.

Some doctors come over from New Zealand for Mozzie and take him back home in a special bed for people with spinal injuries look like a incubator. I went and visit with him before he left, to say I was sorry for what happen.

'Mate,' he say, like he just got the flu or something. 'A couple of weeks and I'll be back on my feet again. And I volunteered for Haiti — you didn't force me. What are you blaming yourself for?'

How about for thinking badly of him earlier?

As far as I know he still paralyze from the waist down, even though the swelling in his spinal cord gone down and the doctors cain' find no reason for him not walking yet.

And Laura, Laura, Laura. I don't hear a Goddamn word from her for over nine months — I mean she could be dead for all I know — then this Christmas card with a sheep lying on a beach in a Santa outfit arrive from her this morning with a note and a check for five thousand New Zealand dollars. Her card is the first item of personal mail I ever receive and it come as a big surprise, though not as surprising as some baby photos I was expecting even less.

DEAR RENÉE,

Meet Angelique Renée Delacross, born 4th December, an early Christmas present for me, weighing in at 7 lbs 2 ounces. I still can't believe I'm a mother and I'm hoping instinct kicks in soon before I kill her by accident. How was I supposed to know you don't pick a baby up by the arms? There's so much more to looking after one than I thought.

So that's my big news. Well, shock, really.

Without doing a DNA test I'm fairly positive that Angelique is Floyd's daughter. She looks like him. And besides, I still maintain a cigar is not having sexual relations. Not enough to make a baby anyway.

How are things in St Luc? Did you find Jolie and the twins? I hope things are working out for you. How's Floyd doing? I hear that he was flown back to New Orleans. Mozzie's in a wheelchair now and living back home with his parents. He's starting to get very depressed/suicidal at the lack of progress, especially as there's no reason why he shouldn't walk. His doctor thinks it's more to do with psychological trauma than something physical. I haven't visited him for a while because the last time was too sad. I preferred the old Mozzie to the new Mozzie. I hate to make the comparison, but he's like a zombie now. From all accounts the only writing he's doing these days is practising variations of his own obituary.

I've just won a big-cheese award for my Mardi Gras photos, so I've enclosed a cheque for you. I know it can't make up for losing the gold, but I hope it comes in useful. Mambo Miranda has been paid back so you don't need to worry about that, and Officer Kneale from the consulate has passed the rest of the prize money on to the driver's widow. It should be plenty for a few years. Apparently she's using the money to go to beauty school so she's got some way of making a living. She sounds like a smart woman, so I wouldn't worry too much about her.

I'm sorry for not writing to you sooner but there was a lot to think about after Haiti. Excuse my French but I couldn't have buggered things up more for you if I'd tried, and that's a lot for a person to live with. I'm really sorry, Renée, and if I can ever make it up to you, don't even slightly hesitate to ask.

Have a fabulous Christmas and New Year. Say hi to the kids.
Love Laura and Angelique

THAT AFTERNOON I catch the bus down to New Orleans and get off at Charity Hospital, never mind if any of Floyd's family is there, because the man got a right to know he a daddy, coma or no coma.

The nurses set the radio in his room to Christmas carols and they decorate the place up with a tree and tinsel and lights. Floyd's hair turn darker from not being in the sun for the best part of a year, although somebody trimming it. He lost a lot of muscle.

I pat his shoulder before I take a seat. 'Hi, Floyd. How you doin', darlin'?' I ask, like he going answer me. 'I brought you some grapes. They in the bag over there. The nurses can take them if you don't feel up to them.'

The only response is the beep, beep, beep of some machine, keeping him alive — probably.

'I got some big news today,' I say, taking Laura's card from my bag. 'And it concern you so I thought I better come on down and let you know 'bout it.'

Even though there still no sign Floyd can hear me, I take the baby photos out the envelope and hold them up so he could see them if he was able to. 'This is your baby daughter, Angelique,' I explain. 'Ain' she pretty? She the spittin' image of you but with red hair like Laura. Look, she the exact same nose and mouth as you. She must be, what, coming up for three weeks soon.'

Beep — beep — beep.

'Now, before you do the math and go jumpin' to the conclusion that Donny just as easily the daddy, without goin' into too much

240

detail, it ain' possible to get pregnant from tobacco. Nuh-uh. You is definitely the daddy.'

Beep — beep — beep.

'Although the way you was carryin' on with that Peace Corps girl right under Laura's nose, I sure as hell wouldn't blame her if things had gone further.'

Beep — beep — beep.

CHRISTMAS DAY COME round and it the worst day of my life so far. Hoover refuse to come on the phone and speak to me, and when I call up Little Sammy and Whitney at they different foster homes they can hardly remember who I am. They more interest in playing with the new toys they got. Jolie call me later from the prison, pissy and in the mood to argue, which is exactly how I feeling, and the conversation don't go too well.

'Mama, when you goin' get a decent lawyer and raise the bail to get me out? I don't belong in here. I want to be with my kids.'

'You don't need bail, baby, you need a miracle. You *rob* a liquor store, for Christ sake. Ain' nobody handing out no medals for that.'

'But I didn't know Alfie had a gun,' she yell. 'I keep *tellin'* you that. I ain' into no freakin' guns shit. I thought we was just going in there to buy cigarettes and beer. I was just as surprise as the damn lyin' cashier, so hurry your useless ass the hell up and get me out of here before I go crazy. This is all your fault — it the least you can do.'

'Might I remind you, darlin',' I tell her, 'that if you didn't gone and sold that journal, for not even close to what it worth, and got yourself exactly where you is now, I could have had O.J.'s lawyer spring you out back in March. You got a bunch of your own blame to face up to, baby, and it about time you made a start. I don't even think I like you enough right now to raise the bail money.'

'Fuck you,' she say, before hanging up on me.

Late in the evening the loneliness get too much for me, and I walk the two mile to the only gas station open and buy a dozen Colts, because, hell, there ain' no visitors coming today, not even my own family.

The phone ringing when I arrive back at the trailer with my arms almost dragging on the ground from the weight of the beer.

'Who is it?' I ask, hopeful Hoover change his mind and want to speak to his mama on Christmas Day after all.

'Are you ready to fulfill your promise to your ancestors, Renée?' Mambo Miranda ask, without so much as a hello or how are you first.

'HOW THE HELL I suppose to afford all that?' I say, when she tell me what is involve in a ancestor feast, a *manje lwa*, something like that. 'The money Laura gave me is for the lawyers — and it ain' even scratching the surface.'

'You're wasting that money if you throw it at lawyers.'

'Oh? And a party for dead people is a better idea?'

Mambo Miranda take a deep breath before she respond. 'If you give your ancestors more than you can afford, Renée, then they'll give you back more than you could hope for. I promise you.'

'And what if I go spend the check on them and they don't? What then? Nuh-uh. I ain' riskin' it.'

'Then your bad luck won't go away,' she insist. 'If anything, it will get even worse.'

'Ain' you a bunch of good news?'

'Renée, listen and try to understand,' she sigh, like she trying to convince a idiot. 'Your ancestors love you. They want to help you but they can't. Why else do you think you're living in a trailer?'

'Because I ain' got no money.'

'Exactly. That's my point. They don't have the energy to help your life. That's *why* you're poor.'

'They sure seem to have plenty of energy for messin' it up.'

'Why should they reward you if you don't serve them?' she ask. 'What's to reward?

'You listen to me,' I say. 'You askin' me to spend money I need gettin' my family back together. Nuh-uh. I ain' going do it. Forget about it.'

'If you think you are lonely today, Renée,' she say, after a pause so long I think she got cut off, 'wait and see what Christmas brings next year if you ignore your promise to them. You'll look back on this one with fond memories. You can't make a promise to the *lwa* and go back on your word. They'll make every day you wake up the worst one of your life so far.'

ANGELIQUE IS AN adorable baby, giggling and laughing whenever someone pays her the slightest bit of attention. She's enchanted by music, listening wide-eyed and rapt to anything from hymns that waft across from the Pacific Island church two streets over to the theme tune of *Home Improvement* re-runs when there's nothing better on TV. It takes ages to feed her, because whenever I make eye contact she looks up and stops sucking.

On the evening of Boxing Day, worn out from a family get-together earlier, and alone with my daughter for the first time since her birth, I lock the front door and arrange myself comfortably in front of the TV to nurse her. For once she feeds without fuss, worn out from the chaos of Christmas — she's been passed around relatives and friends as if she were a party game — and quickly drifts off to sleep when full.

There's absolute crap on TV, so I switch it off and contemplate Angelique instead, trying to guess who she'll be as an adult: what her personality will be, what she'll look like, what she'll choose to do with her life. Right now, less than a month old, she is so little and innocent, so unprotected and vulnerable, that the responsibility of her terrifies me. It's not as if I've done a brilliant job so far — even before she was born I cost her a two-parent family, a delighted father recording her first Christmas on video. I hope to God I'm enough to make up for it.

A new skill I've developed since her birth is I can answer the phone in under a second no matter where I am in the house. So now, when the phone rings in the hall, Angelique doesn't even have a chance to stir because I answer it almost instantly.

'Hello?' I say softly.

'Ma'am, I've got a collect call from a Miss Renée Poupet in St Luc, Louisiana. Are you willing to accept the charge?'

For an instant I almost pretend to be a wrong number. But it's only for an instant. 'Okay, put her through.'

'Thank you. One mom —'

'Laura? That you? Can you hear me, darlin'? Merry Christmas! I got the card you sent me. You sure had yourself a cute-looking baby.'

'Thanks,' I say, aware that I'm grinning like a lunatic with a bag of favourite lollies. 'She's really sweet, too.'

'Oh, that ain' goin' last,' Renée snorts. 'Enjoy the sweetness while you can — Floyd or no Floyd for a daddy. That kid goin' have a personality change some time in the next two to twelve years that going make you wish you got sterilize at puberty.'

'How are you, Renée?' I laugh, revelling once again in her crazy perspective of the world. 'I've missed you.'

'Well, you don't have to for much longer,' Renée says, and titters with what sound distinctly like nerves. 'See, Mambo Miranda said for you and Mozzie to get your asses back to St Luc.'

Mozzie — 'sick of *being treated like a fucking cripple*' — doesn't take too much convincing and, against his mother's strongly expressed wishes, joins us on a plane to Los Angeles two days later. He's brilliant with Angelique, and keeps her occupied and amused when I need sleep, although he's not too happy about the frequent breast-feeding and nappy-changing requirements of a newborn. The cabin crew spoil us rotten on the flight, constantly checking we're comfortable, discreetly assisting Mozzie to the bathroom when he needs to go. On arrival at LAX, we have a rapid, airport-official-assisted transfer to our connecting flight to New Orleans — back to where it all started. It's one day until a brand-new year.

Somewhere over Texas, I'm desperate for a pee and hand a sleeping Angelique over to Mozzie to mind for a while. When I arrive back, she's awake and giggling at Mozzie, who is laughing and reciting something Dr Seuss-ish to her. I smile at the two of them getting on famously, Angelique drawing Mozzie away from whatever dark place he spends most of his time in now.

'Do you reckon she's Floyd's kid?' he asks when I've sat down beside him. 'She looks like him.'

'Yes, she's Floyd's kid, you cheeky bastard,' I snap, snatching Angelique back, making her cry.

'Cheeky bastard, my arse. If she *is* Floyd's kid, it's only because one of his little fellows got there marginally sooner than one of Donny's did.'

'Not that it's any of your business,' I say, rocking Angelique, trying to calm her down, 'but Donny's weren't in the race. So you can you point that finger of condemnation at Floyd instead.'

Mozzie looks puzzled. '*Que?*'

'I'm talking about the fact I wasn't the only direction Floyd's little fellows were swimming in.'

'You're going to have to help me out here,' Mozzie says.

'Where were they swimming?'

'Towards that Peace Corps girl at the Oloffson.'

'Belinda?'

'Yes,' I say. 'The lovely Belinda.'

'That's not what happened.'

'Yes, it is. I'm not stupid.'

'He was helping her write some letters, you moron,' Mozzie says, apparently finding my assumption completely incredible. 'She was trying to raise funding from France to fly some kid with leukaemia over for chemo, but she no speaka da lingo.'

NEW YEAR'S EVE and there about twenty of us out in the middle of the swamps of the Atchafalaya Basin, in some temple on stilts to keep it from the bayou look like a fisherman or hunter's cabin on the outside. The place so isolate, nothing around for miles except alligators and bugs, and the only way to get here is by boat. We leave the chickens and goat outside in the cages we brung them over in until they number is up.

The mambo in charge, Priestess Veronica, is a initiate of Mambo Miranda from a long time ago, when they was both studying at UCLA, though she from Chicago originally and ain' a Haitian. She dress in this white African muu-muu get-up, with a thick necklace of wood and color glass beads round her neck. Apparently everybody got they own head *lwa* even if they ain' aware of it, and Priestess Veronica got somebody call Ezili Dantò. Mambo Miranda make her a gift of a sequin flag from Haiti with a picture of a color Madonna and her baby on it suppose to represent Ezili Dantò. She also brung five bottles of Babancourt, a whole bunch of different dried leaves and roots, and a box of dirt and stones among other things, so hell knows where she find the room for any clothes.

The inside of the cabin is like being back in Haiti. The walls paint up with pictures of saints and crazy-ass symbols, and there a bunch of drums and rattles and party decorations strung up in the rafters. Priestess Veronica got a pole — a *poto mitan* — in the middle of her temple, floor to roof, just like Mambo Miranda, but Priestess Veronica got hers decorate with Mardi Gras beads, glue on to look like a snake winding round it. She got a trough around the base she tip the box of Haitian dirt into, and she give somebody the stones to clean up before she put them in white saucers and pour oil over them. Laura, the baby and Mozzie the only white folks here, and Mozzie looking plenty piss at the indignity of somebody carrying him in and out the boat like he a baby too. There a kitchen, a bathroom, and some cots in the temple — everything a person would need for staying over for the night.

The rest of the evening is busy with preparations for the feast, and we all get to work with cleaning and decorating the place with flowers and leaves we brung with us specially. Folks dusting the altars and all the Voodoo crap on them, tying ribbons and stringing Mexican lights onto things, chopping and peeling vegetables, baking and icing cakes, making jellies, arranging fruit platters, putting nuts out in bowls, making everything look just right. Somebody even give the livestock a bath and spray them with some perfume.

THE TEMPLE LOOKS gorgeous covered in white roses and lilies, their perfumes enhanced by the sweet-smelling Anaïs Anaïs that Priestess Veronica sprays liberally around from an atomiser. There are white bows tied to bottles of decent champagne sitting on ice, and the white-clothed tables around the room are laden with food and gifts and money from Renée.

The ceremony starts off interestingly enough. Priestess Veronica gives the nod for her congregation — a mixture of Haitians,

Hispanics and African-Americans, nearly all women except for the drummers and one of the priestess's assistants — to get changed, and the women reappear barefoot, in simple white dresses and head-scarves, all as meticulously laundered as Communion dresses.

With permission from Priestess Veronica to video the ceremony — for private viewing only and absolutely not for public consumption — I entrust Angelique to Mozzie's care, and move around the temple capturing little dramas like the mambos arguing over what should go where on the altars.

When everyone is finally seated or kneeling, Priestess Veronica lifts a jug of water in four directions before pouring a thin rivulet around the boundary of her temple, leading finally to the base of her glittering *poto mitan*. Taking his cue, her male assistant — whose bright red silk neckerchief adds the only splash of colour — likewise presents a bowl of flour in the same directions as she did. Afterwards, while enough candles are lit to warn ships off reefs, he takes handfuls of flour from his bowl to draw delicate filigreed patterns on the wooden floor: curiously pleasing, heraldic devices of hearts and stars and swords, and other more obscure symbols I don't know the words for.

Preliminaries out of the way, the next three hours are about exciting as watching golf. The congregation are motionless the whole time they pray and chorus Hail Marys or Ave Marias — something distinctly Catholic-sounding — and the ceremony feels like it's never going to end. Mambo Miranda and Priestess Veronica drone on for hours in Latin, French and Kreyol, shaking their respective rattles from low stools by the *poto mitan*, pouring frequent offerings of rum into the trough surrounding it. Finally, a long drawn-out shake of rattles signals the end of the formalities, and events turn distinctly African.

LORD, BUT THOSE women can dance. Don't matter how old they booty is, they shaking it like it only seventeen, matching any speed the drummers care to go at. They make the MTV girls look like somebody just make ninety in a old folks' home. Rum going round like it made of water, and some people smoking cigarettes despite using up the same amount of energy and oxygen as wrestling with a maniac. Everybody singing the same tunes, and they know what dance steps they suppose to be doing and when they suppose to be doing them. Priestess Veronica go round everybody with a white chicken, flapping its wings over the room like it was a feather duster. Even though that poor chicken get its neck wrung shortly afterwards so the *lwa* Legba will show up and get the show on the road, the chicken still meet a nicer end than the other chickens and goat as the evening wear on. It enough to turn a person vegetarian.

When folks get possess by somebody — and you can tell because they get all scare-looking right before, falling all over the place like drunks until it seem like somebody invisible shove them off a curb into traffic — they all want different things to eat and clothes to wear. Some want mirrors and lipsticks, some want cakes and rum, some want hats and pipes, and some want money and capes and sharp weapons to play round with. One time a woman fall to the ground and writhe around like a snake until Priestess Veronica put a cloth over her head and give her a white egg to eat in private. Personally, I glad about that because I don't need to see nobody trying to eat a raw egg with no hands. After folks come back into themselves, they have to go lie down for a while and take a nap. I wonder if Prince le Kreyol going to show up, but Mambo Miranda say he too hot for them handle, and he don't belong at this kind of ceremony. You only call Prince le Kreyol when you got a big-ass problem and it worth the risk of what mood he might be in.

It obvious that everybody alive or dead havin' a wild old time, and the feast going like it suppose to. All the *lwa* turn up one after the other, and they more than please with what I lay on for them. They dance they asses off with full bellies, knock back as much liquor and champagne as they can drink and crack some rude-ass jokes that make everybody cry with laughing, but I still got a nagging feeling about blowing Laura's check on a party. Inside I quietly hoping that I ain' done the wrong thing and the ceremony ain' just a big expensive show for my benefit.

I hoping like crazy that not the case right up until my vision go funny and Mambo Miranda and Priestess Veronica come rushing at me like I was considering jumping off a building or something. Then damn if it don't feel like somebody shove me in the back as hard as they can. I feel like I plummeting through the air into nothing.

GENTLE HANDS CARESSING *me now: soft and caring like my mama's use to be sometimes if she was in the right frame of mind. Folks taking they turn hugging me up a whole bunch of love that make me feel a hundred times stronger. They tell me that I ain' alone no more, that I have hundreds of ancestors going back thousands of years watching out for me now.*

Thank you, Renée. This is a magnificent feast. You have honored us well.

Feel how full our bellies are, how warm we are, how strong we feel. We are very pleased.

Now we can help you.

RENÉE IS MERRILY shaking her stuff with Priestess Veronica's congregation when all of a sudden she lurches forward, staggering around the temple. Amid a great deal of exciting commotion the two mambos leap to help her and prevent her falling when her knees buckle. Supporting her upright, they lead her into a private room away from the rest of us, shaking their rattles as they go, making a big fuss of her.

About twenty minutes later, Renée, flanked by the mambos, re-enters the temple and looks around until her eyes find mine. Despite her possessing an easily read face, what's there now is completely new to me. She walks slowly over to where I'm standing — in no rush whatsoever. All three come to a standstill around me and I lower the video camera nervously.

'Hello,' I say, smiling inappropriately.

'You have the Captain's eyes,' Renée says to me in a flat African voice that isn't hers. Her face is slack, as though heavily Botoxed. 'You look just like him.'

The only response I can summon, considering *my* ancestor kidnapped the woman standing before me and forced her into a miserable life of slavery after raping her, is to say, 'I'm sorry' — and hope she knows I mean it.

'Don't be,' Tumé says, hugging me with Renée's arms, an embrace more comforting than angel wings. 'The eyes are not the heart.'

WHILE RENÉE IS having a sleep, even though the ceremony is still going full swing, I use the excuse of breastfeeding Angelique to go somewhere quiet and try to comprehend what just happened — the two centuries of history just crossed. I carry her outside and find Mozzie sitting on his own at the end of the dock in his wheelchair. He's staring glumly at the silky, satanically black water and doesn't hear me coming until I'm almost right next to him.

'I'm sorry but this seat is taken,' he says when he finally notices me and looks up.

'Excuses,' I smile.

When he smiles back, it's one of the saddest smiles I've ever seen. 'Can I hold her?' he says, nodding at Angelique.

It occurs to me that Mozzie would make Angelique a great godfather. They bring out the best in each other, and he'd argue to the death for her. 'Here,' I say, closing the last of the gap between us. 'Of course you —'

The next few moments are a quixotic agony, panic blurred by some kind of self-preserving brain clamp-down to stop me losing my mind completely. With my arms outstretched to hand Angelique over to Mozzie, I don't see the loose plank of wood jutting out on the dock, and I trip, hurling Angelique literally ten metres into the swamp. The splash she makes is incredible for a little baby, but even as I register it I stay frozen on the dock, doing nothing but making weird wheezy noises. I don't even register all the noise and confusion that follow the splash until Mozzie calls from below somewhere.

Clinging to a post under the dock, kicking his legs to stay afloat, Mozzie holds a screaming Angelique clear of the water. '*HEY*!' he yells again. 'Hurry up and take your baby off me before a fucking alligator gets us.'

LATE THE NEXT evening, after we have a chance to sleep off the feast and the shock of Angelique near drowning, we arrive back at my trailer to find I left the lights on when I went out. Mozzie still using his wheelchair some because his legs is weak, but he make it up the steps on his own without leaning on nobody. Everybody waiting on me to find the key when the door open by itself and Hoover standing there, nearly four inches taller than the last time I saw him.

'Happy New Year's, Mama,' he say. 'I decide I goin' come home — if you still want me.'

I kiss and hug him for a hour straight before he fed up with it and want to order in some food. While Laura go to Jolie's room to put Angelique to bed — she don't seem no worse for wear after her dip in the swamp — Mozzie take a seat on the new sofa I had to buy when the junkies tore up my old one. He set the video of the feast up so we can all watch it when the pizza arrive.

'Did Mama really get possess?' Hoover ask Mozzie.

'I believe so,' Mozzie tell him sincerely. 'It's all in the video.'

'Cool,' Hoover say.

Nobody expecting nothing but pepperoni and olives when somebody knock on the door in forty minutes like the pizza place said they would.

'My shout,' Laura say, getting up from the dining table to answer.

Some other delivery-man standing there with a envelope in his hand. He wearing dark brown overalls like he come to fix a boiler instead, and he seem overly excite at the sight of Laura's purse and his tip it contain.

'You Miss Delacross?' he ask. 'You know a Mr Simeon?'

'You read it,' Laura say, trying to hand the envelope to me. She look like all the blood just drain right out of her.

I pull my hand away from her. 'Nuh-uh. You read it.'

'What if he died and it's from his dad letting us know?'

'Floyd ain' dead.'

And I know that, just like I know I going to get assign a crack Legal Aid attorney shortly and spring Jolie and the twins back to Louisiana. Even if by some miracle the gold turn up now and I could buy my way out of my problems — and I be amaze if Prince le Kreyol ain' on Donny and Bobby's case about it — I going send it right back to Haiti where it belong. Give it to some nuns to buy the orphans some shoes or something. I rather have all my family safe and in one piece here with me instead. Sure we got problems,

253

but none of them is unfixable. I already decide I going to some evening classes and get a job afterwards, find someplace nicer to live. My family is what really important — I realize now. I need them more than I need anything else. Maybe that what the journal was all about. Some kind of test before the ancestors going forgive anybody.

'Please,' Laura say. 'I don't want to.'

'No,' I say, still refusing to take the envelope. 'It ain' goin' bite you. Just open the damn thing.'

Reluctantly she tear the envelope open, and anybody think she freezing to death the way she shaking while she read the note inside.

'Well?' I ask, when she don't tell nobody what it say right away.

Slowly, taking a deep breath, she fold the note up and tuck it back in the envelope. Then, finally, she break into a grin from ear to ear, and I grinning like a fool right back before she even open her mouth because her smile is that catching.

'*Mais*,' she say, in a really bad Cajun accent, 'where is everybody? I woke up and you were all gone. We've got a christening to arrange, us.'